Breaking Steele
Kimberly Amato

Little Crown Media, LLC

To Laura for always being there even if it meant sitting through a bad movie[s].
For the bad movie choices, I profusely apologize.

Contents

Forward

It feels like it's been eons since my cell phone rang. Forever since Officer Garrison drove drunk, killing my brother and his wife, leaving me to raise their son Chase. Years since that same officer went on a killing spree and threatened my family. Months since I killed another corrupt officer to protect them. If you put these events on a timeline, you would see how spread out they are. How long ago this paper trail started. It was only the beginning.

Regardless of the space between events, in my mind they flood together. I can still smell the rain as I watched them lower Keith Garrison's body into the ground. Detective Everts shot him to save my life, but I needed to see it—and feel it—just to make sure. As I hid, covered by the trees, I watched Irving Garrison shed no tears while the casket was lowered. A Latino woman who I didn't care to identify was by his side. Closure was grand, but I felt there was always more to the story, so I kept digging.

You won't believe how much you can truly find out about a person if you spend a little bit of time online. Forget the social media crap. I'm talking about programs that search your name, your contacts, your investments. Everything you do online, I learned, is ripe for the picking if you know where to look for it. With the help of my lead technology expert and Hadley's boyfriend, Logan Pevy, I found the pot of gold.

The older Garrison always had his hands in dirty dealings. Drugs, murder for hire, human trafficking—he did it all. Always one hand in the cookie jar but out just before Mom catches him stealing one before dinner. He's a sly, smarmy, and vile man who puts power above everything else. My mother always said money can corrupt people, but absolute power corrupts absolutely. Garrison is as corrupt as they come, but like any other high-powered man, nothing sticks to him.

That's the worst part of this job, the knowing. Seeing this man free, knowing he is in control with expendable masses below him. You give him a few people in horrible situations with no way out and toss a few hundred dollars their way and they'll do anything. Worse yet, give him a person with that *itch* to murder and you have a scary tandem. That person has no remorse, no feelings, no connections. Everything in their life—bodily functions, intimacy, conversation—it's all a means to an end.

Harry Brandt was one of Garrison's "friends." He was good, but Logan was better, and we beat Harry at his own game. It came at a significant cost. A lot of things in this life do. I wasn't adept at the game being played. It was new to me, in an area where I was weak, but not anymore. Now I know what to expect. Now I'm playing their game. How do you go after a rat? You can poison it and hope it dies. Or you can go in with fire and force it out of its hole.

Logan and I released everything we could find online—real or circumstantial—for the drama-hungry population, trying to flush out our rat.

It only took a few weeks. Social media picked it up first. Some snippets here, then more posts there, but then it became political. Garrison was a well-known political force who donated heavily. His money was invested in candidates who supported his businesses, like all powerful donors. Most were bought with funds but others satiated with physical or illegal desires. Conservatives took to the airwaves, demanding this homegrown millionaire be given a fair trial in the courts and not in the public forum. "Only God can judge," they threw out more than once. Liberals screamed Irving was the face of tyranny and abuse in a Republican-based government. Independents just turned their nose up at both and said if he's guilty, he'll pay. Until the public became involved, the airwaves were quiet. Now, after the "it's online so it must be true" syndrome has taken place, the screaming makes me smile sadistically. The rat is out of his hole.

As I watched my work unfold like a bad remake of a cult classic film, the nagging voice in the back of my head warned me to be careful. I know Garrison's reach is extensive. I know Judge Rufus Killian is in his back pocket. His proclivity toward Garrison's young male trade was as clear as day. We couldn't prove it with evidence, but who needs that anymore? Not when we have the online population. If it's online, it must be true. Take a look at anything trending today and you'll see that's the case.

I watch Logan drink his coffee across from me, the worry plain on his face. He tries to stay strong, but the fear of retribution weighs on him. I wonder if our actions will bring unexpected consequences, but part of me doesn't care.

The rat is exposed, and this time I plan on killing it.

Chapter One

If anything can brighten up my day, wake me from a sound sleep or make the sun shine a little bit brighter, it's coffee. If Frankie could hear my thoughts, she would have one eyebrow raised and a smirk on her lips. I can't help it. Sure, Frankie and Chase make my day every day, but they can't change my moods all the time. Frankie's the same with food. Put her in front of some really good food, and I swear her face lights up brighter than the sun. Give Chase a free weekend with a new video game, a full day at lacrosse practice, or a no-rules day and he lights up like a Christmas tree. The point is, we all love each other, but there are some things that just make each of us a bit happier.

Getting out of a warm bed though, not so much. The bruises on my body from apprehending Harry Brandt might have healed, but the deeper wounds remain. The mental scars shake me when I'm sleeping. The hallway straight out of a horror film still finds me, although some nights I can push them away. I don't have a physical space to divert the negative energy anymore. Frankie saw to that when she ripped apart my basement hideaway. It's now Chase's sports gear storage room. My nightmares simply persist.

"Aunt Jazz?" I hear Chase calling from the kitchen. Their voices were quieter before. They must have thought I was still sleeping. I wish. I slide my feet to the floor and feel the cold wood against my skin.

No dreams linger in my mind. The smell of fresh brewing coffee slides effortlessly into my sinuses and the left corner of my mouth lifts instinctively into a slight smile. Like I said, it's the little things.

Dragging my old, tired body into the kitchen, I see Frankie sitting with a mug in front of her, her glasses perched at the tip of her nose, wavy blond hair cascading over her left arm as her perfectly polished nails hold a piece of paper closer to her face. Her dark gray suit contrasts beautifully with her naturally tan skin. Slight wrinkles in her forehead add to the look of confusion etched on her face.

Chase sits in his normal jeans and a name-brand T-shirt next to Frankie. He's grown up so much in these last few years. I wish his parents were here to see him now. I force myself out of my reverie to clear my throat, announcing my presence.

"About time!" Chase looks up at me. "Aunt Frankie made a fresh pot for you so you could help me."

"The whole pot, just for me," I say sarcastically.

"Trust me, you'll need it." Frankie gestures toward the papers. "I'm considering adding some whiskey to mine."

I give her a sideways glance as she looks back down at the papers in front of her. She holds her mug in her right hand, and rubs her temple with her left hand. If Frankie looks this lost, whatever those papers say can't be good. I pour my coffee, put my normal dash of milk in it, take a deep whiff of the intoxicating smell, and turn to the table. Time to face the music. I take a sip of my beautiful morning ritual and my mouth puckers instantly—it's weak, a different brand, and possibly decaf. I look up at Frankie, who simply smiles smugly in return.

"You've been cutting back a lot. Now we go with none," she says.

"Okay, so I'm here." I sit down, looking at the papers filled with random numbers. "What the hell is all of this?"

"Math homework."

"The bus will be here in a little bit and you haven't finished your homework?"

"Jasmine, we were up pretty late trying to figure it out. It was a parental decision that he needed sleep." Frankie's voice and facial expression remind me there is no room for discussion. She was here while I worked on some mindless but necessary paperwork. I have no right to criticize.

"Point taken." She smiles at me and turns her attention back to Chase. "So, what's wrong with the math homework?"

"I don't get it."

"Well, if it involves Tom or Billy taking two different trains but one leaves earlier than the other and they travel at different speeds, don't worry about it. It won't matter when you're older."

"Jasmine!" Frankie glares at me above her glasses.

"What? It's the truth. It doesn't matter when Billy or Tom get to where ever they're going. We're all slaves to the system and the time schedules, so they'll get there when they get there. You have to plan ahead to ensure you're on time."

"You're silly, Aunt Jazz." Chase laughs. Frankie's face appears calmer as she watches him enjoy breakfast with the only family he's known.

"Your Aunt Jasmine needs to let her anger at getting the answer wrong go." She stares right at me and smiles. Damn her and that smile; it always prevents words from actually forming in my brain. Between her and that kid, I swear this part of my life is not my own. I love it.

"Okay, kiddo, hit me."

"Answer this problem. What is sixty-two plus twenty-six?"

"That's what has you hung up?"

Chase nods simply.

"Okay." I grab a pencil off the table and write the numbers on the page. "First you add the two plus the six. That equals what?"

Chase looks at his hands and starts to count. Frankie stops him, gently putting his hands back on the table.

"This is simple math; you can do it in your head."

I watch Chase bounce his head up and down, counting each number. "Eight," he says proudly.

"That's right; it's eight. Now what is six plus two?"

He bounces his head again before answering. "Wait, it's eight again."

"That's right. So, your answer is what?"

"Eighty-eight."

"Right. See? It's easy when you think about it."

"But that's not how Ms. Mills does it."

"How does she do it?" I look over to Frankie, waiting for an answer.

"You take away the extra numbers from the main numbers. Then you add the extras together and then the first numbers. Then you add them both together."

I look at Chase, confused, and he slaps his hand over his eyes.

"Say what?" My voice sounds like an exaggerated cartoon character.

"Forget it, Aunt Jazz. I'll just get half the points for not explaining my work."

"What's there to explain? It's adding numbers together, not rocket science."

The bus honks outside, and Chase rushes to put his papers in the solid black backpack. He kisses Frankie on the cheek and then hugs me.

"Don't worry, Aunt Jazz. If Frankie didn't understand, I should have known you wouldn't either."

He looks at me pitifully before patting me on the head like a puppy and running out the door.

"Have a good day," Frankie yells after him.

"What did I miss here?"

"Common Core math isn't the math of our childhood."

"What the fuck is that bullshit? It's six plus fucking two. Seriously, kids have more shit to worry about than removing integers then adding by subtraction. It's just six plus fucking two!"

"Tell me how you really feel?" Frankie smiles as she finishes her cup of coffee. My cell phone chirps on the counter. I stand to get it.

"How can I help him if this makes no sense to me?" Frankie shrugs as I grab my phone. "Steele," I say, a little more irritated than I intend.

"I'm sorry to bother you so early in the morning detective," I hear Captain Tyler say.

"Sir, sorry. I was just . . ." *Bitching about the inability of this country to teach math properly*, I finish in my head.

"I don't care, Steele. I need to speak to you in my office."

"Yes, sir. When?"

"Now."

I disconnect the call as the nerves cause acid to roll around in my stomach. Does he know of Logan's side project? Frankie destroyed my basement, but we recreated it digitally. We have a map of everything. All from my memory. Does he know we released the information to cyberspace? This is why secrets never last. They always find a way out of the shadows at the wrong time. Being conscious about who knows what always eats you alive. That and somehow you always manage to let someone down. Like the old saying goes: three people can keep a secret if two are dead.

"Someone better get to work before their boss rips them a new one for being late. You know, with schedules and stuff." Frankie smiles at me with her lighthearted humor.

"You'll be home later?"

"Normal business hours for me. Chase said he was going to try and teach me one of his shooting games tonight. Something about a zombie apocalypse and needing bait." She shakes her head with a slight laugh.

That woman has no idea how much I love her, truly love her. That laugh makes everything go away for a few fleeting moments. I trust her with my life, but if the captain is calling me for this whole Garrison fiasco, I need to finish it. I also can't lose her, but self-actualizing prophecies are my specialty.

***

It's interesting how many people stare at you when you are in deep shit. Like when your siblings know you're in trouble with Mom, so they make subtle noises, point, and stare as you walk toward your punishment. I can see the expressions on the officers around me as I weave through the desks toward the captain's office. They think my eyes looking straight ahead means I don't see them, but I feel them looking at me. Sad really. This is our future: untrained wannabes who will cower to anyone because they would rather not end up on the news. They don't want to be educated or trained. They want the power and the paycheck.

I want justice for the victims. To speak for those who no longer can. This new crop of desk jockeys don't understand that. They see benefits, pensions, and power. I wish they were more like Will and me. We're a dying breed, figuratively and literally. Half of those I graduated with have moved on, moved up, retired early, or lost the good fight. This life can break anyone if it wants to.

I take a deep breath and open the door to face my captain. I don't know what information he has, but I'm sure it will lead to some kind of suspension. As long as it lands solely on me and not Logan. It wouldn't be fair otherwise.

"Jasmine, please sit down," Captain Tyler says calmly. He's lost all his hair over the last year, but his brown eyes can still read your soul from a mile away. Maybe it's the dad bod he's developed since becoming the head of this department, or just his personality. Either way, he hasn't been on the street since I was a rookie detective. At least he shaves his head now instead of that bad comb-over from years ago when we first started going after Garrison.

I sit quietly as I watch him push papers around on his desk. To the outside world it might look like he's working. Hell, he might actually *be* working, but the piles look disorganized and overwhelmingly high.

"I called you in to speak to you about the Garrison case."

Hear that sound of something whistling as it crashes to the ground behind me? That's the other shoe.

"Are you aware of the media speculation about Mr. Garrison's underground dealings?"

"I am."

"And are you aware that some of this information was deemed classified at given points in time?"

"I was not aware of that, no."

Captain Tyler puts down the papers in his hand and stares at me. I know he can see through my lies. He's been around me too long not to see the truth. Like a well-staged crime scene, though, I can be an Oscar-worthy actor. I'm not going to make it easy on him.

"Well, it has opened up a much larger, shall we say, *emphasis*, into various cold cases."

Cold cases? The information released online was mostly financial in nature. Anything else was purely circumstantial. So, how could this have become a cold case issue without concrete evidence?

"The FBI and others have been digging deep into the financials of Mr. Garrison and his companies. In the meantime, the police chief spoke to Judge Killian about his connections, and they want us to dig through similar cases for the past twenty years. See if there's some sort of connection or history we missed."

"Judge Rufus Killian." The man who likes tiny humans who are incapable of consenting. Like I said, smoke screen.

"Yes, is there a problem?"

"No." Damn right there is.

"I've got all the new recruits looking through prior cold cases."

"Then why do you have these on your desk?"

"These cases are specific. These I know are related."

I immediately know what he means. These are the more recent cases. The ones that might have mentioned a connection to a holding company, a person who worked for one, or even a direct connection to Garrison. That means my brother's file is in that stack.

"And you need me to do what, exactly?"

He leans back in his chair and stares at me. I know that look. He wants me to stay out of it. He always wants me to avoid it, but it never happens. Some call it irony. I call it karma. The more I want justice, the more it feels like vengeance. The more it feels like vengeance, the more it feels like the inevitable. And when it feels like the inevitable, the more I feel like I'm falling down the rabbit hole.

"I need you to stay out of the office until this is concluded," he finally says.

"How am I supposed to do that? Are you suspending me?"

"No, Steele. I want you to work as normal, work your normal cases. I just don't want you in your office or on the main floor."

"And if a case leads me to him?"

Tyler folds his arms and looks up to the ceiling, his breath solid and steady. I wish I knew what he is thinking. In one motion, he could remove me from all cases. He could transfer me or take away any case that even hints at being connected to Garrison. I need to finish this like a junkie needs drugs to stay out of withdrawal.

"Jasmine, I'm not a fool. I know you need to see this through more than anyone else. I also know we have to do this by the book. There can't even be the slightest hint of impropriety."

He leans forward and stares right at me. His eyes tell me everything I need to know. I've got free rein.

"They all know. If it's something related to Garrison, you're the detective they call. I'm trusting you and Detective Everts won't make me regret my decision?"

"Of course not, sir."

"Good." He pauses, grabs a file off his desk, and tosses it to me. "This call came in this morning. Bodies are in the morgue, but you and Will should check it out."

"A video game store, sir?" I ask, staring at the notes scribbled on the manila lip.

"Suspected as a front for drug trafficking."

"Okay, what does this have to do with Irving Garrison?"

"It's rumored he's a minority owner, but we don't have anything specific. Yet. But the scene has all the signs of a professional cleanup job."

"He's tying up loose ends."

"Possibly, but it could also just be a bunch of fools shooting up the place. One thing we know for sure is the manager and assistant store manager are dead."

"Garrison's not a hands-on kind of guy," I say as I scan the first page of the file.

"Which is why you are going to look into it."

I nod, stand, and leave the office. I hit Will's number on my cell phone and send him a quick text with the location. Nothing more. My mind is still reeling from what the captain told me. I have to do it by the book, but I get to finish this. I get to hunt down this vermin and end his free rein of tyranny. Power is intoxicating.

***

Looking at the address, I know I've been in this store before. Every time some new game comes out I know Chase will want, I am here in line with all the other parents at Gamer Syndicate. Nothing seems out of place. No direct evidence of a crime except for the police cars, uniformed officers outside, and detectives wandering around. I wonder if the kids watching outside know this is reality or if they're just annoyed we've closed down their hangout.

"Detective, fancy meeting you here," Will says as he falls into step with me.

"I did send you a text," I deadpan.

"Sarcasm, learn it," he shoots back at me with a smirk before walking into the back room.

"Smart ass," I say to no one as I follow him.

The front of the store might have been void of any evidence, but the back room is rife with it. The smell of death when you enter is overwhelming. I stumble a bit as the odor wafts over me. I don't know what's worse, the smell of drying blood or the decomposition of a body.

"Some smell." Will rubs his nose a bit as if that'll make the smell disperse. "Still better than a dead camel in the hot desert sun."

Ignoring his comment, I turn back to the scene in front of us. There's blood everywhere. I'm sure the walls were white as recently as yesterday, but now they're streaked with the sanguine fluid of our two victims.

"Arterial spray," I say out loud, but more to myself than anyone else.

"You've been hanging out with Victor too much."

Will stands next to me staring at the four blood-streaked walls around us.

"Must have been one hell of a fight in here."

"Something doesn't feel right," Will says, looking around the store.

"Well, Victor has the bodies, and we know the crime scene unit took samples of everything under the sun, even if we didn't need it all. That should fill in the gaps."

I walk past Will and carefully avoid stepping in the exposed pools of blood. I'm careful to walk only where the paramedics, crime scene investigators, and others have destroyed the evidence. It's interesting what we obliterate in the name of solving crimes and lives. If scenes stayed intact, imagine how much evidence we might have to go on. We would also, theoretically, have a larger pool of victims. Life is more valuable than crime scene evidence, but sometimes it just pisses me off.

"You, come here." I point to a young officer leaning against the back door.

"Yes, ma'am," he stutters.

"Officer Ramos," I read off his name tag.

"Yes, ma'am." He seems surprised I know his name. I've seen it before; rookies forget they're wearing something announcing who they are. The first step in getting someone to do what you want: call them by their name.

"Were you here all night?"

"Yes, ma'am."

I already knew the answer. It was written all over his face—the bags under his eyes, the shaky hands from too much caffeine to stay awake. His hands fidget with his belt, which appears much larger than his waist. He's greener than most rookies I've ever seen. This could go either way in the helpful department.

"Do you know what happened here?"

"Yes, ma'am." His belt sags on the left side and he pulls it up again.

"Want to tell us?"

Will stifles his laughter, but you have to feel bad for the kid. He's standing with a messed-up belt, and his shoes probably have dried blood on the soles. His uniform shirt is stained with what I can only assume was dinner hours ago. Maybe the bad smell in the back isn't from death but from this rookie losing his lunch.

"My training officer received a call from dispatch around four a.m. The silent alarm was triggered, and we were asked to go investigate. My supervisor said it was normally not a big deal, that this happens a lot. Something about posters falling and triggering the alarms."

He shifts his weight and looks around for his supervising officer, I assume.

"Where is your training officer now?"

"Officer Ali?"

I nod in response. The second thing you learn about people is the nicer you are, the more they offer up information you didn't ask for. Less work for me to do at the station.

"He was bagged and tagged, ma'am."

"He was shot?" Will cuts in.

"Oh, no, no, I mean . . . well, he was . . ." The rookie stumbles over his words.

"Officer Ramos, just take a breath and start over. If Officer Ali wasn't shot, then why isn't he here?"

"He was covered in blood when he slipped and fell into the pool of blood on the floor. Crime scene investigators took him back to the lab. Something about his clothes and not losing anything viable."

"Okay, so we'll talk to him later. In the meantime, can you focus and tell us the rest?"

"Sure. We showed up. Nothing looked out of the ordinary, but the lights were all on. So, we called dispatch to let them know. They called the security company. Next thing, some kid with a key shows up and opens the door to let us in."

"Does this kid have a name?"

Ramos pulls out a small notebook and frantically flips through it. I know we are supposed to have patience when dealing with newbies, but right now I am running out of it.

"Tucker Winslow, nineteen, student at the local city college. He said his bosses always worked late, so he never expected a call from the security company."

"Where is Mr. Winslow now?"

"He was taken to the hospital for possible shock."

"Okay, you get on your phone to Officer Ali and Mr. Winslow and tell them both they are not to speak to anyone or post online before speaking to Detective Everts or Detective Steele. Understand?"

"Online, ma'am?"

"Yes, no social media, emails, blogging, or whatever else people are doing now. You tell Winslow to sit and watch the nurses walk by. Anything else and I will hold you responsible."

"Yes, ma'am." Ramos grabs his belt as he rushes off to make the calls.

"You have to be so tough on him?" Will asks me casually.

"He started to annoy me," I shoot back at him as I follow the blood spray on the left wall.

"What doesn't?"

"Funny old man." I hold my hand up and motion to the spray patterns on the wall. "That doesn't look right."

"What doesn't?"

"The blood pattern. How can it go in two different directions along the wall and still be from one person?"

Looking at the floor, you can barely make out where the victims' bodies were. Both next to one another, as if they were sleeping in bed. Yet, the patterns on the wall show a crisscross pattern. There's also an empty area on the wall with no second stream of blood. Okay, I am either watching way too much crime drama television or hanging out with Victor too much. That man needs to move out of my house.

"I'm not sure what you're thinking, but you look like you ate a bad burrito."

"My brain just got all scientific and less detective for a second. Scared me."

"Victor needs to move out."

I shoot him a no shit look, effectively bringing the conversation back to the crime at hand.

"The spray lines are in two different directions. There's a gap in the second line. What does that scream to you?" I ask.

"There was someone back here with victim one before victim two walked in on them. The bodies were placed on the floor. Nothing original."

I look around the room; if you remove the blood, it looks like an everyday backroom. Extra games, rubber banded and stacked on the shelves. Systems stacked neatly on the floor. A television sits on a box that controls the cameras in the location. Both are turned off. The safe sits under the desk, wide open and still full of cash.

"Too many questions."

"Like why the cameras were turned off?"

"Why come to a game store at night? Why let someone into the backroom after hours? Why is the safe still full of cash?"

"We won't know until the district manager does an inventory to see if there was something else stolen," Will says.

"You come to a store, maybe take a system or two, but you don't steal the easy cash in the wide-open safe?"

"Someone who knows how to kill quickly, stages the bodies, and exits without a trace wouldn't care about the cash."

"So, what the hell else was going on in this back room and who wanted them dead?"

This stinks of a cleanup. You know when they are closing ranks. Professionals take care of the extraneous variables. Anyone who can talk is killed. Papers burned. No evidence left behind.

"You smell that?" Will suddenly asks.

"I'm trying not to," I answer.

There are many faces a Marine has. There's the "I-know-what-I'm-doing-so-shut-up" face. Then there's the "I-can-kill-you-with-one-finger-while-blindfolded-and-my-other-hand-held-behind-my-back" face. The one I fear most is the "get-the-fuck-out-of-this-place-now" face. That's the one Will has right now.

"Everyone out! Now!" Will shouts and starts running.

Without saying another word, Will pushes me out of the back room. His voice continues shouting over the noises outside. People fleeing, rushing out of the room, things falling off the walls, chaos. The sun hits my face, and as Will pushes me to the ground behind his car, my knees scrape against the asphalt.

The heat and pressure of the explosion hits us first, then the sound. It's loud enough to wake the dead. The ringing in my ears dulls the sound of the car alarms and first responder vehicles in the distance. Standing up, the dust settles around me as I survey the devastation. Officers are rolling on their backs, their mouths open, screaming. Looking toward where the front door used to be, I see Ramos's body attached to the cruiser, impaled by flying debris, his head slumped, his shirt soaked red. He never stood a chance.

Whoever did this wanted to ensure there was no evidence left behind. It didn't matter how many innocent lives would be lost in the process. Officer Ramos, with his too-big belt, was nothing more than an extraneous variable. That's the difference between being human and a monster. To an actual human, a life is never considered extraneous.

Chapter Two

Mandatory checkup is what the other officers told me. Make sure Will and I were okay. The blood on my clothes wasn't mine. I know that, but try explaining it to the EMTs who showed up on scene. I told them I tried to help the wounded and that is how the blood got there. Problem with explosions isn't only the casualties; it's the side effects, such as this sound pulsing in my ears.

I normally have excellent hearing. My mother always told me I had selective hearing. She and Frankie used to laugh about my dog-like ability. The two of them even conned me into having a hearing test to prove their point. Turns out it was above normal; I just liked to tune things out. After that, I couldn't get away with ignoring whatever those two ladies would ask me, say about me, and what not.

Unlike now. The dull ringing is annoying, and the voices around me sound like they're underwater. The doctor's talking to the nurse in front of me, but he sounds like he's whispering. If he would just turn around to face me, I'm sure his words would be crystal clear. I can make it all out, but I have to lean forward. It's getting on my nerves.

"Where's Tucker Winslow?" I say probably a little louder than I intend to. Blame the ears.

"Detective . . ." The doctor looks at me with that stern medical face. You know . . . the one that says rest is in your future and not to get too hyper. I didn't listen when I was a kid after knee surgery, and I see no reason to start now.

"Don't give me the you're-in-no-condition bullshit. I've been through worse. I just want to talk to the witness." My voice bounces off the walls, garnering the attention of those loitering in the hallway.

"With all due respect, detective . . ." He holds his hand out in front of him, gesturing to the floor.

"Which means you have none for me. Look, I get it; you see a bad ass detective come in here with some minor ear injury. Then you open up the file on that fancy tablet gadget, and you see a jacket big enough to make a porn star blush. I know you want to be cautious, but trust me, it isn't going to happen. So, just sign some piece of paper that says I can go on my merry way. Then tell me Tucker Winslow's room number, please," I whisper, or at least I think I do.

The curtain to the right of me is pulled back, and Will stands there in all his gowned glory. It takes everything I have not to laugh at the very fit Marine in a rather small gown.

"Make that two of us, doc."

"Detective Everts . . ."

"Like she said, we've been through worse."

The doctor mumbles something incoherently to himself as he storms off. Reminds me of Chase when I tell him Fruit Loops cannot be considered a food group. I turn my attention back to Will just as he bends down to pick up the bag under his gurney, his boxer briefs on full display.

"Dude, there are some things a person can't unsee!" I say, covering my eyes.

He stands, embarrassed, and I slide off the gurney to stand next to him. Grabbing the bag, I shove it into his hands.

"How come they didn't put you in one of these paper things?" he asks.

"I had female nurses working on me," I say calmly.

"So did I." He stops, and I can hear the gears moving. "Oh."

I laugh at him as he fumbles with his pants. We've become so comfortable around one another, we don't care. It also helps that he is happily married and I don't like his plumbing.

"I don't care what your rules are! I have power of attorney, and I want to see my girlfriend NOW!"

I know that voice. It's a bit scary when she uses it on me in an argument. That's when you stop being an ass and listen, or at least that is what it means to me.

"Looks like I'll be interviewing Winslow alone." Will cracks a sly smile. He knows as well as I do that I'm not going anywhere anytime soon.

"Where's your wife? Why didn't she get a call?" I throw back at him. If he figured out a way to avoid the calls from the hospital, I need to know.

"I have a police scanner in my office, Jasmine," Frankie deadpans. I forgot about that. Talk about a gift biting me in the ass.

"You know, when I bought you that thing, it was to make you feel better about my job."

"Oh sure, hearing about an explosion, officers down, calling the captain to find out where you were . . . right, that calms my nerves so much!" She continues to move her arms about like she's translating her words into some foreign language.

"On that note, I will go find out what room Winslow is in." Will looks at me apologetically, but leaves anyway. I'll get him back for this.

"Baby, I'm fine. Just a little ringing in the ears."

"A little?" she says staring right at me. She's trying to tell if I'm lying. I learned a long time ago, you cannot and should not try to lie to someone who is trained to see through bullshit. It's how I learned to say nothing at all about certain things, like Irving Garrison.

"Yes, a little. It's a dull ringing. More annoying than anything else."

"Let's go home. You need to rest." She pulls me toward the nurse's station; I assume to fill out the discharge papers.

"Frankie, I know you mean well, but an officer was killed."

She stops moving, and her gaze fall to the floor. I know what she's thinking, what she feels. She almost lost me. She knows some family is being given the worst news of their lives. Her hand leaves my forearm, and she turns to face me, her eyes filled with unshed tears, her face impassive as she fights to keep her emotions in check.

"I don't like this at all." She pauses, taking a breath or two. "Just promise me you'll be careful. If the ringing gets really bad, please come home. I don't . . . I can't . . ."

A tear breaks free and falls down her reddened cheek. Using my thumb, I wipe it away. I forget how much my life . . . my determination and drive can affect someone so much. In times like these when words are useless. Only actions can heal deep wounds. Kissing me gently, she pulls me into her tightly. I can feel all her fear rolling down her arms and into my flesh. There's an understanding, a feeling, and it's purely magical. Pulling away from her, I look into her eyes and give her a slight smile. She knows I'll do my best to be safe, but not everything is in my control.

"I love you," Frankie says.

"The feeling's mutual."

Will interrupts our moment. "Excuse me. Winslow is in room 302."

I nod and look at Frankie. She lets go of me and hugs Will gently before walking away.

"She okay?"

"Is your wife okay when she knows you've been hurt?"

"That depends. Did I get a chance to mow the lawn or shovel the snow before I got hurt?"

"If Frankie was here, you know she'd smack you, right?"

"Yup."

"I'm just going to say you're an ass and let's go."

Will gestures like a knight leading his royal charges. The more time passes, the more he becomes a brother to me. Like my older brother used to do, Will manages to keep me in line and beat up the bullies when I'm on the losing end. Either way, knowing he's by my side on these cases has helped me keep a somewhat level head.

Walking up to room 302, I see a heavyset older male pacing back and forth. His voice is lower than I can make out right now, but he's obviously having a hell of an animated phone call. He stops when he sees us, hangs up the phone, and holds his hands up to stop us.

"Detective Steele and Detective Everts," I say as I point to Will and myself.

"Jason Miles, District Manager, Gamer Syndicate." He weakly shakes both our hands. I already know by his demeanor he's going to stall.

"We just need to speak to Mr. Winslow and get his statement."

"That's not possible right now. Mr. Winslow was at work when this unfortunate incident occurred. The company wants to ensure that all of Mr. Winslow's rights are protected. Since he is shaken up and under a doctor's care, the company feels that it would be best if our lawyer accompanies Tucker when he is interviewed."

"Tucker Winslow is not a suspect, Mr. Miles. We just wish to know what happened which resulted in the murder of two of your employees."

"Yes, well." He pushes his glasses up the bridge of his nose with shaky hands. "He is still in no condition to speak at this time. When the doctors say he can be released, we will take him to the precinct."

Will hands him his card. "Call that extension at the Forty-Second Precinct; they'll make sure we get to see you quickly with little fanfare. Ask for Detective Steele, myself, or Captain Udall."

Will turns and walks away with me hot on his heels. He's angry at the stonewalling tactics. You can tell by his bicep muscles flexed and pushing against his sleeves. Classic Will. He pushes the elevator button a little harder than necessary.

"Victor might have something by now," I say calmly.

"Yup."

"You knew they were going to protect their assets before the humans who work for them."

"Yup."

"Seriously, Will, what do you expect from a greed driven society that values a game filled with killing cops, going to strip clubs, and being the underbelly of society over the damage it does to the kid's mental state by playing it?"

"Frankie's rubbing off on you." Will finally smiles.

"Chase wants that damn game. All his friends have it, and we refuse to buy it. Caused a bit of a temper tantrum."

"You can't help what other parents do. Only yourself. I'll talk to him, if you'd like."

"He would probably listen to you more than us. We're the evil parental units."

The elevator dings and I follow him inside.

"Your car here?"

"Nope."

"How are we getting to Victor's lab?"

"Borrowing a probie's cruiser."

Ah yes, finding the one probation officer who leaves the keys in the car. Training at its finest. Not to mention it really is one of the best pranks one can pull. Especially when Will goes all Marine drill instructor, reprimanding-the-good-soldier sounding. I guess we all have to find the small things about the job that keep you human.

***

Victor's lab looks the worse for wear as Will and I walk through the doors to talk to the lovely doctor. His face is stuck to a microscope, his hair a mess, and his right hand shakes slightly. Will looks around and points to the table in the corner littered with energy drinks. I can understand his need to move fast. An explosion in the city and everyone screams terrorist attack. One has to work twice as fast to disprove it in order to calm a city that is more vulnerable than most places.

"You two going to come in or stare at my lovely art with empty cans?"

"You've had too many, Victor," Will says calmly as we walk further into the room. I've seen Victor like this before during his divorce. I've learned to back up and just catch him when needed.

"Busy day, detective." He pulls his gaze away from the slide and turns to face us both. He walks over to Will first, looks him over, and nods. Then he turns to me, stops, and stares. He tilts my head to the right with his hand. Finally, he pulls me into a tight hug.

"You promised you'd never do that again."

"Didn't die, just got blown up," I struggle to say as his hug prevents me from breathing.

"Anything on the victims?"

Victor lets me go and spins back around to his slide. He pulls out two file folders and slams them next to the microscope.

"First, you're dealing with a professional, or at least someone who has done this before."

Victor walks over to the first white sheet which covers a body. He pulls it back, showing the pale face of the female victim. The perfectly sliced throat exposes the esophagus and muscle tissue, the skin stained where blood dripped and dried. My stomach rolls, but I force it to settle.

"Fingerprints and dental records confirm the female victim is Tasha Fisher. Age twenty, Caucasian, approximately five feet six inches tall, weight one forty."

"Time of death?"

"The heat was on high so, compounded with the humidity outside, the back room was over one hundred degrees. So, truthfully, I can only make a guess at the true time of death. Somewhere between midnight and three in the morning."

"Killer wanted to make it more difficult." Will slides his hands in his pockets, frustration showing on his face.

"Yes, but there are a few things the assailant could not cover up." Victor takes a pen and places it along Fisher's neck. "The assailant was left-handed. The knife was stabbed into the neck on the right side, then dragged along, slicing shallower as they went across."

Looking over the woman, I have to wonder what happened in her life for her to end up here. Was her life so poor outside of work that she somehow got involved with a bad situation? Was she just at the wrong place at the wrong time? There are so many questions running through my head, and I know most of them will never be answered. My hands curl into fists on the table as I stare at this victim, taken long before her time. My disgust rises with the migraine in my head.

I get attacked a lot for being a cop. I get attacked for being gay. I get attacked for just being in the wrong place at the wrong time. I remember during one case, a perps' family asked me if I had a habit of profiling assailants. We've all got stereotypes for various cases. I'd be lying if I said I didn't. The difference is I don't care what color, religion, or orientation a murder is. Someone's life is over because you decided it was time. For that, I don't give a shit who you are. You deserve to be punished.

This girl's family deserves to know what happened. No matter why she was in that situation, no one deserves to see this. Her neck has been stitched, but I guarantee you no makeup will cover it. When they come to claim the body, no sheet will cover the vicious method of her demise. How can the one who did this not look at this and question who they are supporting?

"There's more." Victor's words bring me back to reality. He pulls back the sheet, revealing the male victim's face, and gently grabs one of his arms. "The bruising on his wrists indicate he was bound."

"She was killed first."

"Yes, it appears he was forced to watch."

"How would you know that, doc?" Will asks for the two of us.

"The fact that his right eye was stained with blood. Upon further testing, it was positive for Ms. Fisher's genetic markers. The beating he took also showcases that once Ms. Fisher was disposed of, the assailant went to work on him."

"Who is he, doc?"

"Joe Connors, African American, age twenty-two, approximately six feet tall, weight was about two ten."

"Cause of death?"

"Well, Jasmine, I can tell you the person who killed him wasn't very creative. The angle is exactly the same but shallower." Victor points to the neck wound.

"Okay, the girl I can understand. Maybe the perp gets behind her, slices her throat, and her body goes to the floor. How do you get the exact same angle on someone who is tied to a chair?"

"That's the interesting part." Victor grabs his laptop, clicks a few buttons, and turns the screen to face us. "The lateral collateral ligament was cut in both of his knees. The victim was losing blood from his wounds, so he couldn't stand on his own two legs. The assailant holds them up in the proper position and kills them."

"Why not just kill him in the chair?"

"Detective Everts, while I am sure I can speculate to my heart's content, that truly is your job. I just know what the body tells me. The girl was tortured and killed. The male watched and was then tortured and killed. This is a very professional hit."

"Well, doctor, call us if you have anything else." Will storms out of the office

"You have to be that harsh?"

"No, but he can't assume I have all the answers."

"No one was doing that."

"The assholes upstairs are. Apparently, I can't fully run the coroner's office and the crime lab anymore. Something about needing to have more eyes on cases."

"Okay, but Vic, you were never meant to run both to begin with. I know you and Adrian were close, but she died, and you fell into her job. So, the powers that be hired someone new. It's okay."

Victor nods, and I turn to find my partner. Before I get to the door, I feel Victor's hand on my arm pulling me back around to face him.

"Before I forget. I found an odd substance under the female victim's nails. The same substance is on the male's hands as well. I sent it to Doctor Brown in the crime lab. She has both of your numbers and will call if anything comes up."

"Doc Brown? Really?"

"Lillian Brown, yes. Don't make a *Back to the Future* joke. First, you're aging yourself, and secondly, she's heard them all before."

"You made one, didn't you?"

He lets go of my arm and mumbles to himself as I walk out of the room, trying to hide my smile. Will stands with his arms folded, staring at the evil elevator. The door finally opens and he walks inside, quiet. I walk in and stand beside him.

"Victor was just being a pain in the ass."

"I know."

"Then what's going on?"

"Just frustrated."

"This is the job, Will."

"You think I don't know that?" Will raises his voice as he punches the wall. I can see his outburst surprises him a bit, but it doesn't faze me. I've been there before. Hell, I'm still there.

"Maybe you need time off."

"To do what?"

"Spend time with the kids and the wife. Remind yourself why you do this day in and day out."

"I know why I do this job, Jasmine."

"Will, the only thing we have that's good in this life are the families we have at home. Sometimes, it helps getting an extra hour or two with them. We both know why we do this job, but without them . . . we'd lose ourselves to the job."

He relents. "Maybe when this case is done, we'll go away. Not until then."

"Then let's figure it out and go home."

"You know it's never that easy right?"

I nod at him as silence falls between us. It could be a fast case; sometimes things move smoothly. Other times, you get more questions than answers. My gut tells me we aren't going home anytime soon. Only people with something to hide hire professionals. Will knows that. He was one of the best snipers the US government had. From what he's told me, his missions were providing cover for those searching for intel, eliminating hostiles if necessary, and never leaving a trace behind. If this person is as good as Victor thinks, we're going to need more of Will's military training than my detective skills.

***

The tech lab looks like it always does. The monitors on the myriad of desks would give anyone a migraine. There are bouncing lines across a quarter of the screen, some movie image in another quarter, and then two other squares are full of more technical jargon. Either way, it is too damn complex for me. If I could, I would go back to a flip phone. Technology, the never-ending availability that comes with it, and the dark web have made me more paranoid of technology than ever before.

"Hello, detective. The usual hot chocolate?" Logan asks from behind me.

"Hot cocoa?" Will questions as he smiles.

"Sure, thanks." I answer, keeping my eyes focused on Will. Logan walks between us and into the main room. His red Converse sneakers are a distinct contrast to the black carpet as his white laces drag along the floor.

"Are we five?"

"No, Will. Frankie cut me down to one coffee a day," I snap before following Logan's previous path. Trust me, right now I would go for the largest latte the world could make, but I can't. My doc mentions I should cut back a little and Frankie goes into protection mode. I get it, be healthy and all that crap. She wants a long life with me and vice versa. Yet, somehow, I doubt my coffee intake is going to bury me sooner than the fucking assholes who don't signal before changing lanes. Or perhaps the idiots who smoke right in front of every damn doorway that I need to go into. Or maybe the drugs they pump you up with every time snot rolls down your face. Hell, there are plenty of other things that will shorten my life span. Coffee is not one of them as far as I'm concerned. If it is, well then fuck it, we all die sometime.

I huff and fall into one of his comfy chairs, waiting to sip on my noncoffee beverage. I can hear Will walk in behind me, close the door, then take five large steps before dropping into his chair. No coffee means heightened senses, I guess.

"Not doing well without coffee?" Logan asks calmly. I think the look I give him answers his question.

Logan places my cup at the edge of his desk before sitting down with his coffee. I can smell it from my chair. Shit, did I mention heightened senses?

"So, what have you found?" Will starts.

"I wish I could tell you I found out enough to solve your case, but all the cameras were disabled in the store."

"The company swears they were in working order." I grab my drink from the edge of the desk.

"Oh, they were, but the manager turned them off."

"When?" Will asks.

Logan puts his cup down and starts typing on his keypad. I take a sip of the hot cocoa and my tongue tastes the most amazing flavor—coffee. I moan into my cup, and I swear the men blush.

"Good hot cocoa?" Will asks.

Smiling at Logan, who continues to blush while working on his laptop, I answer, "The best ever."

"Okay, so I managed to get the video feed from the stores front entrance, registers, and the back room."

A few clicks of his fingers and the store pops up on his computer screen. There are four blocks, three showing footage and one blank. I assume it was meant for an extension. I'll have to ask the corporate cronies when I see them.

It's an odd perspective to view. I see the two managers walking around the store as if life is normal. To them it was, I guess. I wonder if they ever thought about their lives ending in such a violent way. Were they concerned about where they go after all this living stuff we do? I do. Every fucking day.

The female assistant manager closes the front door. She nods to the manager who appears to be counting out the registers. Tasha walks through the main part of the store, stopping every now and again to fix a box on the wall. Both Joe and Tasha look toward the back room. The two of them get a bit animated before Tasha walks into the back room. She opens the fuse box. She must have flipped a switch, because the cameras were cut off right after.

"Corporate see this?"

"Yeah, everything is downloaded when the registers are closed."

"Did the manager have the registers closed already? It looked like he was counting out while she was in the back." Will voices the same question most people would be thinking. They've never worked retail.

"If the store was slow, you close the backup registers about fifteen to twenty minutes before you actually close. Then, you count out register one, but you don't actually close it. Most people pay credit in stores like this, so you rarely have a cash transaction within those last few minutes. This location closes at nine, so download probably started at nine fifteen or nine twenty."

The two men stare at me and say nothing.

"What? I worked retail for five years. Had to pay off student loans somehow. Besides, my brother had a video game addiction, and I was the one who fed it."

"You worked in a video game store?" Logan asks as if I now walk on water.

"Computer store," I mumble. Logan's face falls, and within a few seconds he starts laughing.

"You? In a computer shop? You barely know what's wrong with your laptop when the battery is dead!" Will chuckles, but one stern look from me and he swallows those noises. Logan looks at my stern face. I must be channeling my mother, because the two of them look like I've caught them red-handed stealing a cookie.

"Well, umm, you know you don't really like 'the Facebook,'" Logan states matter-of-factly.

"True, I don't like anything that sucks the life out of society. After the past few cases, do you really think this social media shit is safe?"

"My daughters have all the new stuff out there. I monitor it all," Will adds calmly.

"You're a Marine. If someone hurt your kids—"

"I'd remove them from the face of the earth faster than they could tweet hashtag help me."

There are moments where words fail you. Imagine, if you will, this grown man with muscles bulging out of his clothing. He reminds you of a wrestler, but with his pinky he could remove your life. He's tougher than any living thing on this planet, yet here he is talking about tweets and hashtags. I don't think I can formulate any reply. Chase would have hugged Will's leg and said he was so cool. Me, I'm told I'm old school. Thank the powers that be I can still kick his ass in first-person shooter games.

Shaking my head free of those thoughts, I stare at Logan, who is still smiling.

"Stop it."

His smile fades to a smaller smirk.

"Sure." He types away at his keyboard. "Hashtag help me. I love it."

"So, the feed goes out and is downloaded to the mainframe. Tasha must have flipped a switch turning off the power to the cameras," Will says.

"Which leads me to believe they let someone in the back door. They knew their killer."

"The question is why and who was it?" Will says.

"There were a few stores across the street; I can see if they have any footage. Not sure of the clarity, but it's better than nothing," Logan adds.

My phone vibrates in my pocket. Pulling it out, I see Chase's smiling face.

"Hey, kiddo. What's up?"

"Aunt Jazz, I was wondering if I could go out Friday night."

"Out where?"

"Just to Paul's house."

Paul: good kid, smart, wears glasses, and has a wicked sense of humor for someone his age. He's one of the few of Chase's friends Frankie and I approve of.

"Time?"

"After school?"

"What will you be doing?"

"You know, the usual."

Red flag. He's getting older now, and I know damn well there is more to it than just the usual. What does that mean anyway? Whenever I said the usual, it meant I was hanging out with people my mother didn't like. Either that or my brother and I were going somewhere my mother wouldn't approve. Like drinking on the beach when Grandpa died. Unless we were in a place that served food or coffee, the usual was never a good thing.

"Try again."

"Auntie, you know we just sit, do homework, and play video games."

"Why play video games next to one another when you complain split screen sucks? I mean that was your argument for an Xbox Live subscription, wasn't it?"

"Umm . . ."

Game. Set. Match.

"Jessica and Lily might be there."

If I was driving, I would have rear-ended the car in front of me. He's mentioning girls? He actively wants to spend time with girls who not so long ago he swore had cooties? Where the hell has time gone?

"Aunt Jazz, can I go? Please?"

"Will Paul's parents be around?"

"I'm eleven; of course they will be. We're just going to watch some movies and stuff. No biggie."

"Not yet eleven, thank you very much. So, Lily or Jessica?"

"Aunt Jazz! I'm hanging up the phone now."

"You're gonna have to spill it eventually!" I hear the beeping sound of a disconnected call, and I put the offending device back in my pocket. Chase is interested in girls. Holy shit. Am I supposed to give him a talk? Oh God, I do not want to give him that talk. My mother hit me with that, the birds and bees. I'll let Frankie do it.

"Doctor Brown just called. She has some information for us," Will says. "You okay?"

"Chase . . . Girls . . . Shit."

"Well, yes, they do grow up eventually."

"How am I supposed to . . . I mean I'm his aunt . . . He's not old enough to date."

"He'll ask about sex eventually," Will taunts.

"So will your girls!" Will's face instantly falls.

He changes the subject. "You'll figure it out. Right now let's talk to the new doc and work on the case at hand."

"I'll need coffee after this." I rub my eyes to get the images out of my head.

"Nope, I'm more afraid of Frankie than you. Sorry."

Walking to the elevator, the only thing running through my mind is a simple one. Growing up fucking sucks.

***

I'm not good with new people. My mother called me a social butterfly, but she never knew it was all nerves. I could talk for hours about growing grass if it meant people would include me and not admonish me. I knew better when I got older. People will make fun of you whether you're talking or not. It still doesn't stop the nervous reaction. Like I said, I don't like dealing with new people.

"Jasmine, you okay?"

"Huh? Yeah, sure." I look up at Will who stands holding one of the large glass doors open. I guess he's waiting for me to go inside, but I'm dreaming again. Ignoring his odd look, I walk inside.

Similar to the tech lab downstairs, the crime lab has an all-glass wall behind the receptionist's desk. People move back and forth like ants in a homegrown farm, some carrying evidence, some looking like they are lost, and others just looking like they don't want to be there. In other words, it looks like every other place in this freaking building.

"Can I help you?" the young receptionist says to me. Her smile reaches her ears and her voice is a chipper tone I'm not accustomed to hearing down here.

"We're looking for Doctor Lillian Brown," Will says.

"Of course. If you'll give me a moment, I will get her for you."

"Can we just go in?" I hear Will's voice echo next to me. I say nothing, my voice trapped in the nerves building in my gut. We've never had to ask permission before.

"Sorry, sir, but the doctor has added new rules. No one in without a member of the lab as an escort."

She picks up the phone and I notice her nails are pretty, neat, and short. They match her hair and her outfit. Perfectly in order. I wonder if she has a slight case of OCD. I'm analyzing again. Not only have my nerves made me become a mute, sweaty mess, but now I am acting like a shrink.

"Detectives, pleasure to meet you."

Turning my attention to the glass doors, I find a statuesque dark-skinned woman standing there. Her black combat boots stick out from beneath her baggier jeans. Everything about her screams comfort. I wonder if her personality matches or if she's going to be a pain in the ass to deal with. If I could stand on the sidelines and study her behavior, I'm sure I'd have an answer in a few days. Sadly, once again I am on the short end of the stick. Time is a luxury when you have dead bodies waiting for justice.

"I appreciate you getting here so quickly. If you'll follow me."

The two of us follow, saying nothing. We pass through a set of locking glass sliding doors, leading to a new lab area filled with evidence and more. The colder temperature forces me to pull my arms to my chest to warm up. Doctor Brown looks at me and nods; I hope it's in understanding and not her sizing me up. Or something like that.

After walking the lab mile, we come across a pair of glass doors with a security panel. It looks minor, almost insignificant, but she stands in front of it for a full minute or two. Then Will and I hear some beeping, and the glass doors open to the sides. I swear I am in a science fiction film without the fantasy, the fan fiction, or the cosplay.

"Come in and have a seat."

Will walks ahead of me and quickly takes a seat. Once I pass the threshold, I jump as the door closes behind me. I turn back toward the door and try to calm the idiotic adrenaline running through my veins. I'm a fucking detective with a gun, not a scared little girl. I can handle this. Doctor Brown clears her throat and I turn to face her. Her perfect makeup, pristine skin, hair meticulous, perfect . . . everything. Plaques with degrees from Columbia University and awards litter the wall behind her. So, she's a doctor. This is my case. I'm in charge. I shake my head slightly, wishing the discord would simply fall out of my ears and away from my brain. This isn't a sandbox in kindergarten. We're not politicians jockeying for votes. This is a murder investigation, and this woman is on my side. She's here to help me. I inhale deeply and exhale all my nerves as I sit in the open chair next to Will.

"You texted Detective Everts earlier?"

"Yes, I wanted to discuss with you something Doctor Hayes found on the victim's hands."

"Doctor Hayes?" Will asks.

"Victor," I fill in for him as I take the seat next to him. When Doctor Brown looks at me quizzically, I answer her unasked question. "We all call him Victor. Only his teachers ever called him Mr. or Doctor Hayes."

"I see, well . . . Victor found a residue on the hands of the female victim as well as a small amount on the nose and hands of the male victim."

"Cocaine?" The obvious answer falls from my mouth.

"Initial tests indicate it was a highly pure version, yes. However, it wasn't found in the female victim's blood stream." She pauses and types on her keyboard with a few clicks. She turns the monitor around to face us. The images flash across the screen in succession, but truthfully, I have no idea what the heck I'm looking at. It looks like a weather pattern from whatever Doppler they use now. Either way, I'm a bit lost.

"Doc, I'm not quite sure what I'm looking at," Will thankfully asks.

"I decided to do a scan of the male victim's brain before Doctor Hay . . . Victor did his full autopsy. He's running tests on the brain to verify my findings. I asked him to keep it quiet until we had some answers."

"But you're showing us these images for a reason, right?" I question. I know I can't be staring at the rainbow connection for fun.

"Yes, detective. The brain scan in conjunction with the residue leads me to believe the male was a cocaine addict. There was significant damage to the brain easily found on these scans. Victor also found damage to the liver, kidneys, and the interior of the nasal cavities."

"He didn't share that information with us," I say a bit harsher than I'd like. I'm not used to having two people sharing bits of information when they see fit. I like getting all of it in one sitting, like potato chips. Once you open that bag, it's over.

"I understand that. We wanted to verify our findings before bringing it to your attention."

"How good?" Will asks, suddenly nervous, his leg bouncing.

"Too good for street quality. Whatever these two had on their skin, it was not for the average user's consumption."

"Elite drugs for elite drug users. The bigger question is how did he get away with being a user, having those serious side effects, and hold a store manager position?"

"I wish I could give you that answer, detective."

My cell phone beeps with a text message. Quickly scanning the information in the message, I stand up and put my phone away.

"Time to get some answers from the company who hired them."

Will stands next to me and extends his hand to Dr. Brown.

"Thank you for your time and information, doctor."

Seeing her facial response to the accolade, I finally see a crack in her appearance; she's insecure about her new job.

"You're very welcome. If I find anything else, I will let you know."

"Much appreciated, doc." I nod before heading out of the office.

"You think they're going to be candid about what happened?" Will asks as we weave through the lab.

"Depends. If the company has something to lose, they'll close ranks to protect the greater good."

"You mean their bottom line."

I smack the elevator button and take a deep breath. I know whoever is with Tucker Winslow, they will not allow him to share anything. He's our best chance to fill in the missing pieces. If he talks, the company could be liable for all the criminal activity, damages, civil litigation, and whatever else lawyers can come up with. My gut tells me this kid isn't going to talk unless we can separate him from the suits.

As I sit in the interrogation room, various questions pop up in my head. Will they cooperate? How much can I push to get an answer should they not want to give me any information? What kind of lawyers am I dealing with? Will let's these ideas just flow out of his mind. He always feels he can only control what he can control, so why let the rest bog you down. I wish I could be like that. I have to analyze the equations, face the situation, and basically obsess about it before the individuals in question come in. He's good like that. More and more he reminds me of Henry.

The door opens with a slight squeak, and I fight the urge to jump up to fix it. A woman in a perfectly tailored suit walks in, stoic, briefcase in her left hand, knuckles white from the pressure of her grip, eyes focused on her cell phone in her right hand as her thumb furiously flies over the screen. Obviously, a lawyer trying to act as if her time is more important than mine. Probably on her social media feed talking about how her life is amazing. She steps to the side, ignoring me and the table in front of her.

Jason Miles walks in after the lawyer, his shoulders slumped, face drawn. He's obviously dealing with some kind of serious pressure. He might be a good weak link to break. Possibly. If he was threatened by the big wigs to keep his mouth shut or lose his job, no force or kindness will get him to open up. I wouldn't blame him either. He might be the breadwinner. I don't know him well enough to judge his decisions; the economy sucks for everyone.

Another skinny, tall man walks in. His black slacks are perfectly pressed, his button-down shirt has the top button open. He walks with an air of confidence, like he's higher on the food chain than poor Jason. He's going to be combative. I can tell by his gait, posture, and the arrogant smile he gives me. Typical out-of-touch corporate goon.

Tucker Winslow walks in, his face pale, hands in his pockets, head down. He looks like hell. Normally I'd say he was probably a good actor, but this feels different. He has this emptiness in his eyes; I'm not sure if it's guilt or a post-traumatic stress response. Part of me feels bad for having to put this kid through an interrogation. Part of me doesn't give a shit. Is that normal? Probably. I'm not a vicious bitch, but this kid is stuck between the right thing to do and a corporation trying to prevent a lawsuit. Bodies be damned. They'll break the lease, get a new building, and act like two people weren't slaughtered under their roof. Tucker Winslow is expendable when it comes to the almighty profit.

Will walks in, closes the creaky metal door, and pulls out a chair next to me. The rest of us follow suit. I guess he's going to play the bad cop right now.

"I'm Detective Everts and this is Detective Steele. I appreciate you all coming in today."

"Ava Hayes. We're here as a courtesy, detective. Mr. Winslow did not witness anything and has nothing to add to the investigation."

Right out of the gate she plays the ignorance card. Like they're helping us just by sitting in the interrogation room sucking up our air. It's easy to see Miles and Winslow both know more than they're letting on by how they fidget in their seats. Based on the lawyer's immediate fight tactic, it's either really serious shit or the lawyer is too new to realize they played the defensive card. Considering the company name, the fact that it's close to the holiday season, and major game releases are coming out soon, I'd say they are trying to distance themselves as quickly as possible. Can't have a double homicide with drug implications when you have a billion-dollar game release in a month or so.

"You play games?" I ask Winslow directly. Ava looks at me quizzically.

"What does this have to do with this case?" she drawls, as if this interview is beneath her.

"Just a simple question. Do you play games, Mr. Winslow?" Hayes looks over at the two other men before focusing on Tucker. She simply nods.

"Yes, ma'am."

"You a first-person shoot kinda player or do you like the third-person perspective games? Or maybe you're a racing game or adventure player?"

"I like the FPS games, but I can play anything really."

"See, my nephew likes the first-person shooters. Likes to feel like he's part of the game, I guess. Me, I'm a third-person kind of gamer. I like to see the whole picture. See who's surrounding my character, see the full playing field on the map. You know what's consistent through both types of games?"

The skinny man leans toward his lawyer, and I feel an objection coming. I really want to laugh, but my mother would smack me for bad behavior.

"Is there a point to this, detective?" Hayes leans back in her seat, and I can feel her impatience with my line of questioning growing.

"You might not notice the consistency if you only play multi-player," I continue, ignoring her.

"I don't understand . . ." She tries to continue her argument, but I cut her off.

"I get it, you don't see what this has to do with anything, but Tucker does. Any person who plays the campaign story of video games understands that the main character, the one who saves the day, they always come clean. Their lies of omission, their silence . . . it comes back to haunt them as their team falls apart. Maybe they lose loyalty from mission members and you get the worst scripted outcome. You don't get the best loot or people hunt you down because you went rogue. Or maybe everyone dies because you kept quiet."

"That's enough!" The skinny man slams his hand on the table, getting my full attention.

"That is enough. I don't know what kind of twisting of words you are trying to do, but Mr. Winslow has assured me he knows nothing that would assist your case," he argues bluntly.

"Mr . . ." Will holds onto the last syllable, trying to get the man to admit who he is.

"Boone, Kelvin Boone." I guess he thinks he was James Bond in a former life, or at least in his dreams.

"Mr. Boone, why are you here?" Will calmly asks. He leans back in his chair. He's getting ready to pounce; you can tell from the way the muscles in his forearms contract and relax before he attacks.

"I'm the regional manager."

"When was the last time you worked a shift in this location?" I ask.

"I visited them a month or two ago."

"For how long?" Will counters.

"An hour or so."

"Tell me, Mr. Boone, do you even know what really goes on in the store? Are you sure you can get the best representation of what is going on after a few hours? A visit that I'm sure they are prepared for days in advance. One where they can easily manipulate everything in the store to make everything look ideal? Sure, the numbers overall don't lie, but theoretically they can easily hide anything they are doing behind your back. Do you know all the employees' names at this location?" Will hits the point home.

"I have twenty stores in this district alone; it's impossible to know everyone's names." Boone leans back in his chair, his posture purely defensive. He looks like a kid on a playground who was picked last because he shot his mouth off too soon.

"So, you couldn't possibly understand what was really going on. In-stead, you've probably spoken to some suit in a high-rise apartment. They told you to squash it quickly, regardless of the dead bodies. Then you probably threatened Mr. Miles' job. Hell, you might have let Tucker here feel like this whole case would fall on him. We're not looking for a fall guy here, Tucker. We're looking for the truth," I say, raising my voice.

"Detective!" the lawyer yells, but I'm so angry I don't listen.

"They're lying to you, Tucker. They'll promise you the world to shut you up, but once this case is closed, you're out. They don't want any negative press attached to their brand. Your name's been in the paper."

"That is enough, detective! I demand you. . ." Ava Hayes slams her hand down on the table for effect. Sadly, it's lost on Will and me.

"Ava Hayes doesn't care about you. She's not here to protect you or Mr. Miles. She's paid by Gamer Syndicate to protect their assets. All that matters is their bottom line. You're an afterthought."

"Detective!" Hayes slams her briefcase on the table as she stands up. The room falls silent. I feel the smile grow across my face as I slowly catch my breath. I know I've broken through. I have no idea which one of them will come forward, but I made my point.

"We're leaving," Hayes huffs as she and Mr. Boone stand up to leave. Miles and Winslow hesitate and look at one another. Will stands up and holds his hands out as if trying to stop a fight.

"Let's just all calm down for one second, okay? We're not here to prosecute your company or throw anyone under the bus. We're just looking for some answers."

"As are we, detective," Boone answers quickly, a tinge of bite in his tone.

"Detective Steele will be leaving this interview room and we will continue discussing things on this matter."

"Excuse me?" I ask, confused by this betrayal.

Will stays silent as he motions to the door. Looking over his shoulder, I see the smug look on Ava Hayes's face, and I feel the bile rise in my throat. I hate corporate greed and the almighty dollar. Enough people have died for bullshit, and this bitch was covering up more of the same. I know he's not trying to be cruel; he's playing the good cop. I showed my hand as the bad guy, and he's filling in the rest. I understand it, but I don't like it.

Slowly, I stand to my full height, my eyes boring holes in Tucker Winslow's. I clench my jaw to prevent saying anything more. Tucker finally averts his gaze to the floor. I turn my back on everyone as I exit the room quietly. I have no choice but to let Will finish up while I sit at my desk. Who am I kidding? I wasn't bred to wait at my desk while others work. Unlike the masses of entitled people, I enjoy earning my paychecks.

Chapter Three

It was a hellish morning, and I slept like crap after yesterday's hours of tests, bodies, and everything else. I woke up to an empty bed. Chase was already off to school and there was a note on the coffee machine: "Decaf Only." Frankie knew I needed sleep and that I would probably cheat. Not like I haven't already.

Walking into my other home away from home, I realize how comfortable I am in a shrink's office. Makes me laugh a bit, considering how much I avoid these places in my daily life. Looking up from her desk, the receptionist holds up one finger, signifying "one moment," and I smile in return. She's new, otherwise I would have been waved through. Normally it would have irritated me, but this time it gives me a few more seconds to clear my head. The commute didn't help; damn traffic made me angrier by the minute.

Looking around the room, I can tell it's newly renovated. The medical facility finally decided to fix the cracks in the walls caused by super-storm Sandy. The worn carpets have been replaced with clean hardwood flooring. The walls are a calming light blue. Frankie will hate it if they've renovated her office. She was quite happy with the way it was.

The receptionist grabs my attention. "May I help you?"

"Hi, I'm here to see Dr. Ryan."

"Do you have an appointment?"

"Umm, no, I usually don't . . ."

Frankie rounds the corner out of the hallway at this moment, the amusement obvious on her face.

"Miriam, this is Detective Jasmine Steele. You can let her through any time. Unless I'm with a patient, of course. I work with her on various cases, consulting with the police department," she says, omitting that she's my girlfriend as well. Have to test the waters before true disclosure is given. You never know the response you'll get.

"I'm sorry, detective. I won't make the same mistake twice."

"It's not a problem. You're just doing your job."

Frankie sweeps her hand toward the hallway to her office as she walks ahead of me. I simply nod to Miriam and head after Frankie. Walking past a few closed doors, I enter Frankie's office and smile. Only the floor has changed. I know she hated the carpet as it showed its age. The new hardwood, with a classic rug in the middle, makes it feel homier. The rest of it just looks like a fresh coat of paint, nothing more. I'm sure all these renovations went on after hours with specific designs for all the offices.

"I told them I'd be most happy if they just fixed the minor damage and gave me a new floor. My office is a sanctuary for many patients who need consistency. The hardwood would have been enough of a shock. I don't need to start all over because the powers that be think they know best," she says, reading my thoughts.

"I understand, but I also think a certain doctor didn't want her place of solitude to be screwed up."

Her smile brightens up my afternoon, and she closes the door behind her. Sliding across the room, she sits on the edge of her desk and eyes me. My brain screams many things daily, but right now it's living in the gutter. If my brother was here, he would smack me upside the head, close my mouth, and tell me I'm being rude. He's not though, so I am openly ogling my girlfriend.

"It's impolite to stare," she says, her voice an octave lower than it was a few seconds ago.

"Yeah, well who can blame me? I have a very beautiful girlfriend."

She smiles at my words, and even though I'm not the Grinch, I swear my heart swells with that look. Every single time.

"I know you didn't just come here to have idle conversation."

I sit down on the couch in her office, not trusting myself to be closer. The leather couch gives perfectly, making me feel instantly safe. I never thought about that before, the feeling of the couch. I can see why her patients prefer it over the stiff businesslike chairs. God, I really hate those things. They kill my back.

"Detective, while I truly love your company, I do have a schedule to adhere to."

"Sorry, I'm just a bit scattered this morning. I needed to see you and maybe pick your brain."

She walks over and sits in her matching leather chair. Crossing her legs, she's the spitting image of professionalism. Her demeanor changes, her face less flirtatious and more business. Again, perfect.

"Go ahead," she says.

"Two dead at Gamer Syndicate. Blood spray, but specific. The victims knew their murderer. It was meticulous, planned, and calculated. As of yet, we have nothing much. Victor found drugs on the victims, the company has closed ranks, and no one is talking. The cameras were off. Logan's working on clips from across the street, but so far nothing."

"Well, first, you're never going to that place or any of its other locations ever again. Second, fire rarely leaves anything behind, Jasmine. You can't expect things to magically appear because you want them to."

"That's just it. It's the lack of evidence that's bothering me. Who has the power to make everything disappear? Better yet, who NEEDS everything to go away? Who is being investigated enough where he has to be careful of where he takes a shit?"

"While your assumption that Garrison is behind this might be correct, do you have anything other than your gut to corroborate your hunches?" Frankie asks.

"Not right now, but you know I'm rarely wrong."

"That may be true, but do you really want to destroy the investigation because of a hunch? If you make one mistake, Garrison might be able to use it in his defense. It only takes one juror, Jasmine. Just one."

She's right. I have to be sure. I can't go into this half-cocked like I did last time. It's time to close the conspiracy door and focus on what I have in front of me. My mind recoils at the very idea, but sometimes to see the full picture, you have to take a step back and focus. Then you see the clearer path to the same destination.

The intercom on her desk buzzes. Frankie walks over and picks up the receiver.

"Yes. Okay, thank you."

She hangs up the receiver and straightens her suit jacket.

"I would love for you to stay and chat, but I have another patient in about five minutes. Why don't you bring home everything you have on the case and we'll go over it tonight?"

"I might be really late, but thank you."

I stand, give her a quick kiss, and head to the door of her office. Opening it, I turn back to her and sign "I love you." It's something we haven't done in a long time. Maybe it's time to take a few steps back in a lot of things.

As I walk back into the precinct, I've got this freshly recharged feeling. I don't have anything new to add to the case. I don't have any hope of finding out something groundbreaking at this moment in time, but I at least have some faith that it will come. I've always said people make mistakes even when they think they're meticulous. Everyone forgets to clean the drain below the screws, but a killer remembers that. That same killer could forget to clean under a victim's fingernails. They might forget they've been bitten, leaving DNA in the victim's mouth.

I remember one of my first cases as a detective. The captain and I solved it based on the DNA of a plant and where it grows. The stab wounds pierced the bicep all the way through, connecting with the ground. When they pulled the knife out, some residue was left in the wound tract. We matched that to the killer's shoes. It blew a hole in his alibi, and then things fell into place. We found and exploited a simple mistake. Whoever it is this time will make one. It's inevitable. No one's perfect.

The officer at the main desk grabs my attention. "Detective?"

"Yeah?"

"Someone on the phone for you. Says it's in reference to your open murder investigation."

"Name?"

"Anonymous tip."

"Transfer it."

I take off down the hall to my office. Normally, I wouldn't run for these types of calls. Most of them end up in dead ends or wild goose chases. Right now, though, I'll take anything that might help me see the trees for the forest. I wave at the captain as I rush past him and into my office to answer the already ringing phone. Taking a deep breath, I pick up the phone and sit down.

"Detective Steele, how can I help you?"

"I saw what happened the other night at the store," a woman on the other end offers. Her voice is calm and even.

I grab the nearest pen and notebook. If this caller is telling the truth, she might give me some piece of information that could help. I have to calm down though; for all I know she's just going to rehash everything the news media spewed out already.

"Okay, why don't you tell me everything."

"Alright. The assailant entered the store from the back door. They had a black baseball cap on."

"Anything on that hat?"

"No, ma'am. Just a hat."

"Male or female? Can you describe them?"

"I couldn't tell. I would say they were tall, average build, darker skin."

"And you saw them enter the store around what time?"

"Around closing time."

"Is there anything else?"

"Yes." Her tone changes with that one simple word. The pause in conversation makes my stomach climb into my throat. This doesn't feel like an ordinary call anymore. I toss my pen at the door, and it clangs against the glass. The captain comes in and looks at me, his questioning gaze going from the pen on the floor to me. I scribble a note with one word— TRACE—and hold it up. He darts out, and I listen to the woman breathing evenly on the other line.

"I'll give you time to start the trace even though it's a waste of time. You'll know where I am soon enough."

Udall steps into the doorway and gives me the okay sign. The trace is on. I nod and turn my attention back to the woman on the line. The captain walks in and stands in front of my desk.

"Who is this?"

"Right away with the big questions? No, no. I never play games by authorities' rules."

"I'm not playing any game."

I hear her laughter through the phone, and it chills me to the bone. There's a distinct threat in her register that I don't want to hear again. Ever.

"You're already playing, dear."

"You must be mistaken."

"Really? Are you truly sure of that?"

"Yes, I'm sure. You should know someone tried to force me into their game. He lost," I answer coldly.

"Ah, well, I would beg to differ. Keith Garrison was a novice and yet he made you follow him around as he saw fit. He converted your fellow officer and almost managed to kill you. You would be dead if not for your partner."

My head hurts. She's right; I did play into Garrison's hands. It was the wrong decision for the right reasons. Either way, if you look at the facts, I did play by someone else's rules.

"What do you want?"

"I'm tired of you."

"And this means what to me?"

"You're asking me? You're not a novice at this, detective. We've been here before. You can walk away and let this be. You can keep plugging away like a good soldier and suffer. The question remains: What does it mean to you?"

The color must have drained from my face because I feel the captain's hand covering my clenched one. I have no way to protect them from someone I can't see. The fucking tree and the stupid forest. I scrawl two question marks behind the word TRACE and the captain nods and bolts out of the room. I have a feeling this call is pinging all over the city. She's doesn't strike me as stupid.

"Excuse me, ma'am?" I can faintly hear a younger voice in the background.

"Yes?" Her cheery and hopeful voice returns as she answers.

"You dropped your hat."

The voice is much clearer now, and I feel the blood rushing to my face as my heartbeat starts to race.

"Why, thank you so much, young man."

"Chase, come on!" I hear some other kid yell over the phone.

"I'm coming! Have a great day, ma'am."

"You too."

The captain comes in and shakes his head. I point to Chase's picture on my desk and write *CHASE SCHOOL* in large letters. Before I can do anything else, the captain is out the door again, barking orders. I'm sure she can hear the commotion in the background.

"He's a lovely and polite boy. I have to say you and that woman of yours are doing a wonderful job raising him. Who would have thought two dykes could raise a boy? It's kind of funny if you think about it."

"You stay away from him."

"Or you'll what?"

"Stay away from him." My anger forces my breathing to be shallow, my voice dropping to a threatening level.

"Now you understand. Walk away, detective. Stop digging; tell your little team to let it go. This is so much bigger than you."

There are several things one can say in this situation. Many of them involve threats of removing one's life from this plane of existence. But it's like arguing with a gun activist about protecting society from violence. They don't care about anything you think or do. They only care about themselves. Just like this woman on the phone. She couldn't give a shit what I think. There is literally nothing I can say or do to change that. She wants to do what she wants, when and how she wants it. The best course of action is not to play, but I don't have that option.

"Your silence speaks volumes. I'll be in touch."

The line goes dead. Before I can control my anger, I pick up the phone from my desk and throw it across the room. It smashes against the wall and explodes into many little pieces. I count my breaths, trying to calm myself. Frankie and Chase are safe for now. In this moment, both of them are okay. I say it to myself over and over again, but the fire in my gut won't stop. My family will be safe because I'm going to make sure they are. I'm going to find this bitch and bring her down a peg. Part of me doesn't care if she's breathing at the end of it. We'll see which side wins out.

Walking into the captain's office, I can tell he's in crunch mode. He's holding his cell phone against his chest while he speaks loudly into the office handset. An officer brushes past me and stands stoically, waiting for the captain to acknowledge him. If my brain was functioning correctly, I'm sure I could hear everything the captain is saying. Right now, I hear my mother in my head. "Calm down Jasmine. Let people help you." Tyler slams the handset down.

As I fall into a chair, another voice breaks through my mother's soliloquy. Henry's voice echoes loud and clear: "Protect my son." Those simple three words from my dying brother stop me cold. I have to remove this perpetrator before she removes me. Frankie warned me this was becoming personal, and I kept going. This is the consequence of my actions. I pull my cell phone out of my pocket and load up an encrypted texting app Logan put on it. I shoot off a quick message.

The officer nods and leaves the office. Captain Udall looks at me. I can feel his eyes burning a hole through my soul. He's going to recommend putting us all in safe houses. It's a procedure I don't really believe in, but at this point I have no control. Just like before.

"Police officers have Chase, but the person who called you was long gone. Chase is home and the officers will stay with him until you get there. Frankie's been notified, and she has a police detail following her to the house. I've also spoken to the commissioner. Frankie and Chase will be put in immediate police custody."

I nod. Kid safe. Girlfriend safe. Family safe.

"Jasmine?"

My eyes finally focus on the captain. His face tells me everything I need to know. If the commissioner is already involved, then this case is high profile. She must have known this would happen when she called me. It's her game, and we're playing into her hands. If you know the rules, you know how to manipulate them.

"What if it's a setup?"

He looks at me oddly. Maybe it's because my tone is calm and even. I feel all my emotions swirling inside, but they're staying at bay. Frankie always said she is never afraid of me when I yell. She says it's when I'm quiet she knows I'm really angry. I wonder what she would say if she heard me now.

"Jasmine, I know this isn't what you want. Hell, you've done everything in your power to avoid it before. But this is going to happen."

"She was right, I played right into Garrison's hands once before. What if this is what she wants to happen?"

I lean forward in the chair, the random possible outcomes of my conversations with her running through my mind. There is so much she can gain from any decision we make at this point.

"Hadley's in the United Kingdom."

"I didn't know that."

"It's not common knowledge. She's filming something that the studios are keeping secret."

"She told you, so she might have told others."

"She told me because I'm her friend."

"And you would have sent out the entire police force to find her."

I'm sure I have some lie or something witty to say, but he's speaking the truth.

"That's not the point. She has her own security. No one really knows where she is. It's perfect."

My cell phone rings. I notice the app shows an incoming call from a blocked number. Tyler sits, his hand hovering over the handset of his desk phone. Both of us are ready for another onslaught of negativity hitting us in the face.

"Hello?"

"Hello to you too, stranger," Hadley's chipper voice rings through the receiver. I feel the corners of my mouth turn up slightly.

"Hey, Hadley, how are you?" I see Tyler visibly calm down and lean back in his chair.

"It's cold and wet, but what else is new. I appreciate the small talk, honey, but you wouldn't text me 911 if something wasn't up."

"I need a favor. I need to send Frankie and Chase to you."

"What's happened?" Her cheery voice is instantly gone, replaced by a slight twinge of fear.

"I wish I could tell you, Hadley. I really do."

I hear muffled conversation on the other end of the phone. Hadley's talking to someone and covering the mouthpiece.

"Okay, I'll get the information to you as soon as possible."

"Excuse me?"

"I'll take care of it. You coming too?"

"No."

She sighs, and I sense a small lecture is coming. She's been through this before. Keith could have killed her. What she saw me do—killing James—I don't know if that vision will ever leave her mind. She knows I'm capable of killing to protect my family. It's something I wish she hadn't seen. It's one thing to talk about it; it takes another caliber of person to actually do it.

"Whatever this is, Jasmine, you come home to your family, or I swear to God I will bring you back from the dead just to kill you again."

"Yes, ma'am. Now, go back to building your empire."

"Jasmine, please be careful."

I hang up the phone without answering. I used to say the same thing to my mother all the time when she traveled with her cousin. They would go all over the country, enjoying the open road and being free. She would laugh at me and simply say "For what I have control over, sure." She was right. We only have control over so much; the rest is up to the extraneous variables of people.

"They're staying with Hadley."

"Jasmine, if they're out of the country, we can't protect them!"

"We couldn't protect them here anyway. This is the best option for all of us. No one knows exactly where they'll be. Safer this way."

"I'll have to clear—"

"It's done, captain. It's my family, my call. I'll take the heat."

"No, you won't. I'll handle it, but we do things together from now on. You're on a short leash here, understand? Now, go. Go home and explain the situation. They have some packing to do. I'll call Frankie and break the news to her."

I nod in response. My body moves on its own, and I stand up. It's going to be a long day. How do I tell my family they're going away to be safe, and

I'm not coming with them? I know Frankie's going to fight me. I'm actually glad Captain Udall's going to make the call to give her a heads-up. She made me promise not to pull this crap again, and yet here I am. Hopefully, she understands and forgives me.

I hear Chase rummaging through his drawers upstairs. I guess Hadley arranged things rather quickly. I'm not surprised. She's becoming a big deal with this new film. I'm proud of her and her super-secret project. Beyond the obvious, I don't want to know anything. You can't screw up and spill information you don't have. I duck into Chase's room. He's wearing his favorite shirt from his father's stuff. It's an old, no-longer-dark-black, KISS concert T-shirt with the dates almost worn away. His sandy blond hair looks like he just woke up. He's still skinny, like his dad. I figure that will change once he hits his late thirties.

He turns with some shirts in his hands and sees me in the doorway. He drops the clothes on his bed and stays silent. He's angry. It's something I've learned to see right away over the years. His blue eyes could burn a hole through my flesh with all that direct energy.

"Hey, buddy."

I speak as calmly as possible. He turns his attention back to the chest of drawers and ignores me. I'm sure he knows I won't be coming with him. I'm also sure that isn't going over well. He's going to lecture me. I expect nothing less. He's a smaller version of Henry.

"I'm sorry this is happening again, but it'll be over soon. I promise."

"Don't lie to me, Aunt Jasmine."

Chase slams the clothes onto his bed. His cold tone stings my heart.

"Okay, I hope this will be over soon. I'll do everything in my power—"

"No, Aunt Jazz! You're leaving us behind again! You know Aunt Frankie worries every night you're gone, doncha? You're not gonna get shot or die, are you?"

He turns and faces me, his eyes filled with tears that threaten to fall.

"Hey, buddy, no! Chase, you think I want to send you away? I don't even know where the hell you're going! You think that feels great? I'm going to do the best I can—cross my heart. Right now, that means getting the two most important people in my life out of my life until this is cleared up. I'm sorry if it hurts you, but there's nothing I can do about that."

"You can come with us."

"Honey, you know I have to stay, right? Chase?"

He slumps onto his bed, the fight gone as the tears roll down his cheeks. Sitting down next to him, I open my arms. He always tries to be a big man, but sometimes he just needs a hug. I have to remember he's still a kid. Chase slides into my arms and he wipes his nose on my shirt.

"If you die, I won't ever forgive you."

I say nothing as I pull him tighter against me. What can I say anyway? "I'll try not to die" doesn't sound very confident. I know Chase is mature for his age simply because of all the things he's experienced. His baby fat is almost all gone. He's growing up, and that scares me more than Garrison or his cronies. Right now, though, I hold onto this moment. I relish the small hug and snot on my shirt. His warm breath on my chest and his tears soaking my bra. I enjoy every second because I know there might not be another one. My nephew is growing up, no matter what happens from here on out.

He pushes against me gently, wiping his tears with my shirt.

"Thanks," I say, trying to lighten the mood.

"You better go talk to Aunt Frankie. She's not happy."

Standing up, I move my wet shirt back into its proper position. I lean forward and kiss his head.

"You know you said "cross your heart," and that means you gotta do it no matter what, right?" He whispers this innocently.

"Yes, sir."

I leave him to his packing, and I walk down the hallway to our master bedroom. As I get closer, I can hear Frankie muttering to herself. I'm not sure what she's saying, but I'm sure it can't be good. I'm forcing her to go on an extended break from work. That means leaving her patients with a different doctor they might not trust. It might be okay for some; it could cause a mental breakdown for others. Taking time off is one of the most difficult things to do in her field.

Leaning on the door frame, I see her rummaging through our dresser. Now I know where Chase gets it from. The anger packing. If it wasn't aimed at me, I would find it adorable. She stops cold, and I hear her breathe in sharply. I am one step into the bedroom, but I quickly turn around and press myself against the hallway wall. She found the ring in my drawer. The ring I've morbidly held onto. The same ring that has been kept with my socks for so long that I've never thought to move it. Now she either knows I wanted to propose or that I'm planning it.

"Hey, Frankie, where ya at?" I call from the hallway. I try to sound further away, but I'm sure she knows I'm full of shit. I hear the dresser drawer close quickly. She must have put the ring back. I hope she did.

"In the bedroom." Her voice shakes a bit.

I push off the wall and stand in the hallway for a few seconds. It's like my body needs to hold onto the charade of being further away than I am. Turning into the bedroom, I see Frankie's long curly blond hair covers her face as she places some items into her suitcase.

"Hi," I say. My knees brush against the duvet on the bed, causing me to stop moving. She raises her head to look at me. Her forehead creases with worry, her makeup almost all washed away with tears, her light brown eyes full of emotion begging to be shared. She's still in her dress slacks and button-down shirt from work.

"I know there are so many things you want to say to me . . ."

She raises her hand to stop me. "Are you coming with us?"

I shake my head. "You know I can't." She walks around the bed toward me. Her hands play with the lapels of my black leather jacket.

"I'm not going to lie and say I'm not upset. I don't want this." She looks at her hands as her fingers nervously run along the stitching of my jacket. She lifts her right hand and runs her knuckles over my cheek. She finally looks directly at me. She grabs my hand and holds it tightly, as if I was letting her go forever.

"I need you to be here when I get back, Jasmine. I know I can live without you, but I don't want to. I won't ask you to make promises you can't keep. I won't ask you to back off and come with us. I know how important this is to you."

I kiss her knuckles but say nothing. I don't trust my voice right now.

"Whatever you do"—she pauses and steps closer to me, her breath hot on my lips— "finish it and let us come back to us."

Her lips gently touch mine, and I swear the world around me fades into nothingness. I put everything I can into a single kiss before breaking away and resting my forehead against hers. As I catch my breath, fighting my desire to grab a suitcase and run away with my family, she lets me go. In silence, Frankie simply continues packing. Her hands tremble slightly as she does. Yet, she's still beautiful. Age has begun to catch up with her, but I don't care. Wrinkles, stress lines, white hairs hidden in the blond—all meaningless. I can't live without her.

I watch her zip up the suitcase as the doorbell sounds downstairs. I turn to walk her out, but she stops me. Chase stands in the hallway, his winter coat making him look like he's enveloped in dark-blue bubble wrap. Frankie simply leans forward, kisses me with such passion my head swims, and turns away from me. She walks down the hallway. Chase stops and makes an *X* across his chest and points at me sternly. I make the same *X* and wave bye to him. The two walk downstairs and out of sight. Just like that, my family is gone. I won't know exactly where they are or how they're holding up. I'll know they're safe.

And right now, that's all that really matters.

Chapter Four

My office, my home away from home. My dreary brown walls, chipped green metal desk, boxes of files that litter the corner, and the dry erase board that currently stands empty, taunting me. It's a silly thing, but I like to have an idea of where something begins. Why bother putting all the information on the board if it can't form some kind of map? That's what the damned thing is for. An old whiteboard with the faint shadows of cases gone by. It's been a week of staring at the board. A week of sleeping on my couch at the office. A week of an empty house. A week with no answers or advancements.

Grabbing a black dry erase marker and standing in front of the board, I want to write something. Hell, I'd take anything at this point. I just need to know what went on in that store. It's obvious to anyone with a brain Winslow was hiding something. I don't blame him. He might have talked if those damn suits hadn't been there. My hand mindlessly flows over the board, drawing a question mark, reminding me there are more questions than answers right now.

"Jasmine?" the captain says as he knocks on the door frame.

"What's up, Captain?" I say, turning my attention from my empty board.

"You sleep here last night?" He points to the blankets and pillow on my couch.

"Would it matter? I brought a change of clothes from home and showered in the locker room. House feels too empty with them gone." I turn my attention back to the dry erase board, hoping to change the subject.

"Something on your mind?"

"Always. I'd be dead otherwise." My voice drips with sarcasm.

"Funny."

He stands next to me. "Case giving you issues?"

"I'm just missing something. I know what the evidence says, but until we can connect the how and why . . . it's just a big mess of a film with no plot."

"Maybe I can help. Everts is already in interrogation. Apparently, Winslow and Miles decided to come in on their own, without the lawyers or suits."

I calmly put the marker down, smooth out my black button-down shirt, crack my neck, and smile. Time to get some answers.

"Will you watch? See if you catch anything?" I ask. The captain's brown eyes show surprise at my request. I rarely ask for help—part of my charm, I guess. For this case, it's all-hands-on-deck. I've listened to Frankie, and I trust her. I'm really close to the whole situation, so a fresh pair of eyes can't hurt.

"Sure thing."

Down the hall, I hear commotion. Crossing behind the counter, I see a man demanding to be heard. His voice is angry, his breathing shallow. Sweat beads form on his forehead, and his fists are raised. He's a classic case of someone who will be residing in a cell for a bit. The type who let emotions rule their actions instead of taking a deep breath. I might be out of a job if people were more decent to one another and did what is right, even when it isn't easy.

That's what I hope Winslow and Miles are here for. They've taken the first step by coming back in without their protection. Now it's my turn to show appreciation with an olive branch. Like my mother said to me once, life is a give and take. The givers can't support the takers forever. There needs to be a balance.

Pulling the interrogation room door open, I see Winslow and Miles sitting on one side of the table. I close the door behind me and Winslow jumps. Miles looks up at me for a second, then turns his attention back to Will.

"Sorry, I'm late," I utter, and grab the back of a chair.

"It's okay, we were just getting started," Will says. He turns his attention back to the two across the table. "You guys wanted to speak to the two of us. We'll listen to whatever it is you want to say."

"First, I want you to know that Tucker and I were not involved in anything we're about to tell you."

"Mr. Miles," I say calmly as I sit down. "We both understand neither of you are directly connected. I'm assuming by your statement that you had knowledge of the illegal activity of the store's employees. If you're looking for immunity, we can't promise you that." I've learned the hard way not to make promises I can't keep. Stupid rookie mistakes of a youthful idealist cop.

"I've got a scholarship. If I get in trouble, I'll lose everything," Tucker Winslow says. He stands up and starts to slide into his jacket. I grab a sleeve as he starts to pull away.

"Mr. Winslow, you're in trouble either way," I start. "You were part of the staff. You have knowledge of the case. Do whatever your gut tells you to do. If you can look yourself in the mirror and feel good about yourself—walk out that door. Considering you voluntarily came back here, well, it leads me to believe you want to do what's right." I let go of his sleeve and lean back in my creaking metal chair.

Winslow looks at me, his tired brown eyes staring through me. His young face shows how stress can age you quickly. Straightening his worn coat on the back of the chair, he places his head in his dry, cracked, working-man hands.

"I worked so hard to get that scholarship."

He seems on the verge of tears.

"There's no guarantee you'll lose it, Mr. Winslow," Will tries to soothe him. "I was the first to go to college. How about you?"

"No, just the first to get money with my brains."

The room falls eerily silent. James Miles's gaze bounces between Will and me. His brow glistens with fresh beads of sweat. His left leg bounces frantically under the table as he plays with his hands. I can feel the tension oozing off of him as fast as the sweat darkens his button-down shirt. The smell of his anxiety fills my nasal passages.

"You want to start, Mr. Miles?" I ask.

"I don't know much. I just know what the computer told me."

"What computer?" Will asks, sounding as confused as I am.

"Um, well everything is logged into the main register of the store. You have to clock into the online payroll programs and scan inventory when it's received. Basically, everything is online."

"What did the computer tell you?" Will continues.

"I noticed that when Connors or Fisher were working every other Saturday night, they would stay well after closing. The alarm company would call to verify they were staying late. I assume they told the company they were working late so they didn't send an officer over."

"Okay, so our victims routinely stayed late. How does that help us solve their murder?" Will asks.

Miles takes a deep breath and composes his thoughts. "The alarm company installed new systems on the back doors that were compliant with the fire marshal's new fire code. We'd gotten fines from the fire marshal, so the company insisted on it. Basically, there is a massive locking mechanism where you have to put a key in a lock—with a code—to open it. That disengages the alarm, allowing a person to enter or exit the back room to throw out the trash. At this location, you'd also exit the store through the back door as well. Each night they stayed late, the door would be opened late at night. It would open again a few hours later."

"Mr. Miles," I interject, "I appreciate you trying to help, but this really isn't helping us at all."

"They never let me work those nights or the next day," Winslow pipes up. He slowly lifts his head from his hands.

"Why not?" Will asks.

"They told me the store manager and assistant store manager had to work those days. I knew it was bullshit, but I used the day to study," Tucker says.

"Did you notice anything odd going on?" Will continues.

"James asked me about the alarm crap, but I knew nothing about it. We both noticed there were some odd things going on, but we couldn't prove anything. One day I was working up front and Joe was in the back on the phone. I had to grab an Xbox from the locked room. I propped open the back door and went to grab the system. Joe was trying to stay calm, but you could hear he was really angry."

"Did you catch any part of his conversation?" I ask as my pen flies across the page on the table in front of me.

"Not really, just something about 'it not being part of the plan.' Or maybe that 'the plan's changed.' Either way, he was pissed."

"How come none of this was ever caught on the security cameras?"

"The camera has a massive blind spot. If you wanted to do anything shady, all you had to do was move one step to the left of the camera and you were clear," Winslow says.

"Basically, the entire backroom wasn't secure. I told them they should have an additional camera put in, but corporate said there wasn't room in the budget," Miles adds.

"Either of you notice anything out of the ordinary on the day of the murders?" I ask, not looking up from my notes.

"From a computer standpoint, everything was as it should be," Miles says, calmer than before.

"I worked the morning shift. Joe came in around one and was really high strung. Tasha came in around the same time. She was really upset too. She made it clear she didn't want to be there anymore. I knew better than to ask anything, so I split early. I had a test the next day, so I figured I could use the extra study time. When I left, everyone was still alive," Winslow adds.

A knock on the door stops me from asking another question. The captain peeks his head into the interview room.

"Detective Steele, Detective Everts, can I speak to you for a moment?"

I grab my notes and walk out of the room. Something big must have happened to pull us out of the interview. Closing the door behind Will and me, the captain rubs his temples.

"I need you both to go to the Hudson Container Terminal in Brooklyn."

"Brooklyn? Any reason you're sending us out of our jurisdiction?" I ask, irritated at being interrupted.

"Logan did some digging and found a few cargo containers listed under a Garrison shell corporation. I called the Seventy-Sixth Precinct and they're letting us take the lead. Officers secured three containers. They're waiting for the two of you before anything is opened."

"What about those two in there?" Will adds.

"I'll finish up in there. See if they have anything more to add. You two just get there now. Lights, sirens, I don't care. Call if you need anything. The mayor is screaming at One Police Plaza, so they in turn are screaming at me. So, be safe and let's get to the bottom of this."

He turns promptly and enters the interview room. I see the captain hold out two of his business cards and offer one to each man. "I understand this is traumatic for you two," I hear him say. "Here's my number—my personal number. If you feel it gets to be too much to deal with, I want you to call me, okay?" As the door closes, I can hear him explaining why he sent us away. It's low, but he continues in a tone that is calm, almost inviting. I wish I had that ability in an interview. I'm all business. Will holds out the keys and I grab them. Time to test out the new wheels.

Brooklyn was always my dad's favorite place to visit. He grew up somewhere in this borough, with his egg cream and Brooklyn Dodgers. Every time I drive through and deal with the horrible traffic, I think of my father. The good moments. The horrible jokes and memories gone by. One day I'll bring Chase here to see the Cyclones. Let him experience Brooklyn baseball, the original Nathan's Famous and Coney Island for himself. Introduce him to his grandfather's birthplace.

Seeing the slew of lights in the parking lot, I know we've arrived. A dozen people stand outside a police barricade with their cell phones. I assume they're taking pictures for their social media feeds. Anything to have something go viral and make them famous. I pull over to the side of the road, get out, and walk through the crowd to the front of the line. Will and I show our badges and the sea of blue parts, allowing us through.

I've never seen a cargo yard. I expected rust, rats, and massive amounts of debris—like a postapocalyptic area of New York's past. Instead, it's clean, paved, and the containers appear stacked in an organized manner, the different colors contrasting starkly against the crystal blue sky of this winter day. It's like a massive wall of oversized Legos with larger toys to move the pieces.

"Detectives?" a young woman in plainclothes says to me. Her black hair is pulled into a neat ponytail, her suit perfectly pressed, her face lively and youthful. Obviously, a new detective.

"Detective Steele and Everts," I say, waving my hands between Will and myself. "I apologize for the delay; traffic was unyielding."

"Detective Cole. We secured the three cargo containers. They're in the back of the yard."

She turns in her high-heeled boots and starts walking. If only she knew how impractical those things are. I watch the other officers check her out as we walk by. Each of them does the same body scan: the eyes start at her heels, slide up her legs, then stop on her ass for a few seconds before heading all the way to her face. She doesn't seem to mind, but that'll change when someone opens their mouth about her promotion being gender based.

"My captain said not to open the units at all, but there's a serious smell coming off one of them," Cole says.

"Thanks for securing the scene. I know it's annoying to have someone from the outside making requests," I say as I survey the area. Detective Cole suddenly stops. I look up and see three containers with two uniformed officers in front of them, one of them standing by with bolt cutters. Neither of them looks happy to be out here in the horrible weather, waiting on some Manhattan detectives to take away their scene. The higher-ups might accept it, but the boots on the ground—they never do. These types of cases can move your career forward. They don't need the likes of me, already established walking in to take it away. I hate this side of the job.

"Like I said, we're here to help out," Cole says again as she looks over to the officers. "Everyone, this is Detective Steele and Detective Everts. They've got control of the scene."

I look at Will and my eyes beg him to take the lead on this one. He'll handle it better than I would. My foot would probably end up in my mouth and I'd shit shoelaces for a week. He simply nods, puffs out his chest, and walks over to the first container.

"Officer . . .?"

"Fernandez and this is Baker." The officer with the bolt cutters points to himself then the cop to his right.

"Thanks for keeping the scene clear."

"The containers were easy. The other officers you passed before had the harder job of keeping the yard clear of traffic."

"Understood, thanks."

Will tilts his head toward the first container, "Mind opening them up now?"

Fernandez moves forward, bolt cutters ready. Will, myself, Cole, and Officer Baker pull out our guns. I take a steadying breath as the lock snaps under the pressure of the tool. Fernandez flips the broken lock off, lifts the latch, and pulls the door open toward him. Will and Cole shine flashlights in the container. It's empty. Will opens the other door. I can hear him talking to Cole and the two officers, but their voices fade into nothingness as I enter the container.

I clearly hear the water splashing the pier outside, the birds calling to one another as they hunt for food. The smell of the low tide fills my nostrils. The walls are covered with old, faded paint. A metal railing lines the walls in the middle, most likely to secure cargo for transport. My flashlight beam hits some scratches on the back wall. One foot in front of the other. Stepping over brown stains. Could be rust. Could be caked in blood. The lab would have to test it to be sure.

Kneeling down by the back wall, I see a small hole below the railing. The metal bends outward, so whatever created it was inside the container. Moving my flashlight further down, the scratches come back into view. My breath hitches as I look at the familiar markings. I've seen them before on prison walls. A prisoner counting the days. Someone was locked inside this container.

"You said one container has a smell?" I say. I quickly step out of the box.

"Yes, ma'am," Baker answers me.

"Open it now." He grabs the cutters from his partner and walks over to the third container. He quickly cuts the lock without looking for approval. I'm sure the urgency in my voice made my intentions clear. Tossing the cutters to the side, he knocks off the lock and opens both doors. The impact of the smell is immediate. Baker rushes to the side and vomits. His partner Fernandez is right on his heels.

Will and Cole walk up alongside me. Their flashlights illuminate the scene. Bodies are chained to the railing all the way around—the floor soupy with human waste.

"Call the Manhattan coroner," I say.

Cole walks away, barking frantically into her walkie-talkie.

"This is way above our pay grade, Jasmine."

"Logan said Garrison had some dealings with human trafficking. I think we now know where they were held. Maybe this was where they came in."

"Suffocation? Starvation?"

I take two steps into the container before the smell overwhelms me. I stop in my tracks, cover my mouth, and move my flashlight around. Women, men, and children of all ages litter the bin. One girl lies in the center of the floor, her skin tight to her bones.

"They look like they're mummified," Will says.

"How long have they been here?" My phone rings from a private caller.

"Answer it. Might be the family. I've got this."

I walk out toward the waterfront, taking in deep gasps of fresh ocean air. My phone rings three more times before I answer it, my breath finally normal.

"Steele."

"Red is your favorite color, isn't it?"

I know that voice. It's the same caller from before. She must have a new cell phone number.

"How did you get this number?"

"You can get anything you want with the right . . . shall we say . . . incentive? Tell me, detective, shouldn't the smell have been enough to tell you something was inside? I mean, seriously, did we have to put a massive neon sign on it for you? Slow police work there."

She was watching us. Or still is. I find myself spinning around looking for any sign of a small camera or person out of place. I stop and stare at the security cameras.

"Congratulations, you figured out how we're watching you. Always a few steps behind. How the hell you became a detective is beyond me. Then again, you do have men dreaming of making you straight. I wonder if your untouched-by-male-hands body is what got you this job. Lord knows your intelligence didn't."

"I'm going to find you."

"Of course, you will. You and I are very similar, Jasmine. We both have blood on our hands. I understand my job is getting it on mine. You just pout and cry about those who've died under your watch. You need a thicker skin. Maybe your childhood wasn't as rough as you think it was since you seem soft. Let's just enjoy our game. I think it's your move."

The phone disconnects and I turn around to see coroner wagons have begun to arrive with police escorts. Will touches my arm and stops its movement. I didn't know I had been shaking.

"You okay?"

"That was her on the phone."

I shake my head and dial Logan. He answers in three rings.

"Yes, boss lady. How may I assist you?"

"I want you to trace the last call that came into my cell phone. I want to know whatever you can dig up and find out how the hell they got my new unlisted number." Logan starts to say something, but I disconnect before he can speak. Will looks at me, and I know he understands.

"Everything's going to the lab. They'll break the containers down to the nuts and bolts if they have to. We'll find something."

"They're always a few steps ahead of us. We've got to get better, be better."

"We will, but this doesn't help. You said it yourself; we have to focus on why we do this job. It's all we got."

I turn away from him and head back up to the cars. Detective Cole calls after me, but her voice falls on deaf ears. The words 'you and I are very similar' play over and over again in my head. I know it's a way to get under my skin. I wanted to scream in the phone that I am nothing like her, like in one of those really bad thriller films Hadley stars in, but I couldn't. She's right. I hunt down Garrison and all his endeavors with the fervor of an obsessed fan. I want justice for all those victims, but at what cost?

I'm not afraid of that darker side of me. I want him dead, and that feeling terrifies me. It's an inhuman thought, but it somehow keeps me grounded in my own humanity.

Will is silent on the ride to the lab. He's probably giving me time to cool off, but I wish he would have spoken up about something—anything. Maybe just to get my mind off my obsession with this mysterious woman. Something to get the rage to subside in my chest. My throat burns from the fumes of acid in my stomach. I want this woman found. I want her to pay for all the damage she's done.

The elevator doors open, and I bump into some medical personnel I've never seen before. The room is filled with a bunch of new faces running around like hamsters on wheels. So many people, moving gurneys and carrying trays full of autopsy tools. One person rushes past me with a tray full of petri dishes and small containers. I assume they're heading up to Doctor Brown and her team. It looks like Victor called in the cavalry to maintain order down here.

"Glad you two made it. Come into my closet for a second and we can talk shop."

Will and I follow silently. I've never seen autopsies being performed before. I know it's what Victor does, but seeing people saw into the chest of a dead human is disturbing. The clinical way the doctor removes the breast plate of the ribs, then places it to the side. Organs removed and weighed. I know these people are dead, but it feels so . . . callous. So empty. These were once people. Now they're nothing but statistics, measurements, and theories. In the end, in this place, we're merely statistical analysis to be categorized in paperwork somewhere.

"Have a seat."

Victor's directness jars me out of my inner diatribe. I sit down next to Will in the cramped former closet that serves as Victor's office. Victor sits across from us and kicks the door shut.

"I'm sure you noticed the throngs of eager medical students out there. I was forced to bring them all in due to the sheer number of bodies. Before you ask, Jasmine, all the work will be checked and verified by me. I'll make sure it is all by the book for court purposes."

"Okay. Do you have anything we can go on?"

"Well, not much. We're working on it as fast as we can, but with fifteen bodies, it's going to take a little time."

Will finally speaks. "Anything is better than nothing right now, doc."

Victor pulls a pile of papers from the right side of his desk to him. His black-rimmed glasses fall to the edge of his nose. His dark brown eyes slide back and forth along the pages while his perfectly manicured hands flip to the next file.

"Victims appear to range in age, nationality, and gender."

"Appear?" Will asks tersely.

"We haven't identified any of them yet. We're running their restored prints through all known databases, but it's a long shot and it's going to take some time. That being said, if you take into account that some are

Asian, some White, and some African American, you can easily deduce that not all of them are of the same background. It's a probability thing." Victor pushes up his glasses with his right middle finger. I presume to prove a point to Will.

"So, we really don't have much to go on here," I add. I try and steer the conversation back to the cargo container.

"All I can tell you is what I have from a very preliminary screening of the victims."

Victor closes the file and pushes the pile to his left. He leans back in his chair and runs his right hand over his buzz-cut black hair. Through the window, he takes in the organized chaos outside the office. I swear I can see his dark skin pale as he sees the bodies lined up on metal slabs. Will's phone rings. He says nothing but stands, opens the door, and bumps my chair to leave. I hear him answer the phone and his voice gets fainter as he walks away.

"This one is going to kill me, Jasmine." Victor's eyes lock onto mine and I see a shimmer of water hidden behind his lenses.

"Talk to me, Vic. Tell me what the hell is going on."

"I don't know, but whoever did this?" He pauses and looks back out into the main room. "They are some callous motherfuckers. They can't have a heart or a fucking conscious. I've seen so much death, but this . . . this is just plain vicious."

I know what the evidence is screaming at me like a neon sign. I wish it was different. I wish Victor wasn't confirming my suspicions. I wish I could tell the victims' families, whoever they are, that their loved ones died quickly. That they didn't feel any pain. It's often the only consolation I can offer the ones left behind. Not this time.

"How long were they . . .?"

"I don't know. They could have been there for two weeks or two months. It depends on the temperatures, and if they had any water or any kind of food in that container."

"I didn't see any holes for gathering rainwater or wrappers from food."

"So, estimate a shorter amount of time. Either way, after that much time they had to know they were dying slowly. Each and every one of them sat in their own shit knowing that this was how they would be found. The psychological toll on them might have caused death to come sooner."

"You think they denied themselves food and water since they knew the eventual outcome?"

"It's possible." He looks sadly at me. "It could be they were fed regularly by one of their captors. I don't know. Could be they were poisoned and left to rot. I won't know anything until the tox screens are back. I'm trying to be rational here, Jazz, but my best guess tells me they were left to die with no knowledge of if or when their captor would come back. What kind of person does that?"

"Someone covering their tracks? Someone proving a point? Maybe someone trying to throw the investigation off track?"

My phone beeps and I see a message from Logan. Victor stands up and we walk out of his office together. He quietly moves among the staff working frantically. I follow behind him, my mind so full of rage that I can't silence the screams. I know what I told Victor, but I also know what my instincts are telling me. This was a cleanup job. Someone wanted to tie up loose ends. But why get me and Will involved? Unless they wanted a bigger stage, more coverage, and more people to torment.

Seems irrational to me, but when dealing with a narcissistic psychopath, what is rational? Even serial killers are more rational and more methodical. This bitch who's been calling me, she's just a psycho, plain and simple. She's behind this, along with Garrison. Maybe they want the world to see how they can get away with murder or they want to frame someone else for it all. One thing's for sure: I want them both to suffer for this.

As I walk into Logan's office, the hustle and bustle hits me like a baseball bat to the face. I'm not used to seeing all of these people run around like children on a brand-new playground. People are speaking different languages, keypads are being pressed frantically, and mouse clicks reverberate in my eardrum. It feels like I'm on an episode of a science fiction television show; I'm the clueless one, the woman from another dimension.

The massive television screen at the edge of the office shows crime scene pictures of all the victims, their lifeless faces being scanned by the computer praying for a match somewhere in cyberspace. With weeks of decay, it's a long shot, but it's where we start.

This is where I'm useless. I can't move forward without any information from Logan or Victor. My internal detective is telling me where all these bodies are coming from, and it's rarely wrong.

The smell of coffee reaches my nose, momentarily replacing the smell of death. I grab it thankfully and look over at a tired Logan. His hazel eyes are drawn, his black hair matted and wild. I know he misses Hadley and is worried about her. Without saying a word, he simply motions for me to follow him. I stare at the desks, hoping to see some new information as I walk to his office, my feet feel slow and heavy.

He closes the door behind me and that blocks out most of the cacophony from the techs outside. Logan sits behind his messy desk. He flips open his laptop without even looking at me. His silence is starting to freak me out. He's always so talkative, even in dire times. This is different though; I think he feels responsible. I know I do.

"I reactivated my dark web profile. I know I promised you I wouldn't, but we have no choice," Logan says tiredly. He types away at his keyboard, as if looking for something.

"We spoke about this before; I trust your judgment. At this point, I need all the help I can get," I answer simply.

I know I sound defeated. I'm not sure he's used to hearing me like this, but I really am at a loss. How could someone leave those people to die like that? I've seen many things, witnessed so much, but this is by far the cruelest.

"Where's Will?"

"Not sure. This last crime scene seems to have rattled him. I think he just needed some fresh air. Don't worry, if anything comes up, I'll bring him up to speed. There is this invention called a cell phone, and thankfully I know how to use that." I'm trying to lighten the mood and failing miserably. I'm concerned about Will, but there's nothing I can do about it right now.

"I've been doing as much research as I possibly can," Logan says. "The FBI shut down a lot of the dark web sites we've used in the past. Of course, when one door closes, another one opens, but it's a matter of finding where that door is and who is behind it. Not to mention the software changed. I managed to find the update, got it installed and running. That killed my laptop. Turned out to be a massive virus trying to get into the NYPD's system to find out information. Information about *this* case. Luckily, I wasn't connected to the database here. I managed to shut it all down before it got too out of hand. I formatted it, got everything installed without any issue the second time."

Logan avoids eye contact and keeps rubbing his hands together. His nerves are getting the better of him. He needs more than coffee—he needs sleep, actually—but I doubt he'd listen to me and go home. I wish Hadley were here; she'd know how to help him.

"Okay, all information that was a bit over my head. Did you let the captain know?"

"Yeah, he had no idea what I was talking about. He gave me the number of his contact in the FBI. Since they're working on the Garrison case with us, the captain figured it was in their best interest to let them know what I found. We might be getting a visit soon."

"What did you find out when you investigated the new pages?"

"Not much. It seems the new pages are slightly out of my reach. I'm trying to break into the new coding, but it's a little more difficult. It's using some new version that I've never seen before."

"I guess we start from square one. Have you managed to find anything on the bombing at Gamer Syndicate?"

Logan leans to his right, frantically moving papers around his desk. He grabs a file from the middle of a tall stack of folders, flips it open, and pulls out one page. He hands it over to me and I quickly scan it, unsure of what I'm looking at. It looks like a mind map. The center of the page has Garrison's name on it. From there, there are lines heading off in various directions. Some of them lead to names, places, or numbers. I'm not quite sure at all what to make of it, but if anyone can figure it out or explain it to me, it's Logan.

"I know it looks overwhelming, but I managed to trace some of it. It's rudimentary, but if you look at the map, you can see that Garrison is at the heart of it."

"We knew that already."

"Yeah, but what we didn't know was how it all fit together."

Logan stands up and walks to the front of the room. He flips the lights off, suddenly plunging me into darkness. I guess I'm trying to think of anything other than what's in front of me. For the first time in a long time, maybe ever, I truly think I'm in over my head.

Watching Hadley's boyfriend walk around his desk, I'm a bit confused as to what he plans to do. He cracks his knuckles, stretches his neck, and jumps around a bit. I'm sure anyone looking at us from the main floor would be worried about our sanity. Hell, I'm worried about Logan's. He mumbles something to himself, grabs his laptop, and plugs something into the side. Next thing I know, his computer screen is projected onto his office wall.

"Where are Hadley's movie posters that used to hang there?"

"She thought they were kind of creepy. Besides, I have the real thing now; don't need to stare at fake wall pictures."

"Have you heard from her?"

"No." His voice drips with a sadness which betrays him. "Have you?" he asks while typing on his computer.

"Only when I asked her for help."

I try to keep my voice in check, but I know I fail. I miss my family. There's nothing that a Chase or Frankie hug wouldn't fix. It's stupid and irrational, but I swear their hugs can solve anything.

"I'm sure they're fine," I toss out quickly.

"Okay, here we go." Logan projects the mind map on the wall in a more polished, easier-to-read format. He stands up and grabs his ruler. "This only covers what I've managed to dig up, okay? It doesn't show whatever you've figured out on your own."

"Got it, only web geek stuff."

"So, we both know Garrison is at the heart. That's the easy part. The bigger issue was how he managed to run everything in cyberspace without being caught."

Logan points to a small box with the name Harry Brandt in it—the technological muscle behind everything Garrison tried to do. Current residence: a cemetery outside of town.

"Thanks to Harry Brandt's computer, which we seized in our dark web case, we found out he managed most of the online stuff. He coordinated buys, drop-offs, drug deals, and more. Basically, he was the head honcho for everything."

Looking at the screen, I simply nod. Logan smiles and moves his pointer to another box.

"Brandt had lower-level dealers. They handled the street-level grunt work. Since Brandt's death, their activity has pretty much stopped." He swirls his pointer around aimlessly on the screen. "They're in the wind. So, the drug route has stopped, but we all know addicts find a way regardless. How does this help us?"

"All that's true, and sadly it doesn't. Help us, that is. If we had the line open, we could trace the correspondence. But what we do have"—Logan moves the pointer a little lower— "is this. I found some screen names listed in some messages. I'm trying to decipher who they are. They might be able to help us go backwards from dealer to asshole."

"Okay, but what about the box that says 'enforcers'?" I ask.

"That's where things get interesting."

Logan grabs a photo off his desk and hands it to me. It's of Keith Garrison's funeral. Irving Garrison stands next to a statuesque Latina woman. Her black hair brushes over her shoulder as she holds her purse in her right elbow. Irving holds his hand on her lower back in a protective manner. The way he stands behind her indicates he's done that hundreds of times before. Everything about the photo screams that this woman is romantically linked to Garrison.

"Who is she?"

Logan says nothing. He aims the pointer at the box reading *Enforcer*. She's his muscle. It's not what I expected. She doesn't fit the mold. It's like a female serial killer. They exist but are such a small percentage of the population. It just not the first thing I would have considered. His woman of the week, sure. Killer and longtime lover—not so much.

"Anyone else?"

"Nope. As far as we know she works alone."

Logan taps a few keys on his laptop, and the mapping screen changes. The woman's image—with what looks like a police file—pops up on the screen. I don't read or speak Spanish, so I can't decipher anything.

"Alexa Valez, born in Puerto Rico, near a United States bomb testing facility. According to her file, her father got into drugs and alcohol. He owed a good amount of money and couldn't pay it back. The gang came to the house, raped, and killed her mother before killing her father. She was made to watch. The leader went against the gangs MO and raised Alexa as his own daughter. She became one of the most accomplished and cold-blooded killers on the island."

"If she was arrested before with gang ties, she should have been placed on the no-fly list. Citizen or not, how'd she get to the mainland undetected?"

"Irving Garrison went on vacation searching for new product. She was put in contact with him. He took a liking to her and must have smuggled her in. That's the only rational explanation I can come up with based on the evidence we've got."

"If Garrison is behind this, why wasn't her file expunged? He has his hand in so many pockets, how is this information still readily available?"

"According to what I could find, he burned a hell of a lot of bridges trying to get ahead. That's the only reason he was in Puerto Rico anyway. He took a ton of gang money from all over the country and even Mexico. After not delivering on his promises, they all set out for revenge."

"But he was untouchable at that point."

"Exactly."

"He managed to get her out of jail by using the cartel he was attached to on the island." I shake my head in disbelief. "Then he smuggled her into the country probably with a fake passport or license."

"That would be my guess."

I mull over this for a few seconds. That means she's been here, flying under the radar, for several years. A cold killer like that can't just stop doing what they're trained to do. She must have killed elsewhere. That seems like the next logical avenue to pursue.

"I want you to send me over everything from Puerto Rico, including all the cases that mentions her. Then we're going to see if there's a pattern in her behavior."

"Check all unsolved murders in the area and see if she's been active here?" Logan asks.

"That's our best play, if you ask me. We need to find something to go on. Maybe, if we're lucky, we can find a pattern."

I take the photo, stand, and walk out the door. I want to know who the hell this woman is and why she's in my city. My anger starts to rise as I see all the people around those two who came to say goodbye to a piece of shit. I'll never understand why murderers are given so many chances, appeals, or help from those in power. The victims get to watch, wait, and suffer. I know Keith was a son and friend to some. To those people, Will's a cold-blooded killer. It doesn't matter that he killed Keith to save my life. Cops killed an innocent kid—that's all they will ever think. I can't change it.

Chapter Five

A nger is a beautiful thing. It can help you get results. It can also get you a shit ton of trouble if you step on the wrong toes. It can also blind you. Right now, as I get out of the elevator, it's fuel. It's something to make me want to push harder, go faster, and be smarter than this woman. I have a little more information and it's time to use it. Getting to Puerto Rico is impossible, and we know those gang members won't talk to the likes of me. They have their own code, and they'll play it out. Time to hit up the captain for some more manpower.

Passing by the captain's office, I notice a woman sitting in the chair closest to his desk. Her long black hair must've been straightened as her roots show a slight wave. Her black suit is impeccably pressed and tailored for her figure; she must be someone of importance. Her high heels are much too sexy for this office. No, she's not from here. She's not one of us. At least not a grunt; she's likely government.

As I knock gently at the captain's door, he looks up from a stack of papers on his desk and waves me in. Walking into the office, I glance over to this mysterious woman. I give her the obvious look up and down, sizing her up. I don't know who she is, but I know that if the government sent her, something big is going on. Either that or they're investigating me, the captain, or the precinct.

"Detective Steele, nice of you to join me," the captain calmly adds from behind a stack of papers. As I walk in the room, the woman turns her attention to me. Her dark brown eyes size me up. There's something about her air of seriousness and steely-eyed gaze that tells me this woman's here on a mission.

"I was just coming up from the tech lab. Got some new information I thought I'd share," I say as I focus on the woman in front of me. My curiosity is getting the better of me, and the captain isn't doing anything to quench it.

"Agent Marlow, FBI. I'm here to help you on the Garrison case," she says, extending her hand. I take it in response, but more out of being respectful to my captain than anything else.

"Agent Marlow's been working with the FBI in Seattle. She's been han-dling the Garrison case in Washington," the captain says, flipping through pages of a file.

"I didn't know Garrison's criminal activity extended to the Pacific Northwest," I say, as the new information has piqued my interest. "I thought he was more concerned about the southern borders. That's what Logan found out when we were digging into his personal records. Seems Garrison had a flair for Puerto Rico and its women. He met someone named Alexa Valez. She had a bad history with the local drug gangs, ended up being raised as their strong arm. She met Garrison on one of his trips and they have been inseparable ever since." I hand the file to Agent Marlow.

"So now we have the name, but do we have a face?" Captain Udall asks me. Without missing a beat, Agent Marlow pulls a photo out of the file and hands it to him. He studies the picture; his finger runs along her facial features. My gut screams that he recognizes her, but I don't feel comfortable questioning him in front of Agent Marlow. Before anything else is said, the captain stands and starts packing up his things.

"You alright, Captain Udall?" Marlow asks, concern written on her face.

"Detective Steele, since this case is getting a bit out of hand, I want everyone to stay in one location. Considering how fortified your house is, and the fact that I know you won't leave even if I tell you to, Marlow will be staying with you. I've also told Detective Everts to move his family to a safe house. He'll stop by for a visit to go over things this evening."

"So, I'm back in college with a frat house?"

"Considering your history, I know you'll refuse any help that I offer you. We're lucky that I have extra officers to drive around your neighborhood to ensure your safety. Maybe this time you'll do what I say and be cautious. Now if you'll excuse me, I've got something to look into."

The captain walks out of his office so quickly I don't have time to respond. He has everyone moving in with me, and truthfully, I am okay with that. Maybe with all of us being under the same roof—eating the same food and drinking the same liquor—we will be able to figure this out faster so that I can have my family home.

More importantly, we can solve this before anyone else dies.

"So, Agent Marlow, I hope you don't snore," I say, trying to lighten the mood.

"It's not me you have to worry about, Detective Steele. You won't even know I'm there while you're sleeping. Working on the other hand? I'm a bitch. I've been chasing the money trail, the body trail, and frankly any fucking trail to bring this guy down. Not since the Seattle Slayer have I been so invested in a case," she says, and then grabs her purse and a box on the floor.

"What happened to him?" I ask, grabbing the second box on the floor.

"I don't know. He's dropped off the radar again. When he comes back, I'll catch him."

"And if you don't?"

"Detective Steele, serial killers are very different than the murderers you deal with. The ones I deal with are meticulous, methodical, and never really stop. If he doesn't come back and kill again anywhere, then he's dead inside. My job's done. But they don't go quietly into the dark night; that's unrealistic. They need to kill like you and I need a drink after a hard case. He'll be back; it's just a matter of time."

"It's kind of depressing," I say. I hold the office door open for her. Agent Marlow walks through and shrugs her shoulders, not giving me a verbal answer. I follow behind her, letting the office door close. I wonder if she's right. Are the people I deal with in New York so very different from someone who could kill somewhere else? Aren't all murderers methodical and meticulous? Don't they all have this unwritten need to remove life from everyone? Hell, just to remove the breath of one human being is probably enough to fuel them for a week.

Maybe I'm missing something. I'm sure she'll fill me in when she's ready, but she doesn't trust me yet. I can tell by the way she walks, carries herself, and chooses her words too carefully. The FBI might be off-center, but she's alone. Usually they send them in twos, like Twix candy bars. Whatever her reason for being here, I'm thankful for the help.

***

We get to my place, and I open the door for Agent Marlow to walk inside. I close the door behind us, make sure it's locked, bolted, and chained. I know anyone with desire and will can break in; it's more for my false sense of security than anything else. I grab two beers out of the fridge and hand her one without thinking.

"I assume you drink?"

"I usually prefer wine, but this will do." She grabs the beer, twists off the cap, and takes a long, hard drink.

I do the same and sit down at the kitchen table. She takes the hint and follows suit.

"I'm only here to help, detective," she says, raising her hands in front of her. "Nothing more, nothing less."

"I didn't say anything."

"The silent types never do." Marlow leans back in her chair, watching me intently. "Your body language speaks volumes."

"If you wanted my body, you should have taken me on a date first."

She grins and lets out a throaty chuckle. Her brown eyes ease up on the strength they had before.

"I'm only here to help you. I have no intention of getting in your way," she says before she takes another long drag off the bottleneck.

"The feds don't just send someone to help. They always have ulterior motives. So, what's yours?" I ask her.

"They want to see how you're doing with this Garrison case. If you catch him alive, we want to be able to try him federally."

"Okay. Why'd they send you specifically?"

"He's a serial. Everything he does, everything he thinks, it's all classic serial killer. He might not kill them with his own two hands, but he's a killer nonetheless."

"You not telling me anything I don't already know. You didn't answer my question." I down my beer. Two quick steps to the fridge and I grab two more. I open mine and place the other in the center of the table. I watch her, and she slowly finishes the rest of her beer before grabbing the one in the middle. The cuff rides up on her shirt. I see deep scars on the inside of her wrist. An untrained eye would think she might've tried to kill herself, but the angle seems somehow off. Someone did that to her.

"I've been working on a case of my own back in Seattle. Just like you, I've got a jackass that doesn't understand murder is wrong. No connections, no DNA, no evidence really. He goes into hiding when he feels like it. So, my department head decided I needed a break. My boss knows how good I am at connecting the dots where others might miss one or two. Maybe I can help, and that's all I plan on doing."

"You have anything on yours?"

"Only about thirteen bodies and counting," Marlow says. "Depends what he's in the mood for. He might go for months not hurting anyone and then a body every week for a month. Garrison isn't like that. He's the paper man. He makes sure he has something on everyone; everything is in his control. Even his woman, the Alexa Valez character, it seems she goes and cleans up his mistakes. She's the muscle."

"There's got to be some history on a woman that highly trained. Paperwork, passports, flight manifests . . . there's got to be some kind of a trail."

I grab my cell phone and quickly send a text to Logan. We really need some reinforcements, so I text Will too. Hopefully he's back from his slight mental health day and can focus on work at hand.

"There's a whole hell of a lot of paperwork; none of it really means much."

"It's a trailer full of bodies, and you're telling me there's no evidence?" Marlow asks.

My cell phone starts to vibrate and dance across the table. I see Victor's goofy face staring back at me, so I grab it and answer.

"Hey, Victor," I answer monotonously. It quickly hits me how I could really use some sleep. Who am I kidding? If I close my eyes, I see those bodies curled up crying for help. I've said it a million times before: sometimes the job just comes home with you no matter what you do.

"Jazz, everything's settled down here. I'm gonna come home and bring what little I have. The rest of the tests should be available in the morning, but I don't know what help they'll be."

"Thanks, Victor. See you when you get here."

"Victor? That's the medical examiner, right?" Marlow asks.

"Yeah, that's him."

"Then who is Frankie?" Marlow asks innocently.

"Frankie?" I haven't brought Frankie up. Where did she hear the name?

"Captain mentioned him."

I spit my beer at her as I laugh. It's been a long time since someone's confused Frankie for a guy. I forget how common that can be.

"*She* is a psychologist the department uses on specific cases."

"Crap, sorry. I'm not usually this much of an ass." Marlow's laughing now as well. "Can I claim jet lag?"

The front doorbell rings and I pop up. My hand goes to my gun.

I know who I think should be at the door, but you never know. I nod to Marlow and walk into the living room. I can hear her shoes on my floor close behind me. I creep toward the door. Marlow pulls her weapon and aims it. If it's Alexa, she might get one shot off, but she won't leave alive.

I turn back to face Marlow, and she simply nods. She's at the ready. Taking a deep breath, I pull open the door, hoping for the best. I can feel the stress flow out of my shoulders when I see Logan holding three pizzas in his hands. Victor rushes up alongside him, carrying a case of beer. The two smile at me as if this will be a party instead of a criminal investigation.

"I called from the driveway," Victor says, grinning. I snatch the case of beer out of his arms.

"You're a gigantic ass. I nearly shot you. Now get some plates." Victor pales slightly and heads into the kitchen.

"And you"—I point at Logan— "are not forgiven either. Except for the pizzas. Take 'em to the living room."

***

The dry erase board from the basement sits in the middle of the living room. Frankie would be so angry and tell me to get it back downstairs. If she were here.

One box of pizza is empty and we're halfway through the second when Will walks into the living room. All of the voices seem to die into nothingness as he stands there holding his baseball cap. Logan reaches forward and grabs a beer out of the box and hands it to him. I attempt to toss him some paper plates but end up hitting Logan in the face. No words need to be said. We're his friends, his colleagues, his family; he'll talk when he's ready.

"You must be Will?" Marlow says, her mouth half full of pepperoni pizza.

"Detective Will Everts, Agent Karina Marlow. She's here to give us a fresh look at what's going on."

The two nod at each other as Will dives into the second box of pizza. If he only knew that bacon was the first pie, he'd be angry.

"So, anything new?" Will asks bluntly.

"Not much on the digital end," Logan explains. "Once Valez gets to New York, she goes off grid. There's no credit card usage, cell phones, emails, or anything I could sink my teeth into. If she had anything, it would have been paid for by Irving Garrison. Beyond that, Valez gets paid in cash for anything else she wanted," Logan finishes and meticulously dries his hands with a napkin.

"Two of my ex-Marine brothers work at the shipyard. I asked them for any information on the containers, but it seems they were brought in overnight when neither of them were on shift." Will shrugs.

Marlow places her plate down on the carpet, wipes the pizza oil from her perfectly manicured nails, and stands up. She walks over to the blank dry erase board and stares at it. All of us watch her, curious as to what the agent is going to do. She pops open her suit jacket, removes it, tosses it on an empty chair, and grabs the black marker. Her crisp handwriting screeches across the board as she spells out Irving Garrison. She underlines his name twice.

"The FBI knows for a fact that illegal shipments have been coming into the Hudson Container Terminal for quite some time. It used to be run by the mob, but now the people that work there themselves are for hire. That doesn't mean that all the employees are dirty." She directs her words at Will, effectively stopping him from refuting her statement. "The money that we've managed to follow seems to indicate that every Tuesday and Thursday night illegal shipments are entering the port."

"You're telling us the FBI knows that this has been going on and they've done nothing about it?" Will asks, somewhat incensed.

"Truthfully, we could shut down the illegal operation tomorrow—hell, we could have shut it down five years ago—but that won't help us. These are small fish, and the FBI only likes to hook whales. We've got people who come in, put trackers on the containers, and hope for the best." Marlow continues to face the board. With her back to the rest of us, we're tense and on guard.

"How's that working out for you?" Logan laughs. He probably knew the statistic before the FBI even have the numbers to generate one.

"That's above my pay grade."

"What do you want to add to the board besides his name?" I ask. The way she stands at the board, swinging the marker back and forth, it's as if she knows something but is unsure if she should share. Slowly, gingerly, she draws a line from the "n" in Garrison, to the right of the board. She hesitates; her hand shakes for a moment and she takes a deep breath. Her head hanging down, she writes the name Judge Rufus Killian. She places the cover on the marker and clicks it closed. The sound reverberates off the walls. Just because we had notions that he was involved doesn't mean we were able to prove it.

"Two years ago, we brought down a pedophile ring in Washington State. Mostly young boys, in the most depraved situations, and doing the most . . . unspeakable things. One of the names on the list that sparked our interest was Judge Rufus Killian. Apparently, there had been some preliminary investigation in two other states regarding his involvement in downloading and distributing child pornography. When my partner and I looked into it, each case fell apart. Nobody could make it stick. A few weeks later, I get called into my boss's office. He tells me that I am to stop investigating and hand over all of my paperwork. Considering how hard this case hit me, I demanded an explanation. That's when I was read in on the bigger fish to fry: Irving Garrison and his gang."

"The FBI let a pedophile go?" Logan asks, throwing his pizza down on the plate.

"That's the funny thing: we know he's still downloading, possibly sharing, but he's no longer uploading new videos or new images of his victims. It's as if someone insisted he stop or forced him to. We all know pedophiles don't just cease doing what they're doing, so this had to be pretty big," Marlow says.

"Could be Garrison. He seemed to take issue with Walter Miller assaulting Kaley Johnson. I'm sure she wasn't the first he assaulted," Will adds.

"You're asking us to believe that Irving Garrison is so influential that the FBI has been hunting him for years?" Victor finally interjects, having been quiet for the entire conversation.

"No. I'm telling you the FBI feels that Irving Garrison has his hand in enough illegal activities to put a red flag on his back the size of Texas. He's our focus. That being said, he might just be a single player on a much larger chessboard."

Marlow walks back across the room, sits down, and crosses her legs. She gracefully grabs her beer, tilts her head back, and swallows the rest of it. She looks at me casually, and I can see her brown eyes appear more lifeless than before. It's hard to keep a bright, shiny view on life when you've seen children tortured, raped, and murdered.

"Now that we know where the FBI stands, can we move on?" I take a few swigs off my beer and let the liquid cool my throat. "Do we have anything to go on from the crime scenes? Forensic evidence? Bugs? Something other than some officer losing his lunch from the rancid smell?"

"All the forensics are being covered by Lillian," Victor states calmly as my eyes lock with his. He blushes as I continue to stare at him. I know he rarely calls anyone by their first name, unless he's your friend or involved in something closer than a working relationship. I'm guessing it's the second.

"So, we call the doc and ask if she has anything new for us," Will adds, drawing my attention to him.

My cell phone comes to life on the end table, followed by Marlow's. Seconds later, everyone else's follows suit.

"That can't be good," Victor says, stating the obvious.

"Steele," I answer my phone and focus on the voice on the other end. Everyone answers their phones as well. I cover my right ear to drown out the rush of voices in the room. I know they're probably getting the same information on their calls. The officer on my call speaks so softly all I manage to get out of the call is there's been a murder and the address. There are days like this—a lot of them—in most cops' lives. Days which never seem to end.

"You driving?" Agent Marlow asks me.

"Will, you coming with or meeting us there?" I ask.

"Coming." He nods and grabs his coat.

"Well, I'm driving myself," Victor says, "seeing as how I am going to be up late as hell doing a preliminary autopsy."

Marlow hands me my coat and keys. "Glad you got those few sips of alcohol past your lips?"

"It wasn't enough." I slide into my jacket before grabbing my keys out of her hand. I'm technically not on call, but if they find something related to my case, they call. Simple really. Here's hoping this new information helps open up the case and doesn't just add to the death toll.

***

The silence in the car does nothing to change my mood. Will sits next to me, staring out the window. It's rather obvious something is going on with him, but he's not talking. His face is flat, cold, and distant. I should be his sounding board, but with Marlow in the back seat, I'm not really free and clear to hear him. She's got some secrets; all agents do. Between the two of them, I am happier in the silence.

The drive is lined with elegant streetlamps, no sidewalks. Rows of mini-mansions with paver driveways with built-in lights that line the road. Most of the kids living here have more money than they could ever earn—given to them freely. How many of them will end up like the Garrison kid? Entitled? Angry? Who the hell knows, but I really would like that driveway. Mine looks like shit. I'd be happy with a leak-proof roof, truthfully.

The lights from the police cars up ahead pull me out of my reverie of wants. The dimly lit neighborhood looks like a holiday seasonal display with blue, red, and white lights flashing in time. Marlow leans forward from the back seat and pulls on the back of mine. Will opens the door before I come to a complete stop and is out of the car before I put it in park.

"He always like this?" Marlow asks.

I ignore her question and step outside the car. The police have cordoned off this crime scene more efficiently than I'm used to. Crime scene tape is tightly run from tree to tree. Officers have the press out of the way behind some more tape fifty yards up the road. The few spectators that have gathered are being held at bay as well. Perfectly executed. It makes goosebumps form on my skin. There's only one reason for this much control.

"Steele," Will says to the right of me. My eyes must convey my confusion. He never calls me by my last name without my title in front of it. "We have a problem."

"What kind of problem?" Marlow asks, her voice calm and cold.

"It's best if we all go inside and discuss this. Too many eyes and ears out here."

He lifts the yellow tape and allows Marlow and me to duck underneath it.

The three of us walk past the media as bright white light covers us all. I turn around and see a teenage boy with his cell phone out. He waves at me, turns the camera around, and takes a selfie with me in the background. I don't really care about the picture, more the attitude. This is the future of my country, taking a selfie while a detective deals with someone on their worst day.

I take one step toward the offending spectator but a hand on my shoulder stops me. I turn around and see Will staring at me. His eyes tell me to stop, but his flexing muscles show me how angry he is as well. Surprisingly, it calms me immediately. I nod and the two of us head into the house.

"Marlow?"

"Already inside waiting for us," Will says, his voice devoid of emotion. "You really think we can trust her?" I understand his concern; it's mine as well.

"Right now, we don't have a choice. Let's just keep our noses clean and do this right," I say while trying to keep myself from tripping up the front stairs into the house. An officer protecting the entrance to the house moves to the side, letting us in. Once Will passes, he slides right back to his post.

"Victor here yet?"

"Yeah, he's with Marlow. Jasmine, this is a big one," Will says, as he leads us through a maze of rooms to a den.

There the victim sits, eyes open, the milky white cornea staring into space. Teeth black, probably dried blood from when the victim gurgled his own fluids before death. His suit clean, except for the blood that trickled down his neck from the small hole in his shirt. Everything seems to be in place; even the iPad sits on the desk. Books line the shelves behind him, in alphabetical order and dusted. Besides the fact that he's a neat freak, it's pretty obvious the victim knew the murderer. The place isn't trashed.

I watch as Victor looks over the body. Will talks to the officer next to him, pointing to the entryway. Marlow waits by the body. I assume she wants to see what the medical examiner can share. I turn around, and that's when I see it—a judge's cloak hanging on the back of the door. It all makes sense. This is the body of Judge Killian. Whoever is doing this continues to tie up loose ends, as well as be one step ahead of me and my team.

"Victor, what can you tell me?" I ask simply.

"I'll know more when I get back to the lab and start an autopsy. I can tell you the judge's been dead for a while. He's in full rigor. Cause of death should be obvious and overkill," Victor says, pointing to a hammer sticking out of the victim's head and the possible bullet wound.

"We need to work this place apart. It's possible whoever did this didn't really get what they came for," Marlow says while looking through some drawers in the desk.

Will throws a look over his shoulder. "I think they got what they came for, Agent Marlow. Nothing seems out of place, and the victim's personal effects appear to be here. Most likely they came here with one task in mind."

"With all due respect, we don't know what went on here or what was left behind," Marlow fires back, angrily. "I know this case has been trying on all of you, but we can't allow that to interfere with our jobs. This is a high-ranking judge in the state of New York. His crimes were hidden well, so we need to ascertain who knew about them and why was he murdered. Those two questions that could lead to our killer."

"Whatever you say, Agent Marlow. Just remember I'm not the enemy here. Next time you suggest something, do so clearly and precisely so that we can follow you. After all, we're just the lead detectives on the case," Will says sarcastically.

Victor looks over at me and we shake our heads. This is not going to be an easy case by itself, let alone with two people who aren't seeing eye-to-eye. Will walks past me without saying a word. I assume he's going to search the rest of the house to look for anything that could give us additional information. Marlow's right; even if the assailant came here to kill the judge, there is a possibility that the judge has incriminating evidence hidden somewhere. It's Detective Work 101, but Will's not thinking that way. I have to smooth out the ruffled feathers before it's too late.

"Jasmine, I have to get the body out of here through the back door. I'm having my assistant drive the van up to the side of the house," Victor says.

"Why can't you bring it out the front door, doc?" I ask quickly.

"His body is in a fixed position. I'd have to break everything to get him horizontal, and that might damage any evidence. Honestly, I'd rather just wheel him out in his office chair."

"You're crazy."

"Would you rather I parade a well-respected judge, regardless of his behind-the-scenes sexual endeavors with children, in front of the media?"

"If he was alive, I would say yes. Do what you have to do, doc," I say. I know he means well, but my head is ready to explode. Between the crime scene investigators dusting everything, which is making my allergies flare, and the sandbox war between my two colleagues, this day cannot end fast enough. I just need a little bit of evidence. Hell, I'll take a human hair with no DNA; anything is better than what I have right now. United we stand, divided . . . we are falling.

Chapter Six

Another sleepless night. But it looks like we finally caught a break. Victor's insistence that we remove Killian's body in a fixed position actually turned out to be a blessing in disguise. To do that, we had to dismantle the desk. It wasn't a big deal. It's an upscale Ikea model; a half dozen Allen screws, a couple small brackets, and it came apart.

That's when we found the false compartment behind the drawers. And the beat-up laptop which was inside it. I made sure one of the uniforms on scene hustled all the electronic devices back to Logan while we stayed to help with processing the scene.

Marlow and Will took on the lion's share of that task, walking through the whole house, and came up with some promising leads, but the silence between the two was unbearable. Will has never had an issue with authority before. I'll have to get to the bottom of this soon. The tension finally got the better of me, and I headed back to the station to wait on them to finish up.

Another week of cop drama later and the laptop seems to have finally given up the ghost. I make my way down to Logan's office with a decaf and an energy bar in hand.

Logan looks up and smiles as he clicks away at the dented laptop. "You're just in time!"

As I drop my overly exhausted body into a chair, I smile, remembering how we found the false compartment. Victor was the first to notice it—and let the rest of us know by screaming a horror-movie-watcher scream that made everyone leap. My heart raced for a good minute as he simply pointed at the laptop. Once they got the body out, I looked into the opening and pulled out the laptop hidden within.

"You look like you're having fun," I say as I sip my caffeine-free drink. I know Frankie isn't here, but for some reason it feels like cheating if I have a cup of coffee after promising her I wouldn't. And I am already feeling guilty from the one Logan snuck me earlier. Another difference between humanity and criminals: we feel guilt over what we've actually done, not just for getting caught.

"First the iPad was filled with generic things: e-books, games, his schedule, and his email. Nothing out of the ordinary at all. Now the laptop, on the other hand, is a gold mine. You have no idea the amount of shit the judge hid on here." His brown eyes dart across the screen as his fingers dance over the keys.

"Care to share with me, or are you just going to get off on the wonders behind the criminal mind?" I manage to eek out through my tired laughter. Anyone else would probably be offended by my words, and by thinking I was calling their sanity into question. Considering the content on the computer, they would attack me for calling them a pervert. Thank God my friends aren't normal overly sensitive people.

"Sure, once I break through the rest of these encrypted files. The amount of child porn on here is phenomenal, not to mention the emails he sent with pornographic attachments. I'm running a program trying to backtrack those emails to actual human beings. If I have my way, the FBI will be crazy busy for a while tracking them down." Logan smiles as he looks up briefly from the laptop screen. The light from the screen illuminates his face in a glowing, horror-film sort of way.

"Have you heard from Hadley?" His eyes go back to the screen, but I can feel the emptiness in the words. He misses her. I understand that. Sleeping without my family under the same roof is wearing on me as well.

"Not since she took Frankie and Chase with her."

"How are you handling it?"

"Not well at all. I'd be doing much better if we were closer to solving this case. Maybe if you sped up your fingers, we would be able to move forward a little quicker?"

"Okay, no small talk. I get it. I'm working as fast as I can. Encryption takes time. Or rather decryption."

"Is there anything you can tell me? The smallest thing can be more important than you know," I plead with Logan. I need something from him to divert my mind from my family.

"He had an offshore bank account. It seems to be run by the same people handling Garrison's money. I don't have direct connections as of right now, but they might be in the encryption files. I've got images of several young boys that are in the missing person's database, but they could be from years ago. Once these images are online, they have a life of their own."

"Explain."

"No image is sacred. Once it's uploaded it can be used for anything. Like your social media images for example—"

"I don't do any of that crap," I say, cutting him off.

"You don't, but the regular people in society do. Anything we upload can be right-clicked and saved to a hard drive. You could post an innocent image of your nephew in a bathing suit at the beach. It's innocent in nature, but to a pedophile, it's eye candy."

"Okay, so they can save the image and do unsavory things to themselves. I get it." I throw my half-eaten PowerBar in the trash. I've lost my appetite.

"Yeah, but then they can upload it to whatever database they share images with. Then those people save the image and re-upload it. Then those people do the same. It never ends. It's why most victims have difficulty moving beyond what's happened to them. Remember Kaley Johnson? Walter Miller, another fine associate of Garrison's who wound up dead, sexually assaulted her and documented it. If I search for her, I'm sure I'd still find images and possibly some videos of Walter Miller abusing her too."

My stomach rolls as he talks about the reality of sexual abuse victims. It's a never-ending cycle of hatred for oneself. I always thought once we found where things were going, the victimization would end. I was wrong.

"I thought Garrison had no stomach for that kind of crime. Remember Mr. Miller's rather disgusting demise?"

"How could I forget? I still don't know how they managed to make the body look so full of stuff when all the organs were missing."

"Stuffed it with newspaper, but that doesn't answer my question. How could a man with even a sliver of morality allow a judge to get away with this? Especially when he killed another man responsible for the sexual assault of a young girl he might have sold for a profit later on," I ask again in a firmer tone.

Logan sits up and stops everything he's doing. He stares at the screen. His eyes scan left and right like a subway train speeding by. Suddenly, they stop and he leans back in his chair.

"It wasn't morality as much as it was profit margins. Secondly, Judge Rufus Killian was on the payroll," he says as he spins the laptop to face me. I scan the decrypted email. My hatred for the judge is growing exponentially. If he wasn't dead already, I'd have him do a perp walk and toss him in gen pop. They just love men who rape kids. It's a simple code really. Innocence is to be protected; everyone else is fair game. Killian wouldn't have lasted more than a few hours before being tortured himself. After a day, maybe two, he'd be found hanging in his cell in an apparent suicide that would be anything but. He wound up with a hammer sticking out of his head. In my opinion, he got off easy.

"So, Garrison blackmailed him."

"Yeah, according to the emails, if he touched any of the merchandise, he'd be exposed himself. That and he was promised payment for rulings in his favor," Logan adds quickly.

"I see that. So now we know the judge was in his back pocket. So, every conviction Judge Killian issued—or didn't issue—will be called into question. Fantastic. The bigger question is can we connect those payments to

Garrison's bank accounts? Maybe this other woman . . . Valez? Is there something that can connect the damn dots?"

"Not yet, but this allows me to call our new partners in the FBI and ask for their high-tech, sexy software to work for me."

"You just called software sexy."

"Don't judge. You love Frankie, video games, and cars. I've got Hadley, code, and software. We're even. Now shut up and let me get back to work."

"Okay, I'm gonna head upstairs to the conference room and see what Marlow has come up with. Maybe she can fill in some gaps."

"I'll shoot her an email with what I found," Logan says as his hands and eyes go back to the laptop. "If you speak to Hadley, tell her I miss her like crazy."

"I doubt I will, but sure." I stand and leave Logan to attack the code. It must be a game to him. I mean, why else would you want to sit in a chair attached to a keyboard for hours trying to decipher something that someone doesn't want you to see? Maybe it's an ego thing, like, "I'm better than your security." I'm that way with my job, so I can understand that. I'm glad Logan—his fast hands, critical mind, and slight techie ego—are on my side.

Walking into the makeshift office, I see Marlow leaning back in a chair holding her cell phone in front of her. Her left hand waves around as she talks to whoever is on the other end of the video call. Her smile reaches her eyes, and for the first time, I can really see Karina Marlow as a human being as opposed to a hard-nosed FBI agent. Her brown eyes, highlighted by the slight lines at the corner of her eyes, look so alive and vibrant. Her face is relaxed, her body calm; I'm jealous.

It's rare for me to enjoy the finer moments in life. I can be at the park watching Chase's lacrosse game and yet worry about everyone else there. Does someone have a gun? Is there someone looking at Chase in an improper way? Even at home, I find it hard to break free of the cases I've worked on throughout the day. I'm jealous she can do that. Maybe she has a trick up her sleeve I could borrow. One thing is for sure, I'm about to wipe the smile off her face, and I don't want to.

Opening the door, Marlow immediately leans forward in her chair. She looks up at me and holds one finger up out of view of the camera. I simply sit down and sip my decaf.

"Karina," the voice on the other end says. Her smile widens and she tilts her head to the right. Her shoulders sag a bit as a wave of sadness rolls over her. It's something I feel I shouldn't be witnessing.

"Hey baby, I have to go back to work," she says. "Make sure to tuck the kids in and tell them I love them."

"I always do, love," the man replies.

"Have a great game tonight. I love you, and I'll see you once this case is closed."

"Of course, mi amor. Be safe and don't let that Steele woman walk all over you."

I feel my lip curl upwards in one of my famous smirks. I'm sure me looking up through my eyelashes gives her pause. Her eyes lock with mine, and I can see she's trying to hide her embarrassment.

"I love you, honey, but I've got to go." She hits a button on her phone and drops it on the table. "About that . . ." she begins.

"That I walk all over you? Or is it that I try to pull rank and seem like more of a bitch when I want what I want?" I say with sarcasm pouring out with every syllable.

"If we're speaking truthfully . . . yes."

"Just yes? To which one?"

"That you carry yourself in a powerful manner even if you have no strength left in you."

"You sound like my psychologist of a girlfriend." I laugh a little, but it dies before it gets to be too rich. I miss her. I take a breath to center myself. "Forensic profiling and a lot of undergraduate psychology classes. I'm not just a pretty face."

"Point taken," Marlow concedes.

She stands and walks over to the coffee pot in the corner. "I haven't met this girlfriend of yours, have I?" She pours herself a mug and adds several sugars and a drop of milk. I know what she's doing. She wants to pick me apart, see if she can trust me. If we open up to each other a bit, she'll feel a connection to me. That way she can justify protecting me in her mind.

"No, I sent Frankie away with my nephew." She stops and sits back down in her original chair. Her intense stare pushes my buttons, and I divert my gaze to the windows.

"There's a story there."

"There always is," I shoot back quickly. "I'm sure you've read the file. Let's just say it's safer for them to be away from me until things are settled."

"Fair enough." She calmly sips her sugar-laden drink. "Tell me about Detective Everts."

"Loyal partner, great detective, former Marine, and an exceptional father."

"Who obviously dislikes my interference here."

"Has nothing to do with you, per se. This case is just hitting him hard."

"Maybe he should take some time off," Marlow says tenderly. I hear sincerity in her voice.

"You know the drill. You take time when whatever is bothering you goes away. Then you fall apart." I continue to look out the window. I know my decaf is cold at this point, but I take a sip anyway. Sometimes your body just needs to do things to dispel nervous energy.

"I understand that. I'm here trying to help you find criminals who never stepped foot in my state but pumped more drugs into it than Exxon pumps up its profits and Russian ties."

I stay silent. How does one reply to that? I know the feeling. Garrison is my obsession and yet here she is, forced to help me as her killer roams the streets free. I want to say something, but my mind screams at me to shut up and move on.

"Logan's still dissecting the laptop downstairs. He found that Judge Killian was on Garrison's payroll."

"That's not surprising. Any evidence of specific transactions?"

"Offshore bank accounts, most likely. As for the rest, he's still digging. I was hoping you could take a deeper look with your team back home."

"I'll see if our department can dig into Killian's financials. Maybe something will pop that helps us."

"I doubt it," I say seriously.

"Oh ye of little faith."

"You and I both know anything we find on that computer won't be overwhelming in the way of evidence. We're gonna find exactly what Valez or Garrison wants us to find."

"Very true. We'll have snippets of a much larger image that we can't quite put together just yet. The point is we'll have one thing more than we did before. I know this sucks, and trust me, I want to go home and be with my boys. But this will unravel in its own time," Marlow answers calmly.

"Irving Garrison's son was an alcoholic and an all-around vile human being. He became a cop and worked under my nose. Keith was basically an obnoxious, egomaniacal cop who loved the power. He was everything wrong with the police force *and* in the minority . . . but the press loved him."

I look over at Marlow. Her face shows no emotion. She's just listening without judgment. I don't know why I feel compelled to give her this information. Maybe I know Will might not be able to save me from myself this time. Maybe I need some backup.

"I was getting ready for dinner with Frankie, had the engagement ring and everything. I go to the door and there's a cop standing there. He looked at me with such pity, you know? He takes me to an accident, and

I see the captain waiting. He opens the door and pulls me into a hug. When I looked over his shoulder, I saw my brother's car. That's when I heard Chase screaming at the top of his lungs. I fought my way out of the captain's arms and ran over. Held onto my nephew for dear life once everything was over."

I stop talking and drain the dregs of my decaf. No tears fall down my face anymore. I know I haven't fully dealt with what happened, but I've accepted the fact that it was out of my control. Keith was to blame, and he paid with his life.

"I assume your brother passed away?" Marlow says softly.

"Yeah."

"You're raising your nephew with Frankie?"

"Now I am. Took a long time to get to that point."

"Grief is different for everyone. You have to handle it in your own time," Marlow says as she stands to get more coffee. She picks up the pot of decaf and gestures toward me. I nod yes.

"I lost her for a long time. It wasn't until . . ." My voice fails me, and I stop talking.

"Until?" she prompts gently.

"It's a long story that you already read. Will saved my life that night. Frankie went through hell, and now we're working on getting our life back together."

"Simon proposed after a game of paintball. He was on the opposing team, and I was just out of the academy. I shot him square in the chest. He fell down hard. So, I run up worried I really hurt him. He pulls me down for a kiss, tells me I hit him in the heart, and opens his jumpsuit. He had this white shirt on with 'Will you marry me?' written on it. It was so tacky, yet perfect for us." Marlow places a cup of coffee in front of me. I grab it quickly. "You still have the ring?" She sits back down in her chair and leans back, crossing her legs.

"Yeah, in a drawer."

"What are you waiting for?"

"I don't know. I want it to be perfect, romantic, or whatever. I had it planned before, and I don't think I could do it again. Maybe it's me. Maybe it's the ring. Hell, maybe it's the fear of preparing for the proposal and having something shitty happen again. I don't know."

"You'll figure it out."

"Why are we talking about this?" I ask honestly. I really don't like the darker side of this conversation.

"Because we can? Until I call the Seattle office, there's really nothing much more we can do. So, we're talking about my kids and husband, your girlfriend who should be your fiancé, and how our lives are never how we planned it."

"Realist. I like it."

"We're outnumbered by idiots, power-hungry fools, and religious zealots. I prefer to be abnormally normal," Marlow says.

I raise my mug and smile. "To America!" Marlow toasts my mug gently as they're both still full. It's nice to feel laughter bubbling in me again. Since the threatening phone call, I haven't been able to find humor in much. With the video store bombing, the graveyard in the container, and the murder of Killian, it would be strange if I could. A cop's gallows humor can only take one so far. I'm still waiting for my phone to ring again with some bad news. Right on cue, my cell phone dances around the table with an image of Will and his family.

"Hello, detective. What can I do for you?" I say into the phone, a bit of happiness bubbling out with my words.

"Just curious if you have a few minutes." The seriousness in Will's voice breaks through, and I feel my face fall.

"Where?" He knows I'll be there. Asking me was just a formality.

"Park. Our usual spot." The line goes silent. I stand up and collect some papers from the table.

"I'm going to be MIA for a little bit. If anything comes down the line . . ."

"I'll call you. Otherwise, you're not to be disturbed. I got it," Marlow states while looking over the notes in front of her.

"Thank you," I say, and head out of the room.

"Take care of your partner." I nod my head and bolt out the door. Will's voice was calm, even, and almost emotionless. I know he's reached a breaking point, and I hope he's ready to talk. If I've learned anything in the last few years, it's that internalizing everything makes you lack focus and direction. In other words, you become an all-around asshole. Neither Will or I can afford to be that.

***

It's an eerie sensation walking through Central Park when there is something violent going on in your mind. I remember when I was still a student and 9/11 happened. There was no crosstown traffic, and I had to somehow get home to Frankie in our one-bedroom shithole Uptown. National Guard was everywhere, the streets mostly empty, and Times Square was a ghost town. I remember taking a bus from my internship all the way Uptown. Fighter jets flew overhead, causing fear to crawl down my spine like a spider hunting its prey.

I cut through the park, something I had never done before. The sky was crystal clear, people lying on blankets all over. To this day I wonder what they were thinking, but the kids—they just played like nothing had happened. Their joyous screams as they chased one another or the yelps when their dog almost got away were just the same as any other day. For them, it was a normal day. Their innocence was kept intact while the adults were completely destroyed.

The park still feels odd to me for that reason. Sure, I've been here and brought Chase here. I've had barbecues with Will and our families here. It's a wonderful getaway in the middle of a concrete jungle, but it still has a bit of darkness to it. How can one sit here and enjoy something when there are murderers and rapists beyond the gates? Hell, there's been more than a few in here and yet we play as if there is nothing to fear. I wish sometimes I could shut off the analyzing and figuring everything out just long enough to see the beauty that is around me. Sadly, after all my education, I don't have that luxury.

"Traffic on the west side highway?" Will calls to me as I walk to our favorite picnic area.

"Subways were a bitch," I answer back as I reach him and sit down.

"I thought you loved to drive."

"I figured you would, so I thought I'd save a tree and use mass transit."

"Didn't work out so well."

"No, not on time, and when the hell did the price go up again?"

Will chuckles a bit at my commentary. The two of us fall into a calm silence as we settle in on a nearby bench. In front of us a family plays Frisbee. The dog seems to be a better catcher than the young boy. Reminds me of my brother when we were little. He'd throw the damn thing so high I couldn't catch it. Always tried though, and landed awkwardly on the grass. Sprained my ankle when I was nine. Try explaining that to the doctor in the emergency room. Sprained via Frisbee catch attempt. I miss those moments now.

"I'm sorry my head's been up my ass lately," Will says so low I almost didn't hear him.

"I get it," I respond simply. What else can I say? I'm angry he hasn't been talking to me and putting this investigation at risk, but in the same token, who am I to judge? He's been by my side during the worst, and it's my job to stand by him as well.

"I owe you an explanation," he adds, looking out into the nothingness of the bright blue sky.

"Only if you want to."

"I wasn't born here. It took a few years before I became a citizen," he starts as he shoves his hands into his pockets. I'm not sure if it's to deal with nerves or anger. "My grandmother had this big belief in the American dream. She would always tell me that the Statue of Liberty said to 'bring the tired and hungry'. . . that there would be more opportunity in the United States than anywhere else in the world. It was full of people wanting a better life. So, she planned, filled out paperwork, and tried to get us into the country. For years I watched her do everything according to the law. She went to the embassy with me in tow, asked questions, learned the language and the laws . . . but there were so many people and not enough opportunities."

Will stands up and walks a few steps in front of me. His shoulders slump, and I can feel the tension rolling off him in waves. He turns to look at me, and his face is slightly wet from fighting tears.

"One day, these men came to my house. Demanded my father come work for them. My father owed many people money, and he couldn't pay. So, he left us thinking he was protecting his family. In reality, they just started coming after my mom. So, one day my grandmother grabs a suitcase and starts shoving clothes inside. My mother comes in and grabs me, tells me we have to go. I had no idea what was happening. I was too young to understand. Next thing I know we're in this boat. It was freezing cold, and I was so hungry . . . but we continued to hold on until we got to the shore of the United States. Some men met us there and we were smuggled in. They demanded my grandmother work off the cost of getting us there. Those men were bastards, but she didn't care. I had a chance to make a difference in the world. One day she went to work saying her debt would be paid off at the end of her shift, then she would work for herself."

He rubs his hand along his neck while a fresh set of tears run down his face.

"She never came home. We couldn't go to the police because of our status, but my mother and I knew what happened. My mother moved us out of Florida and up to New York. We worked hard to get our citizenship, and I joined the Marines, all to honor her sacrifice. Seeing those containers just reminded me of her. I needed time to clear my mind."

"I get it, you needed time, I truly do. I'm beyond sorry you had to live through that, but you need to talk to me. I would have understood better than anyone else in the world, and you didn't trust me. We can't work like that, Will. I've got your back, and I always will. Just trust me next time, okay?"

His slight smile is infectious, and I feel my lips curl as well. I want to stay mad at him, but he's one of the few friends I've got. I understand why he hid. Most of all, I've been there as well. I stand up and take one step toward him before I see the birds fly away. A sound. Like a firework, but not quite. A breeze, like someone blew hot air on my neck. Will's smile drops, his eyes questioning as we both look at his shirt. The tinge of red spreads like wildfire from the center of his sternum.

In a flash, he's on the ground. Pulling my jacket off, I punch it into a ball and hold it firmly down. My left hand shakes frantically as I dial dispatch.

"Nine-one-one, what's your emergency?"

"This is Detective Steele, badge number 1207. Shots fired in Central Park near the Fifty-Seventh Street entrance, officer down! I repeat, Detective Evertz has been shot!"

The words feel foreign coming out of my mouth. I look at my jacket as the blood seeps through it, creating a reddish-black color that I normally love on an inanimate object. This though, it's Henry all over again. The phone drops from my hand as I hear the dispatcher continue to talk. My hands push down in tandem, and small bubbles of blood pop along the edges of the stained clothing. My eyes focus on my hands as I feel something hit my arm. Everything in me knows it's Will trying to get my attention, but I can't focus on him right now or I'll break.

Sirens in the distance—a beautiful sound right now. Will hits my arm again. I continue to focus on my now red hands. Every now and again a droplet of water hits them and dilutes the color a bit. My tears do that. I hear the screeching of brakes, and I look to my right. Paramedics jump out and rush over to me. Their mouths move, but I can't make out anything.

The taller one pushes me out of the way, and I careen out into the grass. I watch as they shove tubes into his arms. Bags of fluid held by fellow officers. I wish I knew when they showed up. The team lifts Will and places him on a gurney before running back to the bus. In a split second the vehicle is gone, and there's a massive mess to clean up.

"Jasmine, look at me," a familiar voice says to me. Captain Udall, his voice sounds so muted and lost. "Jasmine." He snaps his fingers in front of my face. "What happened here? Are you all right?"

I know he's asking me all these questions, but all I can do is look at my hands. My blood-covered hands. Will's blood. I have to call Mia and the kids. I feel the captain lift me to my feet and lead me to his car.

"She shot him," I mutter.

"You don't know that, Jasmine," he says unconvincingly. He knows the probability of it being someone else is slim at best. Alexa Valez was here and took a clear shot at my partner. After the bombing of Pearl Harbor, Japan's Yamamoto supposedly said, "I fear all we have done is to awaken a sleeping giant and fill him with a terrible resolve." She is behind this. And she has no idea the beast that she's woken in me.

Chapter Seven

Beeping. I hate that sound. It's the true sound of waiting: waiting to know whether someone's going to live or die. As long it stays a constant, incessant beeping, you've still got a chance. I wonder if Will's heart is still beating. I wonder if he left all of his blood on my hands. It felt like it. With each passing beat of his heart, the blood pushed onto my hands, warming them. I tried to fight back, keep it all in there; obviously, I failed.

Captain Udall has come in more than once asking what happened. For the longest time, I just stared out the window as the nurses collected evidence while the new day dawned. What am I supposed to tell him? Should I mention how Will had briefly checked out while trying to battle his own internal demons? Should I tell them he was sorting things through, getting his head back in the game? One of the best officers I've ever known was just gunned down. Either way, I'm going to need to tell him something and soon.

"Captain Udall said you'd be here," a broken voice says to me. I look up from staring at my hands to see Mia's face.

"Mia, I'm so sorry," I say, trying my very best to keep a steady voice.

"I wish I could blame you; it would be so much easier. The captain told me what they think happened. Sniper." Mia sits down in the chair next to my bed. Her tearstained face looks wrung out. "The doctor tells me I should thank you."

"I don't know what for."

"They didn't tell you?" She looks up at me curiously. "You kept pressure on the wound. He would've bled out in seconds if not for you." Mia shakily raises her hand and rests it on mine. I squeeze her fingers gently, taking all of the comfort that I can from it. I don't know what else to tell her, or what else to say. Thankfully, I hear the doorknob start to turn. A man in blue scrubs sticks his head in the door.

"Mrs. Everts, your husband is out of surgery. I can take you to see the doctor now," the nurse says mechanically. Mia stands and simply nods her head. She looks at me and smiles half-heartedly before pulling her hand free. Once they leave the room, I put my face back in my hands.

My breathing slows, my eyelids close, and I try to remember and focus on the scene at the park. The trees are green; pollen is high. My nose is running a little. There was barely a cloud in the sky. It reminded me of 9/11, everything was pristine; one of the more beautiful days. No one else was near us, but there was a bike chained to a lamppost nearby. I don't remember seeing that bike when we left. Then again, I was very distracted.

I remember the air disturbance caused by the bullet whizzing by my head. I remember the slight breeze coming from the east side of the park. The look in his eyes when he realized he had been shot. I remember not being able to talk to dispatch clearly and precisely. I remember my emotions getting the better of me as they so often do no matter how much I try to contain them. I had no idea what was going to happen. And the time that passed by so quickly. That pisses me off. I should have known instinctively what to do. I should have seen something. All of my training, all that we've been through, and I still have work to do.

"You can't keep beating yourself up about this, Jasmine," Captain Udall says. I don't know when he came into my room, but he's here and I'm conscious. I guess I have to listen to him.

"I'll beat myself up until I know he's in the clear."

"That might be a while. Detective Everts is in the ICU. They managed to take the bullet out and stop the internal bleeding. He's lucky. The doctors say if the bullet was an inch higher or if you didn't apply as much pressure as you did, we'd be burying him right now. The point is, Jasmine, what's done is done. I want to know what you saw, what you smelled, what you heard. I don't care if it was a woodpecker poking a tree or two teenagers screwing in the bushes. I need to know. We need to know. Maybe we can piece together the scene and hopefully the evidence will lead to something," he says, rubbing his temples.

"What evidence was left behind?" I look up from my hands.

"There are some shoe impressions and what looks like a cigarette butt or two in the right area. It's a public park, so we're not sure if the cigarette butts are from the shooter, but the officers canvased the area and this spot makes the most sense. We did find a shell casing buried under one of the bushes they used for cover."

"How does a contract killer forget to pocket their brass? That's a rookie mistake," I say.

"Rare as hell, but I've seen it before. Cops' response is rather quick, so they make a slight mistake. Considering where it was found, maybe she stepped on it, pushing it into the dirt, so she missed it. Maybe it just rolled out of sight. Either way, we caught a damn lucky break, and I don't plan on squandering it," the captain replies.

"Has Doctor Brown started the DNA sequencing on the butts yet?"

"It's on the top of her pile."

"When am I getting out of here? I can't be of any help to her here. Maybe we can prove that Alexa Valez is behind this," I plead with him.

"The doctors think you need a day or two to rest. You checked out on me back there. Nothing I said made it through to your brain. Not that you listen to me on a good day, but you were in shock. It happens to the best of us. So, I'm suggesting that you go home and rest. I don't expect you back in the office until tomorrow."

With that, I swing my legs out of bed and scan the floor for my shoes. On autopilot, I grab my boots and put them on.

"You're not listening to me, Jasmine." He shakes his head. "I don't know why I'm wasting my breath on talking— "

"Captain, we've been down this road before. It doesn't work. I want to be there for Mia and the kids."

"This comes from the higher-ups. You come back to work today, and I'll take your badge. As far as Will's family, trust me—they're not alone. And I'll update you every time there's something to update you about." The captain walks over and places his hand on my shoulder. It feels fake, almost forced. Maybe it's because right now I don't care what he thinks or says. I want to work. I need to work.

"I understand your need to be a part of this. Just understand what I'm telling you: don't come into the office. Stay home with Agent Marlow and clear your head. I'm sure there's light reading for you to do." He squeezes my shoulder twice with a sly smirk before backing away. I'm reading him loud and clear. He just gave me clearance to work the case from home. That I can do.

Udall slips out the door, and I stand and do a quick stretch skyward. I grab my personal items, my gun, and my badge before heading out the door. The hallway is lined with blue uniforms. Mia and the kids sit in the center, huddled together for comfort. Will better pull through, or I think his wife will find him in the afterlife and kill him. Before I know what I'm doing, his family is within arm's reach.

I kneel down to their level and simply open my arms. The kids hesitate for a second before lunging into my embrace. I pull them to me as tightly as I can, showing them all my love and support. I can feel the tears come to my eyes, but I blink them away. This isn't the time for the kids to see me weak. I look up at Mia, who smiles sadly. She knows how much these kids mean to me. "I'm going to find the bastard," I silently promise her.

"I heard you need a ride," Marlow says from behind me.

I feel the kids let go of me and I kiss their foreheads. Standing up, I give Mia a reassuring hug, even though it might not be worth much at all. I pull back and stare at the hallway of blue. It's always a sight to behold, but never one I wanted Frankie to see. You never think this could happen to you . . . until one day it does.

I turn around and see Marlow holding up a set of keys. She tilts her head toward the elevator. I just nod and follow her down the hallway. Nothing needs to be said. No more words. This whole case we've been two steps behind, probably three. It's time we're on even footing. We've been missing something this whole time. Maybe the DNA or the shoe impressions will help. One way or another, it's time to start looking for whatever we're not seeing.

A whiteboard is the simplest little thing. Just a blank slate for the team. Photos, timelines, anything and everything that can help us solve a case gets put on that damn thing. It's always been helpful to see the full outline in the past. It lets me see the bigger picture, the clearer picture, the one beyond the emotions. It's also something you can get lost in, like my basement before Frankie took it all down. You can get obsessed with links, strings, images, and whatever else you can find. Right now, though, it houses an image that I wish I could pull down. Will's picture, connected to a timeline with no discernible connection to anything other than me.

"Yes, sir. I understand that, but we are doing the best we can with the information we've collected."

I hear Marlow talking in the kitchen. Her bosses aren't happy with her or the rest of the team right now. We've got a crooked judge in the morgue. I'm sure there are lawyers lining up around city hall to file appeals for their clients. I'm pretty sure the majority of them will get new trials even if they're truly guilty. More taxpayer money down the drain because some politician saw money, power, and pleasure ripe for the picking. I wonder how many just do the goddamned job like the rest of us blue collar folk.

"Any news from the hospital?"

I look up to see Marlow leaning against the entryway. I simply shake my head in response. Will's been out of surgery for over five hours, and no news is good news right now. "I got an earful just now," she says.

"I heard," I state flatly, my eyes never leaving the board in front of me.

"Well, beyond being ripped a new one for not saving the life of a criminal judge, we apparently have every resource the FBI has to offer at our fingertips."

"Killian was a bastard, no loss there." My disdain oozes out in my words.

"True, but if he was caught, they could cover up all his previous deeds and just make him go away. No basis for appeals for every case he ever presided over, you know? Now? His homicide means paper trails, connections to be made, and a massive number of appeals that will clog an already overwhelmed system. Even if those wrongly convicted get a new trial, they will be buried behind those who deserve to be in prison but can buy their way out. Politics at its finest," she finishes.

"We don't write the rules, we just enforce them," I answer solemnly. I know the feeling when someone is guilty but set free or given a deal to roll on someone else. If you're in law enforcement, you've seen it more times than you can count. We just get the evidence and line up the cases to the best of our abilities. The rest is up to the lawyers and judges. If you're innocent, a good lawyer—regardless of experience—gets you a fair trial. At least that's how it's supposed to be.

"Did they give you anything we could use?" I toss out, trying to change the subject quickly.

"Not yet, but they're digging through all the files for Alexa Valez. It's a connection we hadn't explored before due to . . . I don't know . . . a lack of interest or a missing link."

"I feel like I'm missing something stupidly obvious and it's really starting to irritate me," I say, walking away from the board to sit next to Marlow on the couch.

"It's like when you lose your keys and they're always in the last place you look or in a spot you swear you searched at least twice."

"I think this is a little more pressing than where the hell my keys are hiding."

Marlow stands and walks over to the board. She picks up the black marker, leaves the cap on, and points to the picture of Judge Killian.

"We know Garrison had information about the indiscretions of our illustrious judge. That led us to"— she moves the marker to the image of Valez— "the homegrown hitwoman slash enforcer named Alexa Valez. Her paperwork led us to a romantic relationship with"—she moves the marker again to the image of Irving Garrison— "the head of the whole thing, making a perfect loop." She puts the marker down.

"So, you've basically stated the obvious. My first thought is 'and'?" The sarcasm oozes off my tongue easily.

"My point is maybe we're not missing something exactly. Maybe this isn't about the players we think it is." Marlow raps on pictures of the three for emphasis. "Maybe we have to look more into the connections and the indiscretions rather than the individuals themselves."

"We've already looked ad infinitum into the backgrounds of the three people up there. The only thing we know for sure is that these bastards show no remorse and the three we have on the board aren't running everything. I mean, c'mon, we're having difficulty finding anyone willing to speak who isn't afraid of deportation or their own demise."

"Listen to yourself. You've already looked. The team already searched. Like I said, maybe the damn keys are there and we're just missing them," she says calmly with a tinge of pleading in her voice.

I get what she's saying, and it couldn't hurt. She's a new set of eyes, and it's past time to be transparent with everything we have. I get up and walk over to a box near the front door. Kneeling down, I grab the handles and carry it to the coffee table. Flipping open the top, I reveal all the case files I have collected on Garrison since this whole fiasco began.

"Then let's start at the beginning." I grab my brother's file and hand it to her. "You'll have to look over this one. I know it inside and out. Maybe you'll see something I missed."

"Okay, I can go through all of the older files on my own, but right now I want to start at the video game store. Let's look at Valez and see what she's hiding."

Digging through the box, I pick up the older files and move them to the side. I see Marlow's eyes widen at the sheer number of pages. I'm thorough. Marlow grabs the rest of the file folders, elbows the box to the floor, and places them down. She sits down next to me, grabs the Gamer Syndicate video game store file, and opens it in front of us. Spreading the images out brings me right back to the bloody carnage. Two young people's lives callously erased for selling some illegal substances. You figure they would have known better. If they had a choice in the matter, that is.

"Tasha Fisher and Joe Connors, the two victims found in the back room at the store," Marlow says as she scans the first page of the file.

"Both confirmed to be dealing drugs out of the back room after hours. There was little evidence left; most of the stuff was destroyed in the explosion. So, the hows, whys, and anything else we could think to ask is kind of a mystery," I say, flipping through the few images of the crime scene the team managed to get before it all went to shit.

"Any traffic cameras or another store's security?"

"Logan looked for anything in the vicinity. The front of the store was covered, but not the back. Even if there was anything to see, it would be pointless. Not to mention we wouldn't be able to put any of it into context."

"The employee, Tucker Winslow, he found their bodies?" she asks.

"Poor kid went to open the store and found them in the back room. Called the police."

"Responders?"

"Officer Ramos and Officer Ali. Ramos was killed in the explosion."

"Has anyone contacted Officer Ali?" She flips the page to my photo-copied interview notes.

"Personally, no. He left a statement with the captain and his PBA rep. He's been on desk duty since the incident."

"Why? What did he do to warrant that?" She lowers the file and looks up at me expectantly.

"He hasn't been cleared by psych. The guy walked into the back room and fell in a pool of blood. It's messed him up pretty bad." She nods, accepting my explanation.

She pulls out her little notepad and writes Tucker Winslow at the top of a page with a question mark.

"Why'd you do that?" I ask.

"I understand your notes state he might not be involved, but he was there, so we need to eliminate all aspects of him from the sequence of events."

"You didn't see the kid. He was scared, shaken, his eyes more vacant than any victim I've ever seen. He came on his own to talk to us and basically just filled in some minor blanks. There's no physical evidence to indicate he was involved."

"I understand that, but Garrison and his crew have been one step ahead of your team and the FBI for some time. You don't think they would be prepared for a young kid coming by himself into an interview room? While it might just be the typical actions of a kid trying to do the right thing, our job is always to play devil's advocate."

"We call him back in and ask him some more questions in the morning." I grab the second file folder labeled "cargo containers."

"Gruesome murder scene," I say, shaking my head. "Human trafficking gone wrong. Running theory is no money was accessible to move the assets in these containers. So, they just let them . . . go. To die."

"Why, though? We open the container and find their remains, and Garrison goes down easily. Why allow us to find them all? And why now?" Marlow asks, looking through the pages quickly.

"Tying up loose ends? Maybe he's got nothing more to lose, so he's letting everything fall to the wayside while figuring a way out of the country. There are too many possibilities running through my head to even begin to answer that question clearly."

Marlow is right about one thing: it's true that Garrison is probably acting out of his normal safe zone. The FBI is hunting him. The NYPD has everything locked down tight. He's on the no-fly list. His assets have been inaccessible for over eight months. This is a desperate man who's running out of liquid assets.

"If all else fails, there is always a paper trail leading to something tangible that we can hang him with. Just follow the money," Marlow says matter-of-factly, as if we haven't been trying to do that already.

"Your people have been following the money and where has it gotten them?" I say, letting the disgust linger in my voice a little longer than I would like.

"Hey, I'm not the enemy here," Marlow says, holding her palms out. "I'm just trying to move forward and not keep banging our heads against the wall. If you want to bludgeon yourself, have at it." Marlow slams the file down on the table, stands up, and walks to the whiteboard. She runs her right hand through her hair while her left remains on her hip. It reminds me of Frankie when she's frustrated. Frankie would be able to piece things together for me, maybe fill in the deeper profile.

I grab my cell phone and dial Logan. It won't hurt to have him look through some more things. Maybe the analysts missed something. I might not agree with how Marlow speaks, but her words hold some weight. We might have missed something in the paper somewhere.

"How is he?" Logan answers quickly, immediately thinking about Will.

"No news yet," I reply. Marlow turns around and focuses her attention on me. She folds her arms across her chest as she waits. I mouth Logan's name. She nods and walks into the kitchen.

"No news is good news, right?" he asks.

"I guess. Look, I need you to dig into something for me."

"Sure, beats sitting around here waiting for information."

"I need you to dig up everything you can on Tucker Winslow. I want to know everything about him. Nothing is too insignificant," I say.

"Jasmine, you met with the kid. You think he's involved in this?"

"I don't know anything anymore. I just want to dot my i's and cross my t's. When you're done with that, go over Garrison's money again. He might have something out of the ordinary just sitting in plain sight that we've been overlooking."

"You got it, boss. If you hear anything about Will, you let me know, okay?"

"Will do." I hang up on the call as Marlow walks back in, two beers in hand. She hands me one before taking her place back on the couch.

"Checking on things, huh?" she asks.

"Yeah. Like you said: it's about checking all the loose ends. No stone unturned, right?" I take a long swig of my beer. The cold liquid calms the fire of acid burning my insides.

"Someone from my staff should call me in the morning. Whether they have something or it's just the status quo call, I don't know. One foot in front of the other. It's all we got."

"For right now," I say. I don't know if it's confidence or the beer on an empty stomach talking.

"For right now," she agrees, her voice a little more rational sounding considering our situation. She grabs another file folder as she relaxes deeper into the couch. Following her lead, I reach for a file as well. We might be drunk before we find anything else substantial, but it's worth a shot. It's not like either of us will be sleeping anyway. I need to keep my mind busy until I know Will is out of danger. I don't expect miracles, but the word "stable" would mean so much right now. Either way, it's going to be a long night.

After too many hours of searching and reading and rereading and nothing really popping out at me, I must have passed out. Captain Udall woke me with the news Will got out of a second surgery around three in the morning. He's not out of the woods—he's not even listed as stable—but I'll take it. Marlow had already left to go to the local FBI office and see if she could shake the tree a bit.

Me, I decided to head out and get some coffee with Logan. Looking at my watch, I know he's about twenty minutes late. That's less than usual, which means the coffee I bought for him will still be warm. As I see him running alongside the windows of the café, dodging rain puddles, I have to smile a bit. He always has an entertaining entrance.

"Sorry, I'm late again," he says as he falls into the seat across from me. Dropping his wet coat on the chair, he flips open his bag and grabs a cylindrical device. Logan drops his bag and twists the device in his hands. Placing it in the center of the table, he grabs his cell phone and checks something.

"What the hell are you doing? And what the hell is that?" I say as I point at the cylinder. He simply raises his index finger.

"And we're good."

"We're good with what?"

"Jammer. No tracking, turning on our phones remotely, or other equally nasty tech stuff. Think of it as a nice bubble of protection for our table." He smiles brightly.

"What about the people sitting within earshot? It would be rather simple for them to just make a phone call later and tell everyone what they heard." I smile at him as his face falls. He didn't think of that, but I respect the attempt.

"Well, we're still gonna use it."

"Whatever you say, geek monkey." I sip my coffee and feel the warmth start working its way into my bloodstream. "Will got out of surgery at three this morning, but he's got a long road ahead of him. That's all they told me. Now, tell me what's new in the land of information."

"That's good to hear. Before I tell you the rest, I got a call from Hadley last night." His smile could light up a room. It's rather nauseating.

"How is she?"

"Great. She was doing some action sequences, which was totally new for her. She has a butt double, which bothers me a bit, truthfully." I let out a small chuckle that causes Logan to stop talking and stare at me. I swallow my smile and wave my hand for him to continue. I don't trust myself to open my mouth right now.

"Anyway, she said Chase was loving being on a film set. They have some tutor working with him to keep him up to par with the kids in his grade right now." Those simple words simultaneously excite and soothe me. It's not like I forgot about him—far from it. However, hearing that he's still learning and having a ball calms my soul in so many ways.

"Thank you," I force out. I really miss my family. I don't like this, and the case is taking much longer to solve than I want.

"Frankie's not doing so hot." My eyes shoot up and lock with his. "She's apparently lively with Chase, but other than that, she's hiding out. She doesn't get as involved as Hadley wants her to. She misses you a lot."

"She should consider it a bit of a vacation. She's in some exotic location on a secret movie set with one of her best friends."

My weak voice betrays my intentions with those words. I would rather have her with me here. I want her safe, but I'm selfish.

"They know you're fine, and I shared a little about our case. Nothing too deep, but I thought Frankie might be able to help us with a profile. Plus, it would give her something to do to feel less helpless."

"Smart man."

"Happy wife, happy life," he says. My eyebrow goes up quizzically. "You know, so I've heard." He wrings his hands in front of me, trying to disperse the energy surging through his body. I continue to stare at him, enjoying watching him squirm. It feels very normal, a little ray of humanity seeping through the dark clouds around us. "So, about the case?" He changes the subject and my bubble of peace bursts.

"Did you find anything specific?"

"Marlow meeting us here?" Logan looks around the room for our fellow FBI agent.

"She's at the Bureau trying to see if they've found anything. If she makes it here, excellent. If not, so be it. I'll update her when I see her."

"Got it." Logan pulls a black file folder out of his backpack. He places it on the table before sliding it over to me as he looks around again. It takes everything in my being to stifle my laughter. I feel a smile gracing my face, so I know I haven't succeeded well in covering everything. I open the file as I shake my head.

"What am I looking at?"

"Anything and everything we've got on Tucker Winslow." As I flip through the first few pages of the file, my blood begins to run cold.

"Where was he born? Who are his parents? Birth certificate?" I continue flipping through the file, searching for the pertinent information every child should have.

"I dug into all the usual sources online and then went on the dark web. There's nothing on Tucker Winslow before high school. It's like he didn't exist, or at least that version of him didn't. I couldn't find a previous alias, so he could be illegal or a refuge from another country. Maybe he's been in the witness protection program."

"You've been around Hadley too long," I say as a goofy grin crosses his face. Shaking my head, I turn my attention back to the file. How can someone get into this country without some kind of digital trail? If he did have the papers at one point, where the hell did they go? If he was in some kind of program, they would have created an entirely new persona. All the documents would have been created to protect him. There would be some kind of documentation from birth. This kid has nothing. In this post 9/11 world, that's a huge red flag. My gut says something is *way* off.

Suddenly, another file drops into my arms from on high. Looking up through my eyelashes at the offending human, I see Marlow sipping on an obscene concoction she calls coffee. She shrugs out of her wet coat and hangs it over the back of the chair before sitting. The sugary smell of her caramel, whipped-cream-infused chemistry experiment makes my stomach turn. That could also be the lack of breakfast and stress, but I choose to blame it on her drink. I begin to wonder if there's actually any coffee in there.

"What's this?" Logan asks as he reaches for the file. Marlow smacks his hand quickly. He pulls back as if his mother had just punished him for touching a hot stove.

"Tucker Winslow." She pulls up a chair, sits, and crosses her legs, her slacks pulling up slightly to reveal four-inch, black stilettos. The woman might have style, but those cannot be comfortable. Her one-size-too-small shirt and her perfectly styled hair all screams "I've got to be in control." Yet, yesterday she was calm, relaxed, and more flexible with her thoughts. Today she was with the local FBI. She must feel the need to showcase power and position in front of the men there.

"If you're done analyzing my work attire, detective, we can move forward." She smirks before taking a sip of her diabetic coma-inducing coffee. If Frankie were here, she would have smacked the back of my head for staring, assuming the wrong thing. Blame the degree; that's my excuse and I'm sticking with it.

"Tell me what we've got." I lean back in my chair, drinking my coffee, flipping through the pages of the new information.

"Mister Logan here"—Marlow nods in his direction— "did his due diligence and a thorough job in searching for everything, even those things on the darker side of life."

"How'd you know?" Logan questions.

"Logan, we're the FBI." She lets that sink in for a minute, watching Logan begin to squirm in his chair.

"Can they see everything?" Logan says and fidgets in his seat as Marlow smiles. He leans back, his leg bouncing as his eyes dart around the room. I'm sure he's running through all the various websites he's visited or the video chats he's had with Hadley. I shake my head, trying to remove that image quickly.

"She's kidding, Logan. Calm down," I say as my eyes remain closed, thinking of happy thoughts that don't involve my sister-from-another-mister in bed with her boyfriend.

"Are you? Kidding, I mean?" His voice sounds so innocent and somewhat afraid of her answer.

"Yes, but it was so worth it to see your face."

"Then how'd you know what I searched for?"

"Because thanks to the previous case files, I know your work ethic and pattern. We traced what you did based on your past searches. Couple that with your signature that you leave everywhere, and here we are." Logan closes his mouth and leans back in the chair.

"I think I need another coffee." He gets up and looks around the room once more. I'm sure he knows Marlow is kidding, but he's a paranoid conspiracy theorist at heart.

"Seriously, what am I looking at here?" I pull her back to the case at hand.

"You're looking at everything Tucker Winslow was before he became Tucker Winslow." Marlow reaches forward and takes the file out of my hands. She flips through a few items before pulling a page out and handing it to me. My eyes widen as I look over the document which was missing from the original file.

I start reading aloud. "Emilio Valez: mother is Alexa Valez and the father isn't listed. He was born in Puerto Rico and must have come here with his mother when Garrison brought her here. Why didn't he have to apply for any paperwork?"

"Because Puerto Ricans are full United States citizens. The minute Emilio was born, he had full rights in our country. So if Garrison wanted to fly both of them to New York, all it would take is a simple plane ticket. Nothing to claim, no worries or concerns. He could have been flying anywhere. No one would care."

"Are we sure Emilio's his son?"

"Considering he paid for the kid to go to an exclusive grammar school and an even more elite high school, I'd say he was. Not to mention the documentation from doctors that list him as the father."

"Then why not on the birth certificate?"

"We can only speculate. Maybe Alexa didn't want his name on the form? Maybe she couldn't reach him when she found out she was pregnant?"

"Maybe the cartels controlling the area she lived in would have killed her son?" I suggest.

"That is one of our working theories. However, it falls apart when Emilio and his mother begin making regular trips to Puerto Rico, only to return a few days later. When asked, it was always a family event. She was even quoted as saying 'you know how we Latinos are,' playing up the ignorance of the security agent. Rather offensive, but the agent was unsure how to respond to her comments. Wrong or not, he did what he felt was best and let it slide."

"They were running drugs and he became something of a drug mule."

"Probably." Marlow hands me a few more pages before sucking down the last of her drink. "After Valez's travel, cocaine became more prominent on the street. There were two versions: one very pure and expensive version, then the hacked street version."

"Laced with everything under the kitchen sink."

"Mixed with baby powder, talc, asbestos powder, and in some cases, straight up poison. Anything to make it go further."

"How many fatalities during this period?"

"We saw a notable increase in deaths among sex workers and home-less victims. Sadly, they could never truly tie these mixes to the body." She hands me one case report of a Jane Doe.

"So, because there were so many other possibilities for cause of death it was hard to pinpoint just one. I get it, but my God what this woman went through. Sexual trauma, evidence of long-standing physical abuse, and needle marks everywhere. Why haven't we found this woman's family?"

"Because her teeth were knocked out or pulled out voluntarily, prints aren't in the system, and her DNA isn't on file anywhere. Whoever she is, she managed to pull her tricks and stay away from lockup. It's not pretty, Jasmine, but it's the reality of drugs. Unless we find a specific mixture linked only to his brand, we can't hang these victims around his neck."

"Then we hang the new ones and get justice for all of them," I say, exuding more confidence than I really have.

"That requires digging deeper into Valez, Garrison, and his two sons." Her tone shifts as she almost looks through me. I know what she's referring to, and I'm sure she found the information. I don't need to verbalize everything I've been through, let alone where I made significant mistakes.

"Considering your tone change, I'm sure you found out about my brother. What's the point of rehashing it now?"

She tosses a photo on the table. The full-color eight-by-ten of my body on the floor, Will holding a bloody rag to my chest. It's rather surreal seeing yourself in a photo, knowing the truth about what happened but not really remembering any of it. Will's face looks ashen, his hands red, and his eyes frantic. I look . . . my body looks like death.

"What about it?"

"Keith Garrison shot you, and according to medical reports, you died on the table before being resuscitated."

"That about sums it up." I chug some hot coffee, burning my throat to quench the anxiety rolling up from my stomach.

"I'm concerned about your involvement in this case."

"If the captain hasn't pulled me, One Police Plaza hasn't asked for my dismissal, and my girlfriend thinks it's okay, I don't see why you should be worried. I've been after Garrison since day one. I plan on sticking with it until it's over."

"Jasmine . . ."

"The Seattle Slayer." My voice stops her cold. She knows exactly what I'm talking about. That's her case that she can't let go of. The one that always gets away no matter how hard she hunts him.

"Okay." Her voice is softer but colder. Her eyes telegraph disappointment mixed with anger and hurt. Two strong-willed women fighting for the same justice, yet somehow at odds with each other. Like the rest of our gender worldwide, we put each other down before lending each other a hand. Nature of the beast, I suppose.

"I got you each a refill." Logan arrives just in time to break the tension. "Especially you, Jazz, because once Frankie comes back, you're off coffee for a long time. I guessed on your drink, Agent Marlow. I hope you like it." Logan places a whipped-cream-covered drink in front of Marlow, but her eyes never leave mine.

Logan notices the tension. "Okay, what did I miss?" He picks up the photo of me off the table and falls back into his seat. He looks up at me and back to the photo. I can only imagine what's going through that techie brain of his.

"It's nothing." I grab Emilio Valez's file and the new coffee Logan bought me. I stand up, preparing to leave.

"Detective?" Marlow begins to reach for me but thinks better of it.

"Look, you fill Logan in on what he needs to dig into. I'm going to head to the lab and see if they have anything new. After that, I'm going to scour the cold case files and see if I can connect these cases' victims to Garrison or Valez."

"I can search for that if you want," Logan adds.

"No thanks. Sometimes I just need to sit in a dusty old room and read actual paper. Get a feel for things." He simply nods in understanding.

Without saying another word, I leave the building. Marlow pushed my buttons back there, and I know why she did it, but it doesn't make it right. My mother always told me it was never what I said to her that hurt, but the tone in which I said it. Marlow was almost accusatory, colder and harsher than she needed to be. She could have easily asked me about it instead of throwing a photo in front of me.

As I walk out into the rain, my hand goes to the scar between my breasts. Seeing that picture made me relive the pain, the burning. I can feel the fear of it happening again begin to roll down my spine and goosebumps start to form on my skin. One Valez is good. Valez squared is formidable. They had me fooled. I've been a step behind, but that ends now. Alexa and Emilio Valez don't know it right now, but justice is coming for these victims.

Chapter Eight

The crime lab is a place for answers or more questions. It all depends on the evidence. It's also a place you can waste hours of your life waiting. It's worse than a doctor's office when waiting for your appointment that was scheduled to begin an hour ago. Sitting in this plush chair, I wish science was more like television shows. You know, where the crime scene investigator finds some sort of fluid on a victim's body and runs the test. Within a great little montage, the results come back and the killer is caught within the forty-five-minute show. In reality, we wait . . . we pray . . . we play games on our phone, and we become impatient.

"Is Doctor Brown in?" I ask the secretary for what feels like the fiftieth time.

"Yes, detective, but as I told you, she is in a meeting," she answers matter-of-factly while typing a mile a minute on her cell phone.

"Excellent, thanks." I get up and walk to the doors and wait for them to slide open, but nothing happens.

"Someone will come get you shortly," the receptionist says without looking up from her phone. Just as a snarky reply forms in my mind, the doors open and someone walks out. Quietly, I duck into the lab area, my eyes watching the kid to see if she noticed me moving. When I realize she has no clue I've moved, I shake my head. Great security we've got here. She's like a mother staring at her phone telling her kids to "stay where I can see you."

Walking around the corridors, I watch the people mill about. I wonder what they're thinking, or if this is the only case they're working on. Knowing the reality of our system, there is no "one case," or downtime for that matter. Once a sample is tested, there is another one waiting in the wings. The backlog in rape kit testing is enough to keep this lab running 24-7 for months. It's a sad state of affairs.

Stopping in front of Doctor Brown's office, I see the back of Victor's head sitting in a chair. I hear his voice, but I can't quite understand what he's saying. The doc though? She's smiling brightly. I tap on the glass, and the doc's face falls. I know I'm interrupting, but what can you do? She reaches under her desk, and I assume pushes a button because the doors swoosh open.

"Hey, doc. Victor. How are you both doing today?" I ask as I sit down next to the coroner and across from Brown.

"I was planning on coming to get you when my meeting was over, detective. Is there a reason you couldn't wait?" she says more professional than angry, but ticked off nonetheless.

"Murder, multiple bodies, long-lost son of Garrison's . . . and my impatience. It's been days, doc," I answer honestly.

"Wait, Garrison has another son?" Victor asks quickly, as if his mind just had a light bulb pop on.

"Apparently, he and Valez had a son. Emilio. Or as we all know him: Tucker Winslow. Logan and Marlow are having a powwow right now about it. Maybe they can find a sample of his DNA somewhere and the doc here can test it against the samples we found."

"First, it's been two days at the most. Second, about the samples . . ." Brown exhales a breathy laugh. "Jasmine, the samples are small, and some are so degraded they'll be impossible to test. Unfortunately, when it comes to the DNA, there really isn't much of a case here." Brown leans back in her chair. The frustration rolls off her shoulders in waves, her hands firmly clasped together on her lap.

"I get it, doc. It's just that anything at this point would be helpful."

"Wait a minute. Don't retail employees randomly get drug tested?" Victor pipes up.

"Depends on the company and their policies. Why?" I ask.

"Because if he was tested recently, we might be able to get a DNA profile from it," Brown says, visibly more hopeful as she processes that information. "It's a long shot, but it's possible. I'll call the district attorney on the case and see what he can do. They might have his information still on file with the testing lab."

"Excellent. Anything else I should know?" I ask, trying to get out of the lab and back to my notes.

"We've got the preliminary report on the bullet Victor found in Judge Killian's body," Brown says.

"I thought the gun wasn't recovered?" I ask, a bit confused at the new information.

"It wasn't, but when I was doing the autopsy, I found the bullet lodged in the fourth rib," Victor says.

"Doesn't sound like our killer," I start. "Take out the fact that they used a gun for this victim, but why not remove the bullet? This wasn't a street shoot-out or a drug deal gone wrong. This was a high-level judge that would most assuredly warrant significant press coverage, police scrutiny, and whatever else the politicians demand we do. The first thing I would do is remove anything that could be analyzed."

"He tried. With the amount of blood, it was easily obscured. When I cleaned the body, I found that the wound track had been enlarged. I tried to get a mold of it, but the damage was too extensive to give me an idea of weapon size. All I can tell you is they dug into the man's chest, broke a rib trying to get to the bullet, and failed," Victor finishes calmly.

"We don't have a weapon to compare it to, so how would the ballistics report help here?" I ask.

"Simple." Lillian Brown pulls my attention to her. "The same gun was used in other homicides in our database."

"So, we can dig through some cold cases and see what turns up?" My voice sounds a bit lighter knowing we might finally have a lead.

"I already took the liberty to do that for you." Brown hands me a piece of paper with five case numbers listed on it. "Captain Udall said to share this information with you only."

"Thanks. Victor, can you kick your team into high gear? I need information or anything you can find on the cargo container victims. Maybe we missed something."

"We're still processing them actually. The judge took priority," he says quietly. I know it bothers him that he can't be more on top of the evidence pile right now, but who could with the amount of it. Maybe the idea was to bury us under an overabundance of evidence so we'd miss the smaller things.

"Okay, I'll see if Marlow can get you her people to help out. We need to crack down now." My phone rings, and I see Mia Evert's name on the screen. I nod to the two of them before exiting Lillian's office. After the door shuts behind me, I take a deep breath and answer.

"Steele."

"Jasmine, it's Mia." Her voice is so small, hollow, and lost.

"Is everything okay?" I walk back along the corridor heading for the elevators, my mind focusing on putting one foot in front of the other. If I don't, I might not make it.

"He opened his eyes briefly. Other than that, no change. I promised him . . ." Her voice breaks. I hear her take a few deep breaths and let them out slowly, trying to calm her emotions. "He would want you to know that he's still not awake. The doctors said he's critical, but stable. There's nothing more they can do for him."

"I'm so sorry, Mia."

"Jasmine, please stop!" Mia barks at me. "I've been hearing that all day from whatever officer, Marine, or whoever comes in here. None of that is going to make my husband get up and walk out of here. I promised him I would keep you posted should something like this happen. I've done that. Now if you'll excuse me, I have to call my daughters."

She hangs up the phone before I can reply. The elevator dings its arrival and I step inside. My earlier happier feeling is long gone with the phone call. What the hell does critical but stable mean anyway? It's like saying you're going to hell, but only the left leg since it was possessed. Or better yet, it's like being a Yankees *and* a Mets fan . . . nope, can't happen. You are one or the other; there is no in-between. You can respect all aspects of the game, but not both teams. Either way you look at it, my friend is lying on his back fighting for his life. All because someone decided he no longer needed to live it. His wife didn't matter. His children weren't a factor. There was a human being, a gun, and a choice. I feel bad for whoever the shooter was. They made the wrong choice.

The basement is dark, dank, and all-around gloomy. There are a few officers down here keeping the sealed room cataloged and doing the mundane work associated with this area. I wonder if they prefer it down here. It's quiet, no one is shooting at you, and sometimes people like me come down and ask for help. Otherwise, it's catalogued, entered into the system, and put in the shelving units. The ventilation system is loud as hell down here. It sounds like a bat repeatedly slamming into a wall every five seconds. There's got to be a compromise between needing the most powerful air system and it being quiet enough to think. The constant hammering would drive me bonkers.

"Excuse me," I say to the officer behind a bulletproof Lexan window. It's then that I notice a little silver button with a microphone is embedded in the wall to the right. "Excuse me," I say again with my thumb firmly planted on the button.

The officer, older, with a white goatee, turns to face me. He has the most piercing blue eyes silhouetted by dark circles under them. He gingerly stands up from his perch and limps over to the window. I guess that's why he's down here. Not because he wants to be, but out of necessity. The hierarchy wouldn't want this to be the face of our precinct when you walk in. They want you to see the healthiest and best the NYPD has to offer. At least mine does, and it's all up to the captain. If you're injured or maimed in the line of duty, you work outside the view of the average citizen. Hell, he made me hide in my office for a long time until I could use my arm fully. Before then, I looked like a baby trying to fully understand grasping items for the first time. I am not ambidextrous. Well, I can be, but usually Frankie's involved in that.

"Can I see your credentials?" The officer brings me back to reality as he slides a metal drawer out of the wall.

"Yeah, sure." I slip my identification in the drawer only to watch it get eaten by the old-school bank teller drawer. He holds my wallet up to the Lexan, the picture facing him as he studies me.

"Reason for visiting us in the dungeon?" I place the paper Doctor Brown gave me up to the divider and let him read through it. I don't want to go into too much detail. I know there's a connection, but I'm not quite sure what I'm going to find. If he talks to any of his buddies or radios upstairs, that might get people's hopes up. Or maybe I'm not one to share information readily. I lean more to the latter.

The drawer hits me in the crotch. My eyes lock with the officer's, who has a slight smile on his face. Not a malicious one, but more like my father used to give me when he smacked the back of my head. A reality check—again. Lowering the paper, I fold it back up. I grab my wallet and put it in the inside breast pocket of my jacket.

"Can you help me find these boxes?"

"Since the new updates, everything is clearly marked, but someone upstairs must like you. They called ahead and requested the boxes be put in the last room to the right. Walk to the door." He drags his bum leg out of the office.

I walk over to the large, metal-frame door. The suction of the door alerts me to its opening. The officer stands on the other side. I walk into the room and the icy air hits my face hard. Brisk doesn't do it justice. It reminds me of diving in a dry suit: everything is perfectly warm, but the skin on your face is frozen. The officer pushes several buttons and the door closes behind me.

He starts in on a speech he's given thousands of times: "Nothing leaves here without proper authorization. There are rooms in the back to go over the information in the boxes and a photocopier in the last room on the right. Copy what you need because, I say again, nothing leaves this place without proper authorization."

"I understand. No reason to repeat yourself."

"You say that now, but like everyone who has come down here since the dawn of cold cases, someone always tries to sneak something out. Let me know when you're ready to leave. I'll check you over before opening the door. Now, walk down the center aisle to the end, make a right, walk to the back, and the last room is waiting for you." He walks back into the office and closes the door behind him. He's a stickler for the rules; good yet annoying in the same instance.

I open the folded piece of paper and look at the list of five case files. Looking back up at the rows upon rows of unsolved cases, boxes upon boxes of evidence and what feels like miles of travel between each row, I'm overwhelmed. So many cases without any closure. So many families never knowing what happened to their child. So many women never finding out if the DNA of their rapist could lead to a match in the system.

It's at this moment I appreciate all those around me. Without them, and my own idiocy, my brother's case would be on a shelf here.

As I walk past the first row, I swear I hear Hadley in the back of my head screaming, "We kill so many trees for paper, everything should be digital, and then Logan could have just searched for what you needed!" I know she's right, but that would assume all the evidence was still sitting in the actual box. What if someone snuck it out? Sure, the officer I met seems to follow the rules. He's not the only one working all the time. There's a gaggle of officers stuck down here. A *lot* of people anyone could slip by. A list of people that might not be happy to be down here or not take their oath seriously. Hell, maybe there is just one person in here who just does his job enough to get a pension and doesn't care. I love the blue line, but every job has at least one asshole, a vile human being and dumbass who does the minimal work required.

Walking into my assigned room, I see five boxes neatly stacked on a table on the left wall. Another table with chairs sits perpendicular to it after a small walkway gap. Walking in, I grab the first box and place it on the main table. Might as well start with the first one placed there. I slide the top off and grab the file and the other papers in the box. I don't need to look at all the sealed evidence until something pops from the page. I might just do myself a favor and verify what is mentioned in the paper is in the actual box. Never know when I might need to reference it in the future. I push the box to the end of the table and sit down. Time to read.

"Jessica Banks, twenty-two, Bronx address, reported missing on November 3, 2005. Body recovered April 15, 2010, after a raid on a drug cartel home," I read aloud to myself. "Body found in a freezer, hidden in a secret room with various drugs, street value ranging from one to four million dollars."

"Took us a full week to thaw her out properly." I look up to see Victor standing in the doorway.

"I thought you were going to work on the cargo container victims. We need that evidence, Vic." I raise my voice a little more than I intend.

"I know, but truthfully there is nothing more I can do up there. I have my team working on it, filing all the paperwork, and doing it all by the book. Jasmine, there is nothing more to find. I can tell you how they died, I can pinpoint how long they suffered, but the evidence to put someone away isn't there. I can be of more help to you here."

Victor doesn't wait for me to reply. He just walks in and drops his ass in the chair across from me. He grabs some of the other files in front of me and begins scanning the pages. I want to tell him to go upstairs, but looking over at the other boxes, I know I need his help.

"You said it took you a week to thaw her out? Why?"

"Well, it's not like you can just shove a body into the microwave, defrost it, and then do an autopsy. It takes time."

"Ugh. You have officially turned me off my microwave forever."

"The point is a body needs to be defrosted slowly. We had to put her in refrigeration and thaw her out. That way I could perform a proper autopsy and gather any evidence that was frozen with her."

"According to the paperwork, she was shot by the same gun that killed Judge Killian," I say, flipping through the file. "Was that the cause of death?"

"No," he says simply.

I flip through several pages, scanning them quickly. My stomach churns when I read a line in Victor's report. I look up and meet his gaze. His eyes seem to glaze over, and the torment of past images plays across his face. This is one that haunted him at night for a long time.

"The evidence showed she had been sexually assaulted repeatedly. There was significant vaginal and rectal tearing. Her jaw had been broken similar to incidences in other countries where girls are sold into the slave trade. Simply put, this young woman was brutalized in every way a man can violate a woman," he recites from memory.

"DNA?"

"Rape kit is probably still in the box. It was never tested."

"Why the hell not?" I ask as agitation fills my bones.

"Money? The fact is her parents were both deceased by the time her body was recovered. Without them pushing this case, it went cold." Victor leans back, staring at the photos of Jessica.

"She was found in Brooklyn. One GSW, vicious sexual trauma, several broken ribs, and a broken jaw. Internal bleeding the cause of death?" I ask.

"*She froze to death,*" he states flatly.

"Excuse me?"

"Evidence shows that she was shot, violated, and was shoved in that freezer alive. If I remember the report, it said there was a lock preventing the hatch from being opened. Before you ask, her blood was frozen in the ice below her body. That indicates her heart was pumping it out of her wounds as she was placed in the freezer. I can't say for certain she was awake when she went in, but she was definitely alive."

I grab some paper from the desk and start writing. Name, birthday, lived, location went missing, body found, bullet caliber, ethnicity, and any other information that could connect all these cases. I put all the papers in the box and slide it to the side. Victor stands, opens the next box, and grabs the files inside. He drops the police report on the desk and opens the coroner's report. Leaning back, I open the thinner police report.

I read the top section of the police report. "Mason Fourier, seventeen, male, shot during an altercation on a basketball court."

"Single gunshot to the chest, pronounced dead at the scene. Nothing stands out with this one," Victor says as his eyes scan the medical reports.

"Except the bullet matches the one from Banks case." I add the information from the case file onto the piece of paper next to me. Rolling the chair along the floor, I flip the next three box tops off and grab the files inside. My OCD gets the better of me as I lay them out meticulously, edge-to-edge, on the table. Each coroner report faces Victor, and the police reports are in front of me. We'll see if we can compare notes and get something going. I'd rather not stay in the dungeon longer than necessary.

"Vanessa Goertz, twenty-nine, reported missing January 2007. Last seen leaving a club in Manhattan with her girlfriend, Kesha Williams." The words fall out of my mouth like a teacher discussing a historical war. "Body was found three months later when a construction company bought some abandoned buildings in Nassau County. Body was discovered in the basement stashed in an old freezer." I drop the file on the table and rub my temples.

"Coroner wrote that the power must have been out for an extended period of time. The remains were significantly decomposed. Cause of death could not be confirmed. The bones were severely broken, most likely due to the positioning of the body in the smaller freezer. Based on this report, it seems the coroner basically only covered the basics. He found dental records to match the body and returned her bones to the family. He writes time of death could not be determined either. There were no forensics at the scene, no attempt to recover any evidence from the bones or the freezer. This was sloppy all around." Victor closes the file and grabs the fourth one. "This case is significantly flawed, but why connect it to the others?" he says.

"Kesha Williams, twenty-seven, body recovered in the trunk of an impounded vehicle in Nassau County. Single gunshot to the head. Ballistics matches," I say and look up at Victor.

"Evidence of sexual assault. Vaginal tearing and her jaw was broken. I can only assume for more methods of violation," Victor says, anger slowly pouring out with his words.

"How come no one noticed this? How come this file is here and not in Nassau County?"

"Because they would have to admit they fucked up?" Victor and I look up to see Logan standing in the doorway, laptop under his left arm. "I could have saved you both so much trouble if you had allowed me to search for all these cases online."

"I still believe in good old-fashioned police work," I say while flipping through the final case file.

"That last one is Miranda Watkins, mother of two, killed by a stray bullet in a drive-by shooting," Logan says. "Two jobs, hard worker, and a casualty of the neighborhood. Much like the previous two, Nassau County didn't want to deal with it. The coroner appears useless, and the police officers wanted to clear the scene as soon as possible. Obviously, the construction company had a bid that was rather suspect from the beginning. Then a body shows up, putting a wrench in the building plans. County gets involved and makes it go away. According to the conspiracy websites, since the bodies were both found on the border, they handed them over to NYPD citing budgetary constraints."

"That's bullshit," Victor says. "A child could have written a more thorough report with crayons. There's no detail about the bones, the fluids, or if there were any particulates encapsulated within. This was either a rush job or the individual was inept." Victor's face turns red, and I can see his anger is about three seconds from the surface.

"Okay, so we know the reports were a mess throughout all of these cases. How the hell did we not connect them? Seriously, there is a fucking bullet connecting all of them and yet we missed it?" I add, running my hand through my hair.

"This is the cold case room. We keep it all nice and organized in case we ever need to access it, but we never expect to," Logan explains. "You can put the blame squarely on money and desire, or lack of either. The fact is the money isn't here for us to chase ghosts, Jasmine. And if someone doesn't have a bug up their ass about a particular case, it winds up in purgatory down here. I've got all the tech in the world, but I use it to catch the bad guys. I can pull all the camera footage, tracking, or whatever else you need, but without a rape kit being tested, we don't have a smoking gun of DNA for a conviction."

"So, Nassau County shuffles it to us and we bury it in the basement." Victor rubs his temples in disgust. "This bullshit is out of hand."

"Nature of the beast. Not enough of the good guys to handle it all. Let alone the bad seeds within our ranks who like to straddle the lines," Logan answers.

"Okay, enough with the grandstanding. I know you didn't come down here to have some philosophical conversation with us, so out with it," I say. My patience with these cases is running thin.

Logan sets his laptop on the table and flips it open. The screen illuminates and a map comes into view with blue and red dots on it.

"The blue dots are where the victims went missing, and the red ones are where the bodies were recovered. Now in the case of Kesha Williams, her recovery can't be included in this theory. She could have been dumped in a car and the police towed it to their impound lot. Everything else fits though."

"Explain," I state quickly.

Logan leans forward, and his fingers fly across the keyboard like Chase after he's had too much sugar. Another set of colored dots appear on the screen. They almost match up entirely.

"The purple ones are the new bodies we've found. The green ones, known activity of Emilio Valez or, as we know him, Tucker Winslow. The orange ones were suspected deals that Garrison has been connected to via FBI and dark web surveillance. Now, this could simply be a mother taking her son to work," Logan finishes proudly.

"Or a son starting to take over the family business," I add.

"Is that enough for a warrant?" Victor asks.

"Seriously?" I pause. "I don't know. It should be. I'm going to get this over to the captain and see what he can do. If we grab Valez junior, then maybe mama will come out of hiding. I need copies of all your findings." I look up to Logan.

"Already emailed. Securely, of course. Once you get to Cap's, you can print it out there. Go. Now. Victor and I will put all this back."

I don't hesitate to bolt out the door, leaving the two men to clean up the mess. This could be the break we're looking for. Grabbing my cell phone, I send a quick message to Marlow with Captain Udall's address. I don't want to deal with the wrath of the FBI by not keeping her in the loop. Hopefully, they've found more information about the case, because in my heart, I know this isn't enough. It should be enough to at least get a search warrant for Tucker Winslow's place. I mean, Emilio Valez's place. Keeping his alias straight is going to give me a headache. I just want this over soon. My phone vibrates, and I look at the screen. Blocked number, but the message makes me smile. Two words I so desperately needed to hear: "Love You." It could be fake, but I'm going to choose to believe it's her. I need it to be.

When I get to the ancient, five-story, pre-WWII building, I see Marlow leaning against the wall. Her cell phone is glued to her ear, her hand in her hair, one high heel placed firmly on the brick wall behind her and one on the ground. If I didn't know better, I'd say she looked like she had gone a few rounds with her friends at the Bureau. Walking up to the building, I notice there's no doorman. I push the buzzer and wait in silence.

"Call me when you have something." She angrily pushes the end call button. "Sometimes I wish I could just slam the phone down like we used to."

I laugh in response.

"Showing your age, agent? Besides, you can still slam your phone down. You just break it and get a new one."

"You realize you sound like my oldest son, right?" Marlow says as I press the buzzer again.

"There's a difference though. I pay my own bills." I press the button again, getting impatient. "He said he was heading home."

Marlow pushes on the door, and it easily swings open. She looks at me, and a slight concern creeps up on me. "How long you think this has been broken?"

I hold the door open and look at locking mechanism. Seeing a few new scratch marks, the hairs on the back of my neck stands up. "These are fresh," I point out.

"Okay, so one of the people in the building might have forgotten their key and broke in."

Staying calm, the two of us walk through a second broken security door. My foot taps on the warped cream-colored linoleum floor as Marlow presses the elevator button. The dilapidated elevator struggles to open as we step into it. The creaky old doors shut as the box shakes every few feet as it moves up to the fifth floor. Finally, with a sound like a dying animal, it dings and the doors open onto the floor. Walking down the long, wavy, warped hallway, I first notice the utter silence. Either no one's home or everyone is sleeping. No parties. No kids screaming. No dogs. Nothing.

Marlow knocks on the captain's door. No response.

"You mind if I do this?" She holds up a lock pick set.

"Why didn't you show me that downstairs?"

"Those were security doors; this is the captain's door. We can be responsible for one of our own, just not all five floors." I simply nod in response and watch her go to work. Kneeling down, she keeps her eyes focused on the lock as she pulls out the appropriate tools.

"I first learned to do this in the fifth grade. My dad taught my brothers and me. Became a bit of a game to see who could break out of Master locks faster." The door clicks. "I always won." Marlow gently pushes the door open. I step inside with her behind me. My feet stop short at the edge of the living area. My heart beats faster, and I feel the coldness creep in. The door closes behind me, and I hear her heels clack to a stop next to me.

"Oh God," Marlow says. Captain Udall is splayed out on the floor.

Mechanically, I walk over, careful to avoid the pool of blood, lean down, and check for a pulse. None. I look up at Marlow and shake my head. She immediately pulls out her phone and calls it in. I feel the subtle vibration in my suit jacket pocket and reach for my phone, the ringtone sound of my nephew's voice for some reason never registering with my ears. It's as if they've shut off.

"Steele," I say trying to compose myself.

"Detective, good of you to take my call," Valez whispers through the line. I wave my hand in the air to get Marlow's attention. When she turns around, I point to my phone and mouth "Valez."

"I need you to put a trace on Detective Steele's cell phone right away!" she says quietly to the agents on the other line.

"Just wanted to say how sorry I am for your loss."

"Was it you or Emilio?" I hear a soft gasp of surprise on the other end of the line.

"Aren't you the clever one? Detective, you should know my son does what he's told. Beyond that, he is a good boy. He also knows how to send a message. One the boss hopes you will understand. He figured leaving one body in a coma and one on the floor would make himself clear. Apparently, it's not clear enough. Just walk away, detective, or I will watch you bleed to death, slowly, myself. Maybe I'll be called a hero for killing a cop with a grudge. Times have changed, and so has perception about your lovely wall of blue."

"Maybe, but I doubt people are stupid enough to believe a tale from a drug smuggling whore who happens to kill people for fun."

"Oh, Jasmine. It's never fun. It's always business. If that makes me a monster, you're in that classification with me. Or does the murder of a fellow officer by your hands not count?"

I look over at Marlow, who swings her hand in a circular motion. She wants me to keep her talking on the phone. For what reason, I don't know. It's the digital age; traces should be almost immediate. Talking is not what I want to do right now. Talk is cheap. I want to find her.

"Tell me where you are and you can decide for yourself what kind of monster I am."

"Not yet, detective, but soon. I promise." The line goes dead.

"Where is she?" I ask as I put the phone back in my pocket. She hangs up her phone and looks up at me. Her hand shakes slightly as she composes herself.

"Police are on their way there now. Victor and a team are headed here," Marlow says calmly.

"I asked a question."

Marlow looks at the captain's lifeless body. "At my hotel. Probably in the lobby."

"Or in your room. Meant to scare you." I pause a second, letting the information sink in. "Wait a minute, you've been crashing at my place, captain's orders. Why the hell do you have a hotel room?"

"I had no intention of staying with you until Captain Udall insisted. He can be rather persuasive. Then I just kept it as a backup in case your place was compromised."

"Instead, she found where your place was and is taunting you."

"I've had worse. Nothing I can do about it, so let's process this scene before the higher-ups get here and kick you out."

She walks away from me into the small kitchen as she puts on a pair of gloves. I look down at Captain Tyler Udall; his unfocused, cloudy eyes stare right back at me. Kneeling down, I look over his neck wound. The shiny white of bone glints at me through the torn flesh. Looking down at his hands, I see they're bloodied and bruised.

"He put up a fight. Not that I'd expect anything less," I say solemnly.

"That's good. We might have DNA."

"We will. Captain would ensure we did," I say plainly.

Standing up, I look around the place. Blood splatter, probably from arterial spray, litters the walls in an almost abstract art design. There are no empty spaces in the spray or the pooling blood. A laptop sitting on the half wall that serves as a kitchen counter grabs my attention. It's powered off and covered in blood. Might have shorted out.

"Killed him from behind." The coldness pours out with each word.

"Detective, if you need to leave, I can handle this until the crime scene unit arrives," Marlow says.

"No," I say. "There's no void in the blood on the wall or the floor. So, Emilio comes up behind Tyler and slices his throat."

"But he would have been covered in blood, no?" Marlow questions. She walks behind me, her heels allowing her to almost be at my full five-foot-nine frame. One hand covers my mouth while her other motions across my neck. She's right; his hand should have created a void of some kind.

"Unless the captain didn't anticipate it or was incapacitated."

"A BOLO was released with Emilio's image stating he was wanted. We added his alias of Tucker Winslow."

Looking around, I see the captain's cell phone on the small, blood-covered end table. Marlow follows my gaze and sees the device. Walking around the pool on the floor, she picks up the phone with her gloved hands. The once white phone has red in the grooves, the side buttons, and screen.

"I'll bag it and bring it to Logan. See if he can get anything off it."

"Assuming the captain didn't read the email, Emilio might have contacted him," I say, grasping for straws.

"It's possible. This was the only witness to the game store murders. Udall wouldn't be doing his job if he didn't offer to help."

"But why at his place? Captain wouldn't do that. Rule whatever number: never bring them to your private residence. We have safe houses or public meeting places for that. Why was he here? What was he doing that ruffled Emilio's feathers?" I ask.

The door opens and several uniformed officers carefully stream in. Victor walks right in behind the officers, his hand up behind him to stop his assistant. I can see the young woman standing in the hallway with a gurney and a black bag. Victor stands over the captain's body and looks around the room. His face is stoic, almost cold. Standing next to him, I simply place my hand on his back for comfort.

"I want you to lock this scene down tight. When the crime unit gets here, ensure they document everything in this place. I don't care if it's a piece of dust from the floor. I want it all. Make sure this gets to Logan in tech, understand?" I hand him the bagged cell phone. In the background, I hear Marlow barking orders.

"Steele, we have to go." I turn around and look at Marlow, who has car keys in her hands. "We'll take my car. The officers can bring yours back." I take my keys out and place them in the hand open in front of me. Doesn't matter who takes them; I'm in no shape to drive anyway. "Vic, I want Logan going through every bit of tech in there. If his fridge has a television, I want to know what the captain was ordering, got it?"

"I got it."

"Emilio or Tucker or whatever the fuck he goes by now . . . I want to know why he was here. I need answers," I say, my words coming out rushed and cold.

"Steele, they can handle it," I hear Marlow softly say behind me. Looking at Victor, I know she's right. His eyes focus on the scene around him, presumably taking it all in. Our leader is gone. My surrogate father is gone. There's nothing I can do to fix it. Turning around, I follow Marlow to the elevator and push the button for the lobby.

"Where are we going?" I ask as we step into the elevator.

"The hotel. Valez left me a message." Another creaky elevator ride down, and the door dings and she confidently walks out into the night air. I follow in time, like the military marching to their new assignment.

"What kind of message?"

"In one of my other cases, it would be a body, or parts of one, a bomb, or something else to grab our attention. Sadly, this time it's an envelope."

She unlocks the car and the two of us wordlessly get inside. The message left for Marlow was meant to be subdued. I'm sure of it. Udall was the real message. They can get to any one of us at any time. I thought Will was their warning shot. Maybe he was and we didn't listen. Either way, they've stepped beyond me just wanting to bring them down. Now the entire family of blue will be hunting them down. I doubt anyone will blink an eye if an officer removes either of these people from the plane of existence. They better hope Marlow and I find them before someone else does.

The silence during the trip over continues as we walk down the long hallway past various police officers. They stand against the wall, just staring like we're two dead women walking. It's either that or they feel so horrible they can't look me in the eye. I prefer the former.

"Agent Marlow," a man in a black suit calls to my associate. He's tall, and he leans over Marlow as if trying to show his dominance. His dark-black, curly hair brushes the collar of his too-small jacket. His triceps pop when he holds his arm straight down at his side. He must spend a lot of time in the gym, but that, combined with how he leans forward, makes me immediately not like him. Maybe it's just sticking up for my temporary partner, but he's one to watch.

"Agent Sharp, what's going on here?" Marlow waves her arms around, focusing on the large assortment of government personnel.

"Suspicious package found in your hotel room with sensitive material? Protocol."

"You're full of shit. This is overkill, not to mention there are concerns over access to my hotel room." Marlow walks past Sharp, and I follow silently behind her. Sharp leans against the wall like a puppy who's been scolded. "Everyone out," Marlow's voice booms across the room. Her motherly tone manages to get everyone to pay attention as they scurry out of the room. She slams the door closed after the last lemming leaves. I wonder if she can teach that to me. It would come in handy when Chase won't get off his damn Xbox and go to bed.

"I know this is a 'Captain Obvious' question, but how would she have gotten in here?" I ask, looking around.

"Someone with determination? There's a way . . . but Agent Sharp was stationed in the adjoining room," she absentmindedly throws at me.

"And I haven't met him before, because . . ." I trail off, waiting for her to answer the question.

"Because his instructions were to strictly monitor the situation," Marlow says as she looks around the room. Her words are chosen carefully, but her tone is unconvincing.

"You're telling me an agent was sent with you and told to not engage? This is the United States government. If you told them you couldn't use the restroom, they would create a team to discuss it. Then you'd have one guy with the duty to watch you poop, another to analyze the process, one to study the product, and then an entire department to discuss the report." Marlow stops looking around the room and stares at me. She raises one eyebrow slightly higher than the other in what I hope is amusement.

"I cannot confirm nor deny that the protocol you stated would be accurate." She nods as she says those words. She's following my lead, regardless of the negative weight sitting on both our shoulders.

I head into the bathroom. The sink is immaculate. The soap is still sealed in the cheap plastic bag it shipped in. The bottles of shampoo and conditioner seem to have been unused. Nothing seems out of place.

"Everything was locked in here. FBI files, information on various financial dealings—this is where I had my team send everything." I hear Marlow talking from the other room. I turn to reply, but a reflection in the mirror grabs my attention. Stepping closer, I lean over the vanity to get a closer look. A light-colored film rests on top of the glass. Could be something, might be nothing.

"Everything was left unguarded?" I ask Marlow as I walk back into the main room. She's lying on her back, gloved hands on the foot of the bed with her head peering underneath.

"Sharp was supposed to be here. Like I said, the team should have been in here working." She slides out from under the bed and sits up. She spins on her butt, faces the foot of the bed, and falls on her back. As she looks under the dresser, she slides her hand along the exposed edges.

"What are you doing?" I ask as Marlow slowly climbs up from the floor to stand.

"Being thorough. If Valez was in this room, she might have left a bug behind. Maybe the bug was in here before she entered and then I wonder who placed it. Could be an inside job."

"Or it could be left from someone who stayed here before you."

"True, but unlikely. Until you look around, you never know," she says as she walks to the entryway door. She flips the light switch a few times. The lights flicker as any normal human being would expect. Marlow reaches into her pocket and pulls out a small Swiss Army knife. Flipping it open, she unscrews the light switch faceplate. A small amount of white dust drops to the carpet like the dandruff on Agent Sharp's jacket.

"It's just my normal routine. I prefer to check things myself." She looks at me as she pulls the cover off the light switch. She starts to unscrew the actual switch as she continues to talk. "Kind of like when I'm watching my sons play basketball. They're such good kids, but my youngest can't play the game to save his life. So, I go in prepared for him to ride the bench." She pulls the switch forward, moving the wires around. "My husband, he's the coach, tries to teach him all the time. It just doesn't stick. I go down to the games and watch my boys play. When the game is done, I have to be equally proud of them no matter what. So, you have a routine or you just stay prepared for anything." She pushes the knife into the hole in the wall. When she leans back, she pulls out a small, square, black box from the hole in the wall.

"I get it. I'm starting to learn that with Chase. You have to be ready for anything with kids." I continue the pointless conversation as she places the square black box on the dresser. She opens a bag and slides it inside without cutting the wire and shoves it in her front suit pocket. After that's done, she quickly starts putting the fixture back together.

"Trials and tribulations. Sometimes you think you're doing things out of character, but in reality, you just need to see where that action leads." She nods to me as she places the last screw into the switch plate. I know she's referencing the bug. Normally an officer would handle it and get it back to our tech department. The fact that she's put it in her pocket means she's as concerned about the individuals outside in the hallway as well as the ones we know about.

I grab the evidence bag with the manila envelope in it and place it under my arm. Marlow opens the door and walks outside. Sharp stands there almost anxiously, waiting to see if Marlow's going to say something. Instead of saying anything, she pulls a clipboard out of another agent's hands and signs something. I assume it's the chain of evidence for the folder. She smiles and pushes past Agent Sharp. Saying nothing, I follow her down the hallway and out of the hotel.

Silently we walk to the car, faster than how we entered. Marlow, as if on a mission, gets into the car and cranks the engine. I jump in the car before she can take off without me.

"Mind telling me where the fire is?" Considering the previous scene, my heart can't take much more shit today.

"Text Logan," is all she says to me. I do as she asks and notice I have a missed call from Will's wife. Hitting the app on my phone, I play the message.

"Jasmine, the officers here are saying that Captain Udall was killed. Was it the same woman? Is Will safe here? He's starting to show some improvement, and I'm scared at how the news might stop that. I'll move him if I have to. Please, tell me someone is close to catching her." The message ends. Close, no. Eventual, fuck yes.

The precinct is quiet, empty, and cold. It's obvious everyone is on edge from the death of my captain. The air is charged with negative energy, and it makes me want to run away. While in the hotel room, I could focus on the task at hand. I could ignore the events seared into my mind from earlier this evening. Now, being around this somber place, it's impossible to avoid it.

Walking into Logan's little basement arena, the energy feels so different than upstairs. People move about like always, investigating, talking—living. Like when I was little and I missed school. I asked my mother why the teachers gave me work to do. She told me that the world didn't revolve around me. She wasn't being mean or malicious, just honest. Life moves on. The people down here know all about the captain, but he wasn't their boss. He was just a person they spoke to on occasion. That doesn't mean they're bad people, just a different circle.

"Jazz, Karina, how are you two holding up?" Logan comes up to us and wraps me in a hug before I can answer. Considering Frankie, Chase, Hadley, and Will are out of commission for various reasons, this is more welcomed than I care to admit. Letting go, he steps to the side and pulls Marlow into an embrace. The woman has been stoic and almost cold since the hotel, and it's as if a switch has been flipped within her. Logan lets go of Marlow and takes a step back, looking at the two of us.

"We're doing as well as can be expected," I blurt out, wanting to move this conversation further along.

"I understand," Logan states simply. "I haven't had a chance to look over Captain Udall's things yet. His phone is being cleaned before we can try to access things. His laptop is on my desk."

"That's not why we're here," Marlow adds. "Can we discuss this in your office?"

Logan looks at her questioningly but motions for us to follow him. Walking through the rows of desks used to be entertaining; now I find myself a bit irritated. I wish these people would slow down, maybe stop. Show some kind of reverence for a decorated officer who was murdered, but I have to remind myself of reality. There is a job to do. Walking into the office, Logan sits at his desk and looks at the two of us anxiously.

"You have that jammer?" Marlow says. Logan shrugs, opens a drawer, and pulls out the device. He clicks it on. Marlow pulls out the bug from her pocket and drops it in front of him.

Logan quickly picks it up and brings it closer to his face for inspection. If he had a jeweler's loupe, I'm sure he would have used it. His face, riddled with intrigue, stares at the little device.

"You know what it is?" Marlow asks.

"Item, yes. Make and model, no. This is new."

"What do you mean new?" Marlow asks as she sits down. I follow suit.

"I mean I've never seen this before. Considering I work here and am a nerd for all things tech, I can safely assume this isn't readily available on the market yet."

"Which means keep it under wraps until such a time as we have more information."

"Karina, I appreciate—"

"No, Logan, you don't. The captain is dead, Valez was in my hotel, and all of a sudden there's a bug there. I want to know why, how, who, and whatever else you can dig up."

"Is there a possibility another agent put the bug in there to keep tabs on you?" I ask, already knowing the answer.

"Anything is possible, but I'd rather not question why my own department would be spying on me." Marlow stands up, fixes her jacket, and promptly leaves the office without saying another word.

"She's green, huh?" Logan asks me.

"No, she's a long-standing FBI agent. She just has too much faith in her job and the people around her. I don't think she's ever had reason to question those around her. She's from Seattle."

"I don't think it matters where you're from; assholes and criminals are everywhere."

"Where there's a will, there's someone who will kill. Keep me posted on everything, okay?"

Logan nods as I walk out of the office. Agent Karina Marlow, the tough-as-nails protector of the law, stands near the slow-as-hell elevator. The way she leans from side to side makes me feel bad for her. This has to be the first time someone in her inner circle might have undermined her. I finally catch up to her as the doors open, revealing an empty car. We both step in, and she pushes the floor for the garage.

"Wine?" she mumbles.

"Red," I answer as the doors close and end our conversation. It's going to be a long night.

Chapter Nine

The room smells of sweat and blood. The salty droplets roll down my forehead, along my cheekbone, and down my jaw. An errant one ends up along my upper lip and slips into my mouth. My mouth guard, protruding forward, protects my teeth from the fist flying through the air. A glove whizzes past my guard, connects to the padding, and sends the saltwater mixture flying off my face to the floor. I twist my body, bend my right arm, and shift forward, my gloved fist connecting under the ribcage of the man opposite me. I hear the gasp. His mouth guard falls to the floor. My weaker left hand swings full force from the side and connects squarely with his head. The man falls to his knees, his hand raised. He surrenders, and I back away.

Two other officers in gym clothing help him off the mat. Neither will look at me. I'm sure my anger is palpable. It's been four full days and Captain Udall's body lies at the funeral home now. Tomorrow's the full "pomp and circumstance" funeral at the cemetery. The public viewing was yesterday; today is immediate family only. His family is refusing to let any of the "blues" in. I look around, my eyes seeking another opponent. Everyone turns me down. I guess taking out three officers in a row is a bad thing.

The speed bag hangs from the wall, begging to be beaten. I oblige. One punch. Then two. Then three in order. Now a rhythm, beating the life out of whoever harmed my family. Dishing out the inner rage I feel building up inside again. This isn't where I wanted to be. I promised Frankie I wouldn't go down that rabbit hole, yet here I am. She's not here to make this pain go away. No one is. I sent them all away.

Will is here. He's lying in a hospital bed, the tube removed from his throat recently, and he's improving slowly. His wife sits by his side. His two daughters alternate who takes care of her. They haven't called or asked for help. Yesterday, they made it clear I was to focus on the case. It's what Will would want and what they need. So, I'm here clearing my mind. Focusing on the punches. Dealing with the pain in my hands and right shoulder. Pain means I'm alive. Sore means I'm healing. Sweat means my heart is beating. I have to hold onto that. Captain Udall won't ever be able to again. I owe it to myself, and him.

"What did that bag ever do to you?"

"It happened to be here," I answer.

"Want to hit something that can fight back?"

I turn around and see Marlow in full gear and skintight workout cloth-ing. She pops her mouth guard in and eggs me on. Looking around quick-ly, I can tell the male officers are entertained by her and the prospect of a cat fight. I walk back to the main mat area and turn to face her. Before I can look her in the eye, my head snaps back to the right side and I fall to the floor face first. The smell of the mat fills my nostrils along with the scent of blood. Sucker punch. Looking toward her, I see her bouncing on her feet.

One swift motion with my leg and I knock her to the floor. She lands on her ass hard and rolls slightly. Her hand runs along her tailbone, and she laughs through her mouth guard. I let her stand up. I want to beat her fair and square. Her left leg flies at my head, and I barely manage to block it. It's not going to be a fair fight. I know that now. This bitch has skills she didn't share with the class.

She smiles at what I can only assume is a look of surprise on my face.

Her gait shifts to her left leg. This time I'm ready and catch her leg midair and land a square punch right above her belly button and toss her leg to my right. Marlow spins around and stumbles backwards. She holds her left gloved hand over her stomach.

"Illegal punch, Steele," she mumbles through the plastic in her mouth.

"And your kick was legal? Above the belly button is legal in boxing," I reply just as horribly.

"Keep your hands up and feel the emotion rolling off you into each punch," I can hear the captain in my head saying. "Just focus, Jasmine. Watch their eyes, not their feet."

In a blur, Marlow connects with my face and then my right side. Several blows and I reach forward, grabbing her around the waist before pushing her backwards. Looking down at my irritated skin, I know I'm going to be purple in an hour, maybe two. As I bounce on my feet, she comes at me again. I feel rather than see her fists. The flurry of punches between the two of us must be a sight to see. My biceps burn with every thrust forward. The sweat rolls into my eyes, mixing with tears as they roll down my face. Her fist connects with my face, and I feel the instant pain below my right eye.

My body hits the mat hard. I just lie there. Every muscle hurts. My hands hurt. My eye hurts. My head . . . my head feels clear! I feel the floor shift next to me, and I see Marlow lying face up, on the floor. Her lip is split, bleeding, and already swollen. Her head gear did nothing to protect her pasty skin from my blows. We must look like a sorry pair.

"Better?" She spits her mouth guard upward and the bloody thing falls to the floor with a splat.

"I'm fine. You?" I mutter. I push the plastic out of my mouth and into my hand. I see her eyes are a little clearer than before. She needed this as much as I did.

"I think you actually are fine. Yeah, I'm good. This waiting game has been weighing me down. Along with my unsolved caseload at home, it's been a bit stressful. A *lot* stressful." She stares at the ceiling.

"I get it. Hopefully, Logan has something for us."

"Excuse me, detective?" I hear a voice near me. The young officer looks at me as if waiting for my permission to speak again. Maybe it's the blood on my face and gloves.

"Yeah?"

"Doctor Hayes asked for you." I nod and wave him off. He scurries away quickly. I must scare him.

"Doctor Hayes?" Marlow asks.

"Victor. He's all professional when sending messengers. All by the regs, but for all intents and purposes, he is known as Doctor Hayes." I roll to a sitting position and stretch my neck out, and crack it side to side. I stand and pull off the boxing gear and dump it in a "to be cleaned" bin.

"Wanna shower and be out of here in twenty?" I ask.

"Not with you, but thanks for asking. I'll see you out here in twenty minutes." She laughs as she walks into the locker room. A few male officers snicker near me, and I know they've heard the conversation. I tilt my head menacingly and stare. They shut up.

"That's not what I meant!" I call after her as I head into the locker room.

That familiar feel of death is on me as I walk into the room. The cold, chemical smell hits my nostrils, and my stomach tightens. It's a smell you never forget or get used to. At some point you just stop noticing it. First, you start with Vick's Vapor Rub under your nose. As time goes on, you move to a generic lotion. Then its tissues jammed up the nostrils. Before you know it, you're here standing like I am, with nothing on your face to block the odor of death. In some ways, it might become comforting, reminding you that you're still alive. And on other days, it reminds you of the vile and heartless underbelly of our society.

Seeing people you know on the slab has ways of changing your view of this room. It used to be just a room where victims were brought in. You feel horrible, but there's a detachment from it. My nephew put it in perspective; you don't see a cow die or be butchered. You just eat the burger. It's a crude comparison but a similar idea. I hate this room now.

"His body isn't here, Jasmine," Victor says from behind me as I stare at the wall of frozen lockers. The numbers where my family members have rested call my eyes to them.

"I know."

"Where's Karina?"

"Wanted to check in with the bosses in Seattle." I turn from the wall of containment units to face Victor. He looks tired and drawn. "How have you been holding up?"

He walks over to his assistant's desk and sits on the stool. His right hand slowly filters through the hair on his head. The longer strands rest against his scalp, staying there briefly before falling back to their previous position. His hands have a slight tremor I haven't seen before. This saga of never-ending torment is taking its toll. One would have to be a psychopath for it not to.

"As well as can be expected. It's not easy doing an autopsy on the body of someone you know. Then, I've got the bigwigs hanging over me every move I made . . . It was difficult to do my job."

"I'm sorry," I say in response. There's nothing else I can say to make it better. We all know that this is a higher-level officer's murder. Those are scrutinized just like the high-profile media cases—the ones that make every news station every hour, every internet video, and splash and trend all over social media. Those are the only cases more scrutinized.

"That's why you couldn't be down here when I was done." He looks up at me with sadness in his expression. He feels guilty for me being on the outside looking in. If he only knew. Walking to the slab nearest him, I lean on it for support.

"Nothing to feel bad about. It's the nature of the beast. Garrison has his hands in so many pockets; people are trying to cover their asses. Make sure they're not in harm's way, you know? When this thing totally breaks, when Logan delivers his full report to the FBI . . . who knows what other chips might fall? No one wants to be on that list or on this slab. Can't blame them for acting like billionaires chasing tax breaks. It's inevitable."

"You and your analogies." Victor chuckles a bit before shaking his head at me. "You're crazy, you know that?"

"Of course, she does. I'm sure she enjoys the idea of it," Marlow says as she walks into the room. "Sorry I'm late."

"What did they say?" I ask.

"Agent Sharp had checked in with them before Valez left me the files. They want copies. I have Logan sending them everything."

"Including the bug?"

"Bug?" Victor butts in, but I silence him with a wave of my hand.

"Not until we speak with Logan. I can't share information I don't have."

Marlow shrugs and turns her attention to Victor. "Someone left a bug in my hotel room. I don't think it's from the two suspects we seem to be unable to catch. I think it was an inside job on my end."

"And you willingly said all of that in my morgue because you thought it was safer? You realize there are cameras everywhere?"

Marlow smiles at him before turning her attention back to me. She wants them to know she's looking into it. If the NYPD does share all their information with the FBI, they'll know about this conversation soon. Then they will confiscate the bug from Logan downstairs before we even get there. That means it's an insider. It's impatient and impulsive on Marlow's part. I hope she has a good reason for it.

"What can you tell us about any and all of the bodies that have come through here?" I push the conversation back to the original case at hand. Victor spins around and logs into the computer on the desk.

"The container autopsies were all completed, with many hours of overtime and manpower. Sadly, DNA records and identifications might take a long time. The majority of the victims we were able to ID were immigrants. They showed significant signs of physical abuse. Some of the women suffered sexual trauma. We can assume by the injuries none of it was consensual."

"You're sure?" I ask.

"With that level of decomp, you can never be sure of anything. Based on the evidence Doctor Brown and I discovered, we concluded it was almost a certainty. Several of the men had severe rectal tearing. We can't conclusively say how the wounds occurred, but three of the men bled out from their injuries in the container."

"Doctor Hayes, how did they die?" Marlow asks.

"What I thought before I can now confirm. The majority of these victims slowly died of terminal dehydration."

"Christ. How long?" I say.

"For the elderly, probably within a day or so of being locked away. For the younger, more physically fit victims, it was five to seven days. Maybe longer."

"That sounds horrible," Marlow pipes in.

"Normally, dehydration is considered a pain-free way to die. Many have stated terminally ill patients are in a vegetative state or a calm one. They feel no pain as they pass on." Victor takes a slow deep breath and pauses. "But, in this case, there is the mental torment of knowing what is to befall you. They were locked away. No fluids. No bathrooms. Disease was beginning to form in the cells of the dead. It was a horrific way to die. It was no better than the gas chambers of World War II or the Pig Basket Massacre—in fact, probably worse. People who can do . . . this, who are capable of harming people as casualties of their own mind's bullshit . . . they need to be put down."

Victor turns back to the computer and brings up another file. I see Captain Udall's face smiling back at us. Various awards, accolades, and honors are listed below his image. He was a decorated officer. He was an honorable man and an even better friend. We had our differences and butted heads on numerous occasions, but this one . . . this one cuts deep. Just to know he's gone. He died doing what he loved. But I'm sure that means absolutely nothing to his wife.

"The captain was in very good health for someone his age. His neck was cut, severing the major arteries, resulting in his death."

"That explains the visual of the scene," I say to Marlow. It was obvious what happened, but confirmation is what we need before we can move forward.

"Anything else we should know about?" Marlow asks Victor.

"He had defensive wounds. A lot of them. If Emilio Valez or whatever his name is did this, he took a beating. Severe bruising to the captain's knuckles on his left hand. Bruising to the sternum, ribs, and a lacerated kidney. He also managed to break his right hand on the assailant's mouth."

"How can you be so sure of that?" I ask curiously.

"The upper front teeth left an indentation on the skin and bones. Doctor Brown is investigating the residue on the skin as well as the swab of his teeth."

"Good for you, Tyler," I say under my breath.

"I'm not sure skin residue will help all that much. According to the FBI and the NYPD, the DNA of our two wanted individuals is not in the system," Marlow says as her cell phone rings. She quickly answers it. "Marlow." Her face goes slack, and she turns to lock eyes with me.

"What?" I whisper to her. She waves me off and points to the doors. I assume we're on the move.

"Thanks for everything, Vic. Tell the doc if she finds anything interesting to give me a call," I say in a lower tone as I follow Marlow out to the elevator. I catch up to her just as she hangs up the phone.

"What's up?"

"They confiscated everything," she says as she walks in the elevator. I think I catch a glimpse of a smile mixed with a grimace on her face. I numbly walk in alongside her and watch the doors close. Shit just got real.

You ever try to catch up to someone who is walking like they're on a mission? You have to walk twice as fast, almost run. I've got three inches on Marlow in height, which translates to approximately eight inches more per stride, but damn can she motor when she wants to. She's already out of the elevator and is pulling open the doors to the tech's lab before I've even taken a step outside. Walking twice as fast as a normal human being should, I manage to stay two desks behind her. She's in Logan's office, but I manage to catch up to her before they can talk. The office is a mess.

"Love what you've done with the place, Logan."

The sarcasm drips from my lips. How did we go from a slightly-more-complex-than-we-would-like-it case to the Feds coming in and taking everything?

"They took all the main stuff and even my backups," he says as he scoots onto his stomach and crawls on the floor under his desk.

"Logan, you called me, so can we please get on with it? I assumed they would be watching. I hoped it would be swift, but even by Bureau standards this is a bit nuts," Marlow says as she looks around the office. It basically looks like my nephew ran in here on a sugar high and destroyed the place.

"Done!" Logan screams from under his desk. His hand pops up from the floor and waves us toward it. This kid has been acting a bit nutty in recent days, but this has to take the cake. The two of us walk to the other side of the desk, and we see a smiling Logan on the floor. He holds his finger up to his lips while his other hand points to the floor. I slowly make my way to the floor. This body is tired; it recently took a beating in the ring and is riddled with previous injuries, so it takes a moment. Once seated cross-legged, Marlow and I wait patiently for Logan to say something. He pulls out that trusty little jammer, flips it on, and drops to the floor.

"Because I'm a good tech and an even better conspiracy theorist, I have a backup for my backups." He smiles at the two of us.

"Paranoid is a bit more accurate," I tease him. "Is there a reason we can't sit in those comfortable chairs by your desk?"

"Cameras and lip reading," he calmly answers as if it it's common knowledge.

"What did you find?" Marlow interjects, bringing us back to the case at hand.

"There were several documents in the folder left by Valez. I'm still investigating who the people are, but it's like a who's who of the political realm. There are bank accounts, connections to bills our government passed to ensure pharmaceutical companies made profits, and that's just the beginning. I'm digging deeper, but this is everything you need to make a case against Garrison and put him away for many lifetimes."

"Why would she leave that for me?" Marlow asks.

"Maybe to make a deal for her son? She had to know what he was up to," I answer bitterly.

"Maybe, but that doesn't make much sense," Marlow replies. "Why give me more information that could assist me in putting her away for life?"

"Unless it was a deal for her life as well," I add. I see Marlow's eyes widen.

"Turning over as an informant." She shakes her head in disgust. "If she has information that was worth a clean slate, the government would give her anything."

"They went after Snowden. What makes her so special?" Logan counters.

"Snowden released information the government didn't want the general population to know. He broke the golden rule of politics and power," Marlow says.

"What was that?" Logan asks.

"He refused to keep his head down, do his job, and shut up. Blowing the whistle only works in the movies—not in the real world. He should have gone through the proper channels," she answers.

"Even at our level, we all know those avenues aren't always honorable," I throw in. "Hell, all it takes is one corrupt cop and the rest of us are painted as villains. Not to mention the peons are always the scapegoat when things go south quickly. No one cares about a mayor who releases orders to force a crackdown on things in a specific way. They only care about those who enacted it. Just like anything else, who you see is who you blame."

"If she was switching sides, why clean up the mess?" Marlow asks. "Why kill those kids in the store? Why the containers? Why be involved in any of this to begin with? Why not just flee to another country with your son and break away? I'm sure she had enough money to handle it."

"There has to be more to it than that," I add, shrugging my shoulders. "Anything on the bug?"

"The bug that you found wasn't meant to spy on you at all," Logan answers.

"How can you be so sure?"

"Because this model is known as the Q-Bug. It has a forty-eight-hour standby time but only a seven-hour usage time. It's rechargeable, but that would have been pointless if they were tracking you."

"So, who planted it and why is it still a concern?" I say.

"Yes and no," Logan replies. "The bug has a SIM card that was connected to a cell phone via code and text message. It's also virtually undetectable as it gives off no major markers of a bug. Whoever placed this in the wall wanted to be able to record the smallest whisper from thirty-five feet away. This baby has virtually no distance limitation," Logan gushes.

"You sound envious, Logan," Marlow says. Her frustration and anger seep out with her words.

"About the tech? Hell, yeah. About why it was there? No, not one bit."

"Can you trace the SIM card?" Marlow asks.

"I tried, but the government spoiled my attempts."

"Anything recorded?" I ask.

"Not at all. This specific model was meant for the person to listen to the conversation from their cell phone. This wasn't meant to record," Logan says.

"Why put it there then?" I ask Marlow.

"To pay attention to the person they knew was in the room? To listen in on a deal gone wrong? Or to put me off the real bug?"

"You're starting to sound like Logan," I say as Logan keeps nodding at Marlow.

"She has a point, Jasmine. Why would they put a bug like this in there? First, they would have to have access to the room at all times. Second, they have to know who is in there and when. They have forty-eight hours, but if you are unsure of when someone will enter, that's not a lot of time. And most importantly, it doesn't record a damn thing. So why this bug? Why put it in the wall?"

He's right. This is too shoddy. It doesn't fit into the mold of what the FBI would do in a case like this. If they were waiting for Alexa Valez, they would have put a bug in which recorded all the time. Then it would have been spying on Marlow as well. They had to know our fugitive would be in there. They had to know she would leave something behind. Yet the question remains: Why this bug and why these two days?

"I think it's time we sit down with Agent Sharp," I say to Marlow.

"I'll handle that. You need to focus on your eulogy for the funeral." Marlow stands and heads out of the office before I can argue with her. I look at Logan, whose expression is more somber now.

"Jazz . . ." Logan starts, but I wave at him to shut up.

"Forget it."

"I know Agent Marlow left, but do you want to discuss the captain's things?" Logan sheepishly asks.

"Tell me," I say, emotionless. I'm truly not sure if I want to hear this.

"He has several files on the Valez family in Puerto Rico. He was investigating those that came to this country and settled in our area. He had notes in file folders on his laptop with names, locations, investment properties. Most in Brooklyn, some in Queens. I assume he was trying to find a living relative willing to speak to him. Most he contacted were deceased or unavailable every time he called. He wrote the letters AA, BD and eleven thirty p.m. on his calendar yesterday."

"A meeting he missed," I say solemnly.

"There's more. His cell phone showed several calls to a group of officers. All of them were undercover following you, Agent Marlow, and Emilio Valez, aka Tucker whatever. There were several text messages sent to him discussing locations and more. His computer outlined his suspicions about Emilio Valez but laid out no specific proof."

"If they were following Valez, how did Valez murder the captain in his own house?"

"That's the thing. I was looking at the footage from his laptop, and I think he had an idea," Logan says, typing away at his keyboard. I'm beyond confused at the moment, but there's nothing I can say until my brain processes everything. He turns his laptop around and plays a video.

Udall stares at the screen and waves his hand as he smiles. He leans back in a chair and takes a deep breath. "I think this is it. After this case, I'm going to retire. I've still got a few years in me, but I want to live a bit. Go places with my wife, maybe paint the garage like I've been promising Sandra. Either way, I think it's time."

There's a knock at the door, and I hear him say "Just a minute" to someone off-screen. He walks out of frame, and I see his gun sitting on the coffee table. A gun we didn't find at the scene. Emilio Valez enters and looks around the room. His body language is off. His white shirt is untucked, his jeans and jacket dirty. He's not standing aggressively; he's almost shaking as if nervous. Udall enters the frame with his back to the laptop camera.

"What can I do for you, Tucker?" Udall asks.

"You told me to call you if I ever needed anything," Emilio says, his hands twitching.

"I told you to come into the precinct. This is my home. How did you find me?"

"I just needed to talk to you, and the officers wouldn't help me. That bitch was out to get me. I know it." Emilio rubs his head as if trying to clean something off his scalp.

"Steele? She was just doing her job," Udall says, defending me.

"Nah, she knows too much. You think I wanted to be a part of this shit? You think I like cleaning up after my father? That fucker didn't even know I existed, but all of the sudden I'm his golden boy." His hands keep shaking.

"What about your father? Who—"

"Don't act like you don't know what I'm talking about! She told me you all know; that FBI bitch figured it all out!"

"I don't, okay, but why don't we go downtown and talk. We can make sure you're safe. Your father can't hurt you anymore," the captain says soothingly.

"Of course, he can." Emilio laughs. "Irving Garrison can't hurt me? Mom was right; it's about time I make my own path." Udall's eyes get wide as it all becomes apparent to him. Emilio pulls out a knife and lunges at the captain. Udall easily dodges the motion and holds his hands up. Emilio looks over to the gun and back to the captain.

"Pick that up!" Emilio tells him.

"I don't need it. You're just confused and scared. I can help you." Udall tries one more time. Emilio hangs his head, and I can hear him mumbling something to himself.

In a swift motion, Emilio comes after Udall again. This time he manages to cut the captain on the arm. Udall looks at his arm quickly, and I can tell his demeanor has changed. I knew he wasn't going to pick up the gun. It's not his way. He was trained to use a gun as a deterrent, but he hated it. If he felt he could disarm and restrain someone without it, he would. Emilio comes at him again, madly slashing the air. The captain jumps back each time. On the last movement of the blade, he grabs Emilio's arm and hits the elbow joint hard. The sound of the knife hitting the floor rattles the speakers.

Emilio head-butts the captain, forcing him back into the half wall the laptop was resting on. The screen wobbles but settles. The two men fight back and forth, exchanging blows. Udall tosses Emilio across the room, and he lands on the coffee table, shattering it into pieces. The gun skitters away.

"I'm gonna say it again, Tucker! You don't have to do this! I can help you. All you've done so far is get into a friendly fight. I'm sure my neighbors have already called the cops. When they get here, I'll twist the story that way, kid. Just don't do this," Udall pleads with Emilio.

Emilio stands up and rubs his hand over his bloody lip. He wipes the fluid onto his jacket and takes a deep breath. In a flash, he hits the captain in the face with the gun. Udall turns and spits blood on the camera of the laptop. He hits Udall two more times the same way, leaving the captain breathless and barely holding on. Emilio bends down and comes back into frame with the knife in his hand.

"You can't help me, Pops. Don't worry, this is just business. Always is." He reaches around and slices Udall's throat. No hold of his head. No disruption in the spray. The blood rushes out along his skin. The captain grabs his throat as he tries to fight the inevitable loss of life. Emilio walks away out of frame. You can hear the door close as Udall fights to stay alive. His free hand punches the keyboard, but nothing happens. He turns to walk out of frame. The gurgling sound hits my ears and makes me nauseated. The gurgles slowly die down until I hear what sounds like a body hitting the floor.

Logan stops the video.

"He tried to call 911, but the blood loss was too great," he says sadly.

"That's why the phone was covered in his blood," I say.

"I'm so sorry," Logan whispers.

I say nothing to him as I stand and head toward the exit. Even after all this information, I don't know what to think. I need to focus on the next task. I have a speech to write. Marlow is handling the interview of her colleague. I need to come up with something witty and compelling for a funeral. I'm not good at this kind of thing. Hell, I rewrote a KISS song for my brother's eulogy. I know he would have loved it. The rest of the family, not so much. It wasn't for them though. It never is. It's a salute to those gone by, so fuck those who don't like it.

Standing outside the captain's former office, my heart skips. It feels like yesterday I was in my most uncomfortable suit trying to make an impression. A first-time detective, with the desire to change the world and the fashion sense of a newborn baby. His laughter as I tried to sit down in the chair and not rip my pants. The outfit was so tight in the wrong places, but he never made me feel worse for it. Udall knew this was what I had in my closet from my thinner days. He didn't really know me, but he knew me well enough to expect I wouldn't go shopping for new threads. I always had the "If you last more than a week, you can buy more clothes" attitude.

My first shift Udall drove me around. Apparently, my new partner's kid was in the hospital and he wanted to make sure I learned the 'Tyler Udall" way. We went over all the paperwork, the processes, and all the mundane, day-to-day things which went with being a cop in his precinct. I remember he showed me to my first desk in the main area—an old, green metal monstrosity with a top right shelf that liked to stick. Nothing fancy, but usable. That was his mantra: anything can be worked with. You just have to find a way. Except when it came to my suit. He took me shopping that night and insisted I buy some clothes that actually fit. Apparently, jeans and T-shirt didn't work with a dress coat either.

Sitting in his chair, looking around the small space, it's heartbreaking. The walls once littered with awards seem empty. The frames of cops he'd met throughout his career are gone. He was never one to brag about who he knew. In fact, he preferred to show off the faces of all those officers he respected. I remember there was an image of a Port Authority officer in one frame. That man's image was the biggest of them all, and I asked the captain why it was there. He told me, "That man was a hero, did his best to save lives in New York's darkest day." I spin the chair around to look out the window—his window—and the ordinary view over a few brick buildings makes me smile.

That was my boss. While others in charge had images of the mayor or some commendation ceremony covering their walls, Captain Udall had ordinary men and women. He was such a contrarian to the rest of the people I know. If someone said jump, Udall would have a conversation about it and why it was necessary. He'd hold a door just because he could. He used to tell me nothing happens because people just sit around waiting for it. We have to seize life but do it in a way so we don't prohibit others from doing the same. He's the reason I am the way I am today. At least on this side of the badge. He made me a good cop and, I hope, an even better detective.

"Can I help you?" I hear a voice from the door to the captain's office. I turn around and see a man wearing jeans, a Yankees baseball cap, and a Cutter and Buck polo shirt. He's holding a box overflowing with items.

"I should be asking you that," I answer with annoyance in my voice.

The man walks around the desk and drops his box on the desk in front of me. He stares at me, as if challenging me in some way. I have no idea who he is or what the hell he wants. I just want him to get out of Udall's office and let me wallow in peace.

"Thomas Zeile." He holds his hand out in front of me. "Your new captain."

Those three words cut through my chest faster than a knife through a tomato. Udall's been replaced that quickly? Who the hell thought this was a smart idea? We should all be given time to mourn and work through what we're feeling. I don't expect a month, but two weeks would have been nice. This guy shows up after four days and expects me to be cordial? Fuck him. I stand up and bump into his hand. He retracts it as he smiles at me. I walk around him and stand in front of the desk. He pulls out the metal nameplate paperweight and places it on his desk for me to see.

"I know all about you, Detective Steele. Your reputation precedes you."

"Don't believe everything you hear," I say.

"Of course. Then again, they were all good things. Personally, I think it's all bullshit," he says as he places a picture of a woman and a baby on his desk.

"Excuse me?" I cross my arms defensively. I don't know what this guy is trying to do, but I don't need it right now.

"I think your reputation is shit. You get the job done so everyone loves you, but you're arrogant, impulsive, and loud. I respect your results, but from now on things are going to be run a bit differently." He sits down in the captain's chair and looks up at me.

"With all due respect, sir, my skills are just fine. My actions are my own and my results speak for themselves."

"Yes, they do. I agree with you on that. You manage to close cases that most people wouldn't touch. Even when you have one sitting on a shelf in cold storage, your notes and investigation skills are impeccable. That was never in question though."

"Then what is it?" I ask.

"The attitude. The inability to take a back seat. The fact that you get too involved in some cases to the point of putting your team at risk. You run headfirst into battle without looking to see if you have backup. You wouldn't last five minutes in a war zone."

"Good thing we're in New York then," I answer smugly.

"That's where you're wrong. The streets out there are our own version of a battlefield. We fight crime, guns, drugs, and homegrown terrorists. We have the best and worst in the world walking through Times Square any given day of the week. You need support, detective, or you're going to be pushing tickets for the rest of your career."

"That would never happen. My jacket is full of commendations to prevent a demotion. Not to mention the union would have a field day. So, *captain*, I don't think I will ever be pushing tickets again. Maybe ride a desk if I piss you off, but never tickets."

I lower my arms and place my hands in my pockets. I'm not going to let him scare me or get under my skin. He might sit in that chair, but he will never be Captain Udall to me. I have to deal with that and so will he. Thomas Zeile has some big shoes to fill, and he might break under the weight. For Udall, I will adapt and thrive. I won't falter.

"Good. That's what I want to hear." He places his feet on the corner of the desk.

"What?" I answer, a bit lost as to the direction of the conversation.

"I want you to be on your toes. I want the best in my division, and I won't stand for anything less. You're still impulsive and your arrogance is on display for me right now. You'll follow orders though, and you will get results. You won't have a choice because I'm in charge now and that's the way it is. Are we clear?"

"Yeah," I say as I turn around and head for the door.

"I know the funeral is tomorrow, but I expect the file on the Garrison case by the end of the day. I want to go over everything."

"I'll get it now." I want to leave, but one question keeps nagging at me. "How did you get assigned here so quickly?" I ask bluntly. My back remains facing the new captain.

"High profile case, quick turnaround. Crime doesn't stop so we can mourn one of our own. It's not pleasant, but it's the reality." His voice is even and calm.

I walk out and head back to my office. The cold reality of change once again slaps me in the face like a cold winter snowstorm. Life moves on no matter how hard we try to hold onto it. I wish I could say otherwise, but I don't think this is going to be an easy transition for me. I feel it in my gut.

Chapter Ten

Dress blues. Starchy, unrelenting, uncomfortable. I feel the weight of the badge hanging on my chest. The weight of other medals and bars only making me more cognizant of where I am. I am aware of the tightness of these shiny, black shoes. I walk in step: right, then left, then right, left. The frozen ground is unrelenting and painful underfoot. The wind whips around and smacks me in the face with reality. The sun beats down on my skin but warms nothing on this frigid day. Reality and Mother Nature have unknowingly conspired to make the day worse than it already was.

The silent and somber procession follows the box to a hole in the middle of a cemetery, a dirt-brown scar which stands out in a field of fading autumn grass and granite headstones. The dirt is covered by some green tarp made to look like AstroTurf. The metal folding chairs have been placed perfectly in a row, awaiting the arrival of the family. One by one, they fall in line. Officers of all ranks and positions stand alongside. Row by row, the chairs fill up. The flag covered box rests above the depths of nothingness. The brushed aluminum cranks hold it suspended and stretched to the limit of its capacity.

I hate these places. And I hate these things, and I hate people in boxes, and I hate watching families weep, and I most of all I hate why we're here today. Rationally, it makes sense to me, but I can't logically wrap my brain around it. Good people die while the truly vile in society seem to thrive. Tyler Udall wasn't one of the bad guys. He wasn't dark or vile. He was a good man, a former soldier with a heart as big as his city. Yet, it's his body in the box. The skin will dry out, mummify, and be nothing more than an artifact for future generations. Either that or he'll be dug up and burned when no living relative can complain. Space on this planet is more and more limited, so why not reuse space by evicting the old tenants? One way or another, this is not, nor shall it ever be, a pleasant experience.

The priest stands tall in his stark, black uniform, leading the dead to the promised land. His long coat tries to fight away the coming blast of cold from invading the warmth like I am in my heart. The pages of his book flip in the breeze as the prayer falls from his lips, forever lost in the air around us. He finally closes it and inhales deeply. He's going to go off script and speak from the heart, something I'm sure he's done countless times before.

"Captain Tyler Udall was a man of the people," the priest begins. "He was a man of his faith. He was a devoted husband to his wife, Sandra. Looking at their life together, one would say it was incomplete without children. Tyler, however, would always disagree. He and Sandra referred to all of his officers as sons or daughters. They fully embraced and loved every one of you here today. Each and every one of you is a living testament to the man that Captain Tyler Udall was. Henceforth, the way you live your lives, the way you perform your duties, the way you treat your fellow man, all of these things will continually reflect . . . him. You're his legacy now. You're the ones who'll show, by their actions, the man that he was. He is being accepted into the kingdom of heaven to be with our heavenly father forever. There are no tears, for he has passed on to a greater pasture. Amen."

The crowd mumbles an *amen* and there is an uncomfortable silence. Sandra turns around and her eyes catch mine. It's my turn to speak. I extract myself from the crowd and move around the hole in the ground. I stand behind the podium and angle the microphone to the proper height. This move is more about wasting time so I can get my breathing under control than needing the microphone adjusted. Once that's settled, I pull out a stack of index cards.

"Sandra asked me to speak today because I've known Cap my entire career. Apparently, it was in his will that I stand here and tell you all about him. I personally think he wanted me to give this speech as a final lesson in public speaking."

I take a breath as some of the people chuckle slightly. My nerves, and a sorrow and a torment I can't run from, slowly creep to my chest, and I feel my heart begin to race. I look over to Sandra, whose eyes harbor so much pain but still manage to show a deep love for us all. She gives me the strength to continue. I look down at the cards and flip them over. Frankie often says, "You speak from the heart, you'll open yourself up to healing." I hope she's right, because otherwise I'm going to sound like a fool.

"I stayed up last night writing this speech, trying to pry out the right words to say. Agent Marlow must have thought I was mad by how many times I recited it while she tried to sleep upstairs. I wanted it to be perfect. I wanted every word to have the proper inflection, emotion, and purpose that it deserves. Not because I'm overly obsessive with anything I touch, but because he deserved it."

I take a breath and watch Sandra's face. She is who I need to speak to; the rest of them don't matter. They are the block people in the background of a badly coded video game.

"When I was just starting out, I was beyond green. I hated paperwork and felt that trees needed to survive longer than we did. I remember telling the captain that if we didn't kill trees maybe people would stop killing each other. He didn't dignify that with a response. He just placed a pile of papers on my desk and sat down next to me. Sandra was waiting on him for hours that night, but he was by my side. He forced me to do all of my work properly. Lesson one: you can't skate by doing shoddy work and relying on talent. Sometimes you have to work hard doing things you hate to be a well-rounded person and police officer."

I shift my weight from left to right, stare into the faux veneer wood on the face of the podium, and swallow thickly.

"When I became a detective, Cap walked me to a new desk. Which, of course, was broken." More scattered, knowing chuckles from the crowd. "It was rusted, the top shelf barely opened, and the light didn't work. He told me he'd make sure the lamp was fixed or replaced. I remember looking at that desk and being in awe of it. Sure, it was a horrible piece of shit, but it was *mine*. This one I had really earned. I sat proudly at that desk, working with it to the best of my ability. When I hit my one-year anniversary, I came into the precinct and there was a shiny, new, puke-green desk with working drawers and lamp. I'll never forget Tyler patting me on the back and telling me I had earned it. Lesson two: you will be repaid for hard, honest work if you put the time in."

A single tear slides down my face, but I do nothing to stop it. If I don't show attention to it, maybe people will ignore my tears. As more begin to fall, I exhale and inhale, trying to steady myself.

"Cap was always there for me in the darkest times. When I lost my brother and my sister-in-law, Cap was there at the scene. He told me the truth and didn't sugarcoat it. He walked me down the aisle of the church at the funeral. Not because he wanted to, but because I needed him to. And it was something I didn't need to tell him—he just knew. He almost carried me to my family's plots as their boxes were lowered into the ground. He kept me standing upright as I greeted everyone who came by afterwards. He pulled the liquor bottles out of my hand when I had too much to drink at the wake. He and Sandra let my nephew Chase stay with them when my world came crashing down. I could never thank them enough for that."

I smile through my tears at Sandra, who has matching tears of her own.

"Tyler Udall was a man who put his life behind others. He would help you by lifting you up. He would push you to be the absolute best person you could be. He never left you alone to fall. He was the ultimate support in that trust exercise. If you dropped back, he'd catch you. There was no other man like him in my division, and there never will be again," I finish.

The officers in my division mumble in agreement. Captain Zeile walks over to me and hands me one of the police radios. This is going to be one of the hardest things I've ever had to do. Taking a deep breath, I press the button on the side and begin the last call.

"Dispatch to 7403."

I release the button. Nothing but static hits the microphone. I press the button again.

"Dispatch to 7403."

Releasing the button, I once again hear the sound of static. I press it again.

"Dispatch to 7403," I say one final time, waiting for the response I know will never come. I press the button down one final time with a shaky hand.

"No response from Captain Tyler Udall. Badge number 7403 is out of service after forty-four years and eight months on the job. Although you are gone, you will never be forgotten. Rest in peace, our friend."

I release the button and hand the radio back to my new boss. The color guard walks around and removes the flag from the casket. As they begin to ritually fold it up, I walk toward the back of the pack. I hear the orders for the firing salute to begin. Seven shooters, aiming to the sky for the tribute. They perfectly time three shots each as the sound echoes across the cemetery. It's the final stage of the funeral. This makes it real, but the gun salute means it's over. Tomorrow people will expect us all to go back to normal like we're robots. It's the circle of life. Following the motion of my fellow brothers in blue, I raise my hand one last time to salute my surrogate father. I promise myself right then that I will always be the human being he was proudest of.

Sandra walks up to me and opens her arms. The woman knows me so well. I lean forward and feel her warmth envelop me. Her lips press firmly against my head before she releases me. Her hand caresses the side of my face with a painful smile. Just like that, she passes by me and into the limo waiting nearby.

The steam from the cup rises and I find myself staring at it, watching it trail upwards and fade into nothing. Sometimes when the door opens, it dances around as if it's alive. It's my third cup. The first to be consumed while it's hot. Frankie wouldn't be happy with the large amount of caffeine I've consumed. I think she'd give me a reprieve considering the situation. I miss my family. I miss Chase so much it hurts, but it isn't safe yet. I need them safe for my own selfish reasons.

"You ought to buy stock in the company if you're going to come here so much."

I look up to see Logan carrying a ridiculously large cup of something. Lord knows what that boy drinks. "Wanna try it?" He takes a sip from the oversized straw.

"No thanks. I'll stick to plain, ordinary lattes. Thank you."

"Your loss. Nothing like piles of mocha, caramel, and whipped cream infused with about five shots of espresso and blended perfectly with ice."

"Are you describing coffee or a dessert? Seriously, whatever happened to ordinary coffee?"

"Went out of style when the man bun came to pass." I open my mouth to reply, but he holds his hand up with that insane drink. "I know what you think of that hairstyle. Let it go."

"How's the lab?"

"We have a huge case with lots of number crap coming up, so things are a bit crazy."

"What's it entail?" I ask.

"Tech billionaire. He never paid his taxes and claimed questionable deductions."

"And that's different from any other rich person because . . .?"

"Because he wasn't the one doing the taxes. Sure, he benefited from them, but the company behind his filings was lying through their teeth. On top of that, he managed to get bank account numbers, et cetera, all legit, right? He needed them in case he had to pay taxes or bills whatever. He had an almost undetectable algorithm that removed a minuscule amount of money from the accounts for every transaction the client made. Then it was all transferred to an offshore account that we have no control over."

"Skimming in the new world."

"Precisely." He takes a sip of his drink and looks at me. "The funeral was nice."

"As nice as it could be."

"Marlow wasn't there," he adds.

"She's working on the case and didn't really know the captain well. Can't blame her. Funerals are one of the worst things we do in this life," I say before sipping some of my now lukewarm coffee.

"She's been involved with this Garrison case almost as long as you have."

"Explain," I say flatly.

"Based on her email and search history . . ."

"You hacked a federal agent's email?" I say a little louder than I mean to.

"Jesus, just tell everyone why don't you?" He looks around nervously before leaning forward. "I just wanted to see what we were getting into. Considering she ran off yesterday to talk to that other agent. So, I did a bit of digging."

"And?"

"She's clean. Like really clean. Apparently, she uncovered a lot of back-door dealings when the new Seattle tech boom started. Various permits were given without having to go through the rigorous process. There were reports of police ignoring the underhanded dealings on the streets, et cetera."

"Someone had the locals in their back pocket. Sounds familiar."

"That's the point. She and Sharp blew it wide open. Problem was, all those implicated either retired, fled, or mysteriously disappeared before any charges could be brought against them. Many were protected by the local unions, so no one had to, or desired to, talk."

"When was this?" I ask.

"Before the information was leaked to the social world via the internet." Logan leans back, smiling at me.

"So, they came here as a team to get their hands on Garrison, the head of the dragon," I say as my mind processes the information.

"You're getting there," he replies.

"But she's been more focused on getting closer to Valez and her son. Well, now her son is going to prison for murder whether she tries to help him or not."

"Yup." He sucks on that straw, and it makes a slight squeaking noise as it rubs along the plastic lip of the lid.

"The bug freaked her out and made her want to speak to her partner in crime. Not because they were spying on her, but because he wanted to know why Valez was in Marlow's room."

"One more for the gold." He's patronizing me on a day I'm not in the mood for it.

"They're both here to bring Alexa Valez in as an informant. Not unheard of, and she alluded to it before, but it doesn't make it any easier to swallow." After the words leave my mouth, my body runs cold.

"And you win first place. That is exactly where my head went after reading the correspondence. Whoever brings Valez in gets the big money. The rest of us get Garrison and her son. That's it."

"Which means the corruption goes much higher than we have clearance for."

"Could go all the way to the top. Maybe even the Illuminati are involved. Better yet, Valez knows the names of the ruling class. You know, the ones who own all the power and money in the world. The ones who start wars to create more profit for themselves. When inventors die or mysteriously disappear and all their research dies with them, it's these people—" Logan says as he continues his conspiracy rant.

"Anything on this AA or DB from the calendar?" I ask, cutting him off.

"I found a cousin named Anthony Amica on the Upper West Side. He's got a rap sheet for various drug possessions with intent to sell. He's also been involved with some not so nice mob characters." Logan slips me the address on a piece of paper.

"Paper?"

"Less traceable."

"Get back to your office. I've got a lot to think about and a new partner to confront. Keep digging on everything—and I mean everything, Logan.

I want to know if Valez has contacted Agent Marlow or Sharp recently. If there's anything, you'll find it," I finish.

"If I disappear without a trace—" Logan starts.

"You're not getting paranoid—I mean more paranoid—on me right now, are you? Please, just go back to your office and keep digging."

Logan stands up and leaves me alone in the coffee shop. Marlow's been hiding some information from me even after Captain Udall insisted we be open with her. This is why I've always hated working with government agencies. If they have an agenda, it's their way or the highway. Damn anyone who gets in their path.

The Upper West Side, where the air is richer along with the prices of everything. Walking around the corner bodega Logan gave me the address to, I wait for the customer buying his Lotto ticket to leave. Once he's done, I walk up to the counter and pull my jacket to the side, showing my badge.

"I'm looking for Anthony Amica," I say calmly so as to not alarm the guy.

"I don't know him. You have the wrong place. I don't want any trouble." He raises his hands and I lower my head. Why is it people automatically assume you want trouble when you show your badge?

"No trouble. I need his help. Nothing bad." I try to reassure him.

The man's head turns to the left and he points one finger at a super tall, very built and imposing figure in the back stocking shelves. Taking a deep breath, I head to the giant and pray he is the nonviolent reformed type.

"Excuse me, Mr. Amica?"

He turns and looks down at all five foot nine inches of my height and smiles.

"Yes, ma'am. Who might you be?" His deep bass of a voice would make my brother's old bass tubes sound pathetic.

"Detective Steele. I was hoping you might be able to help me with something?"

He holds his massive hand out to me, and I accept his offer. His fingers engulf mine in a firm handshake.

"Pleasure to meet you. We can talk, but not here." He holds his hand up in the air, getting his boss's attention. "I'm heading out back for a smoke."

The guy behind the counter nods, and Anthony pulls me by the hand through the maze of shelves to a hidden back door. My gut is a bit torn here. He doesn't appear to be threatening me, but he has a firm grip on my hand, is leading me to a dark alley, and I doubt I can restrain him. This is not a good situation.

The door swings open, he swings me around, and my back hits a brick wall. I'm going to have to disinfect my coat when I get home is the first thing running through my mind. The small, square-shaped area has a narrow one-way exit to the street. Not sure how any human being would fit through it, but if that is my way out, I'll have to make it work.

"Why are you looking for me?" he asks, his tone deepening if that is even possible.

"I need information on a murder case."

"I don't know nothing." He pulls out a joint and lights it. He inhales and looks at my face. "What? You gonna arrest me?"

"I doubt my cuffs would fit," I say sarcastically.

Anthony stares at me for a few seconds before he exhales. He then chuckles a little bit before turning his attention to the blue sky.

"I need to know if you were meeting someone at eleven thirty p.m. at BD."

"No, and anyone who said I was is a liar. I was at home with my kid who's sick."

"Do you know the Valez family?"

"You know I do or you wouldn't be asking." He continues to keep his focus on the sky as he enjoys his joint.

"Alexa Valez is wanted for questioning . . ."

"I said I don't know nothing." He pinches off the end of his joint and turns to head inside. "I've done whatever I need to . . . to take care of my family, detective."

"I understand . . ."

"No, you don't." He pulls open the door slightly. "Those people are not my family. I don't talk or do shit for them. They leave me be."

Anthony walks inside and leaves me in the cold alley wondering what the hell just happened. I grab my phone and dial Logan.

"Any news on double A?" He sounds tired and stressed to the limit.

"Dead end, so keep digging," I say before hanging up the phone. We need to find who the captain was meeting. For all I know it has nothing to do with this case. It could have been a personal trainer or a party planner for his anniversary—anyone. Sanity is screaming at me to find out.

The poor punching bag recoils crisply from my right fist. As it moves back toward me, I wallop it with my left. This is what I need right now to help me process everything. No more jumping before looking. Now it's beat the shit out of a bag and let my brain marinate on everything going on. Let the words, information, and conversations filter through my mind so I can sort out the fact from fiction. Like dealing with politics on television. Sometimes you have to watch a debate, then search for hours figuring out what was real. In the end, you realize all the candidates are lying sacks of shit and no one is truly good. So, you vote for the lesser of two evils. That's my brain right now. Figuring out which person is the least evil.

"Back at the bag again?" I hear Marlow's voice, and it breaks me from my silent process. I ignore her and continue beating the bag. I pour every last ounce of anger into each punch. Better that than the words from my mouth. "You ignoring me, Steele?" she adds.

"Nope," I say as I throw a right hook so hard it pops my knuckles loudly. Shaking my hand a bit, I remove my glove to make sure nothing's broken. Marlow walks around in front of me and places her hands on both side of the punching bag.

"I wouldn't do that if I was you," I say to her, my words filled with disdain. My eyes burn into hers as I put my hand back in my glove.

"You think I'm afraid you're going to hit me? We've been there before. You didn't do that much damage. At least nothing that makeup can't cover," she sarcastically throws at me.

I punch the bag, and she bounces back a bit. I continue the barrage, watching her struggle to keep up. I have to admit it feels good.

"I spoke to Logan," she says. I get a little cross-footed, and my punch is weak. "He attacked me for undermining his friend and the integrity of the department."

"That about sums it up," I say, walking away from her and over to the water fountain. Leaning forward, I take a sip and close my eyes. The cool liquid quenches my thirst, and also my need to feel something.

"You have a right to be angry."

I stand up, push past her, and march back over to the bag. I want to ignore her. I want her to go away. Apparently neither of those are going to be an option. I need her help as much as she needs mine.

"Start talking, and don't lie or leave anything out," I say as I punch the bag.

"I came across Valez's name during the investigation in Seattle. We had no idea how she was connected, but we knew she was someone Garrison kept close. Real close. She was in every photo, video, you name it. So, we did some digging and found out her history."

"Logan said it was pretty easy to find," I say and swipe a glove over my sweat-drenched forehead. "He did some digging on his own and found all he needed to know about her. And you acted like this was all new information." I continue to punch the bag harder, my anger coming to the surface again.

"You found what the Bureau wanted you to find. Just enough for you to be on her tail, but not enough to connect her to crimes."

"You knew about her son then?" I stop punching and turn to look at her.

Marlow rubs the back of her neck and walks over to the gray cinder block wall near the door. She leans against it and slides down to the floor. I can see all the fight roll right off of her and dissipate. In that moment, she looks more human than she has in a long time. The anger slowly moves out of my pores with the droplets of sweat. I walk over to the wall and sit on the floor next to her. Slowly, I remove my boxing gloves. It gives me time to plan what I'm going to say next.

"We never knew he was that violent. I never saw an image of him as an adult. There were baby pictures, but that was about it. Even with the age progression imaging software, there were too many unknown variables. He looks nothing like them. Jasmine, if we had . . . if I had known . . ."

"You weren't here when we had him in interrogation. You weren't around when we got the case. If you were, then I'd hold you responsible, but this isn't on you. This is solely on him. He chose to kill a police officer. He sealed his fate, and I pray to everything that's holy you aren't going to get him out of it."

"No. We sent a BOLO to every department in the tri-state area. If he's in the area, we will find him and hold him accountable."

"And his mother?"

Marlow exhales loudly next to me. I'm sure she's trying to form her words carefully and not upset me. But the thing is neither answer is going to work for me. I see the benefit of bringing her in as an informant. I also want her to rot in a prison cell for the rest of her life. Well, that's a lie. I want her dead. She's a murderer, plain and simple. There's no nice guy underneath we're going to uncover.

"My orders are to turn her if she wants that. Agent Sharp thought he would get a nice promotion if he brought her in before me," she says simply.

"So, what? He bugs your place on the off chance that you'll be there to talk to her?" I ask.

"No, he answered a message left for me at the hotel's front desk. She said she would be at my hotel room that night. He activated the bug when she showed up. He answered the door and from what I was told, she wasn't thrilled to see him," Marlow says as she runs her hand through her hair.

"Why would she be? I don't like the woman or respect her, but he set her up," I add.

"Exactly. She apparently made enough noise that neighbors complained and a member of our team was notified. The agents entered the room and ignored her. Hell, some of them say they never even saw her leaning against the wall. Once Sharp was busy dealing with his mess, she walked out the front door and into the world. She left the file for me."

"Sharp and your team suck." I laugh a little bit.

"That's why the entire team is on a flight back home and I'm still here."

"The FBI is quick to cover things up."

"Probably." She ponders this for a bit. "I don't know. I just go by what's in front of me. I have several agents who were ill-equipped to handle being out in the field and are being put behind a desk, pending a review. The missing piece for me is still the information on the bug."

"Logan said it didn't store any kind of sound. It was simply so he could hear it. Considering he was in the same room, that's a bit foolish."

"Sharp admitted to modifying the bug. It recorded everything to his cell phone. That's why they made sure to confiscate it the minute they knew I had it," she fills in.

"If Logan had more time, he would have uncovered everything she said, and if it was valuable, we could have used it to bring her down. He hasn't even had time to look over the documents we left him."

"My boss already confiscated them," Marlow says. "Before you question why Logan didn't mention it, I doubt he would have noticed. He was with you at the funeral when they went in. As far as the bug, I doubt it's that. I'm more concerned it was more names that the government didn't want released to our level of personnel."

"Those papers must have said something good for you to want them so bad."

"From what I've been told—and take it with a grain of salt—it's all the financials of specific individuals we already know are connected to this whole case. It also has information about Garrison and his dealings, payoffs, and more. It proves one major thing: he isn't the head of the dragon. Who that is, of course, is way above my pay grade."

"Are you talking shadow government conspiracy crap? That is not really up my alley. Let's just stick to what I know, which is Valez wanted to protect her son, Emilio. What happens if we find her? What are you planning to do? How far are you willing to go?" I ask bluntly. "I need to know if I'm watching my back from her or you or both."

Marlow looks at me with a shocked expression. I think my words hit home, and not in a good manner.

"You don't have to worry about me. Valez, she's a wild card. She might feel slighted and not want anything to do with us. Hell, she might want to roll over on everyone, but what she wants in return might be too high. I'm not the boss in charge of what is or isn't. I have a job to do. My first order of business is to help you capture Garrison and Valez. After that . . ."

"We have to let you take her," I say and shake my head.

"She'll never face a minute of punitive time," Marlow says. "Her son, if caught, is all yours."

"You think she'll go for that?" I laugh as I ask what I assume is a no-brainer type of question.

"Valez is dead if she goes to prison. The gangs she screwed over along with Garrison will kill her in a day. Two at most. Men aren't treated the same way. Emilio and Irving will put the fault squarely on her."

"She'll take it for her son, but not for him," I say with a bit of question in my voice.

"Trust me, she'll do it for both of them. She's not a bad woman underneath all of the . . ." Marlow spaces out a bit as if trying to find the proper words.

"Murder, deceit, blood, torture, thievery, and more? Whatever you say, Karina. She shot my fucking partner and called to taunt me about it. If she pulls a gun on me, I'm putting a bullet in her." I stand up and walk away, but she stops me at the door with her voice.

"I expect nothing less. Just remember we aren't sure who shot Will. Considering her son's actions of late, there's a bit of doubt," she says to my back.

"One of us is wrong. The evidence points to you. I pray you're right, cause otherwise we're gonna be walking into a world of hurt." I walk out of the gym without allowing her to reply.

I didn't say it exactly, but Marlow knows how I feel—that this is all a crock of shit. Valez deserves to be in prison along with the rest of her family. I don't care if she's dead in two days. Frankly, she brought that upon herself. You can't ask for immunity or safety or whatever. It's like the person who cries in court begging for forgiveness. Were they remorseful for what they actually did or just for getting caught? Most times it's the latter rather than the former. I wish it wasn't that way, but that's humanity for you.

Standing in my office, I stare at the dry erase board. The lines now connect all the players together. Everyone's on there, and part of me wants to put Agent Sharp along with the bungling idiots at the Bureau on there as well, but I'm at work. If Frankie were here, she'd have psychological profiles of everyone. I'd know what to expect. Right now, I'm going off my education that I haven't used for a few years. Literally, we're waiting on the lynch pin. Once we have that, everything falls into place. One by one they'll all fall. Then my girlfriend and my nephew can come home.

"You reek like bad socks, Steele," Captain Zeile says from behind me.

"Was working out in the gym, sir," I say, my attention remaining on the board in front of me.

"I smell that. You could have showered before coming upstairs and gracing my nose with your presence."

I walk behind my desk and sit down in my chair. I watch as he takes a seat across from me and crosses his legs. This conversation is going to take a bit. I can already tell by the way he's looking at me. He points to my New York Mets pennants that hang on the back wall behind my desk.

"Such a big wall for so few banners. I doubt I'd have the room," he smirks. I remember his baseball cap. He's a fucking New York Yankees fan. Great. That's all I need. A man who counts as having twenty-seven rings, most from a time when there were sixteen teams or less. Bring up the eighties and most Yankee fans feign ignorance. Don't get me started on the steroids or Roger Clemons throwing a bat at Mike Piazza. He better be a decent fan and not an arrogant asshole.

"Anything I can do for you, boss?" I say as I grab my joke zombie medical needle pen, clicking it over and over.

"Straight to the point, I like it. I was looking over the file you so graciously dropped on my desk. I also came to an agreement with the FBI. There are certain files that they can't decipher. It turns out Mr. Pevy is amazing with this technological aspect and is willing to assist them. Anything pertaining to the case in New York we will be able to have and use to our advantage. Anything else, Mr. Pevy will ensure gets to the FBI alone."

"Logan is excellent at his job, and I'm sure will make the FBI quite happy."

"Yes, well, we want Mr. Pevy to stay with us. Let's hope he doesn't make them too happy. Beyond that, have you run down through the case yet?"

"Agent Marlow and I have been through this several times. We know Garrison is connected to all these individuals on the board if not more. The problem is we have no definitive proof putting him or Alexa Valez in direct contact with him. The district attorney won't touch this with a ten-foot pole without something more concrete."

"We have a dead judge," he says. "We can easily put them away for that."

"He was a pedophile and in possession of massive amounts of child pornography. Not only that, but all of his cases would be considered suspect. Garrison's people ensured he was given a pass on his predilections for a verdict, dismissal, or silence. You pick one," I say, confident in our evidentiary discovery to this point.

"Well, according to your notes, Valez was in charge of her son, who is wanted in connection to several murders. Including one of our own. He should be our focus."

"He is, sir. Agent Marlow put out an APB throughout the tri-state area. If anyone sees him, we'll find him. Valez is the key to everything. My instincts tell me she's playing us, and the system, to her advantage," I add.

"Knowledge is power, and she has information we all want. Puts us all in a difficult situation. If the feds want her, they're going to take her no matter what we do. Technically, this case should never have even been in our hands. All of these crimes crossed state lines and yet here you are working it. Tyler Udall must have thought very highly of you to put his career in jeopardy for you and your team."

That stops me in my tracks. Captain Udall stuck his neck out for me with the FBI? That explains a little bit more about Marlow and her team being here, but why? To allow me to bring this all to a close? Why didn't he let me in on everything he was working on? None of this makes sense.

"Captain Udall was having Winslow Tucker, who we know now is Emilio Valez, followed, but the officers assigned to him say they lost him. Considering everything we know, I can guarantee you that something is off. I don't want to say the officers might be on the take . . ."

"But they might have noticed something that seemed out of place. You won't be able to talk to them, so let me handle that. I'll make sure to keep you out of it. Anything else I should be aware of?"

"My nephew Chase and Doctor Francesca Ryan are in hiding with associates of mine."

"The captain had that information in his file, but I appreciate the candidness. I can assume that your relationship with Doctor Ryan won't be a problem, correct?" He stands up and rubs his hands together.

"No, sir. It hasn't been and never will be."

"I'll let you know what the other officers say. Considering everything that happened, they might have just kept their mouths shut. I prefer to err on the side of innocence," Thomas says as he walks to my door. "One more thing, Steele. Just because you have a great baseball player on your team, don't enjoy them too much. They always seem to play better as a Yankee. So, when you're ready, we'll welcome you to our side of town."

Before I can say anything in response, my new captain walks out of my office. He might have meant for it to be a little ribbing between friends, but we aren't there yet. It's a little like reminding the teams who have never won anything about that fact. No one wants to hear that shit. He's just trying to get my mind to focus on something else. I don't have to like it, but I get it. My gaze falls from the doorway to the image of Frankie, Chase, and me on my desk. I miss her so much it hurts. Captain Tyler Udall once said that life was always meant to be lived, not merely survived. Maybe he's right and it's time for me to do something for myself. It's time to deal with the item in my sock drawer.

Chapter Eleven

Hospitals are the most sterile places on the planet. And more people die from infections within those walls than anywhere else. I hate these places. White walls, bright fluorescent lights, the metronome beeping from all the machines. A beep to remind you a person's still alive. The patients might be awake, but the beeps are still here. As I walk down this endless hallway, I see family member after family member sitting next to beds, and I know what they're going through. I wish all too well that I didn't.

I walk into Will's room, and it feels more colorful than the rest of the place. Balloons block most of the view out of the window. I wonder if they want to be as free as Will's spirit is right now. The horizontal ledge of a heat vent showcases an abundance of get-well cards. Some random stuffed animals fill up what little space is left.

Will lies peacefully after what I have heard is a long day of stretching from a very good-looking nurse. The tube might be gone, but he's not fully conscious yet. He is sometimes awake for an hour or two, but then he's out again for another twenty.

He's got a contraption on his finger and an intravenous needle connected to a bag. All normal things, and yet very disturbing to see. Sitting down in a chair next to his bed, I take hold of his hand.

"I know you can't hear me, but everyone says to talk anyway. So, I'm talking. This case—our case—is driving me crazy. Every time I think we're one step ahead, the FBI or some twist occurs and throws things sideways. Now Valez might not be the one who shot you, even though my gut tells me it was her. Then we have these cold cases all connected to the gun that shot Judge Killian. No one knows the location of the gun, and I get the feeling it's been lost in the shuffle. For all I know it's not worth investigating at all. Then the captain is murdered, and we find video, and it's that Tucker kid. . . who's really Emilio Valez and is Irving Garrison's son."

I lean back and find myself laughing a bit. Not too loud, thankfully.

"How crazy does this sound, partner? It's like a bad soap opera. I guess I wouldn't be surprised if Valez was secretly married to one of Garrison's cousins after divorcing Irving. If this was on television, we'd be in the running for some Emmy awards."

I laugh to myself a little louder this time. The beeping of his machines brings me back to the reality of the situation. Did they just start going at a faster rate? I'm not sure.

"He seems to respond to laughter more than just people talking to him," Mia says from behind me. "Or when the nurse comes in to stretch his limbs."

I look up and gesture with my hand to offer her my seat. She shakes her head and walks in, coffee in hand. She calmly sits down in the chair next to me. Her face is worn, her eyes drawn and puffy. I doubt she's slept soundly in a really long time. Between the kids, school, and being here, I don't know how she's still standing.

"What have the doctors said?"

"He's on the right path. His brain is healing, slower than we'd like, but healing. No matter what happens, we're looking at a long road. Physical therapy, police psychologists, and whatever else the job requires him to do."

"Maybe he'll retire?" I say. I don't mean it though. I can't imagine working every day without him around. Damn him for being such an integral part of my family. This is why people work alone.

"He'd never give it up." She sips her coffee. "When he was overseas, I used to think about all the danger he would get into. He still never talks to me about his nightmares. He needed a purpose, and being a detective gives him that."

"I'm sure he will when he's ready." I try to reassure her.

"No, he won't, and that's okay. He doesn't think I notice the change, how happy he's become . . . since meeting you. He talks to you. He opens up to you. He needs someone that he can trust like that in his life. I know I've been harsh on the phone, but he's alive because of you."

"He was shot because of me," I say, my voice wavering.

"No, honey, he was shot because some lunatic in this world wanted to hurt both of you. Will is alive inside because you help him find hope again. He loves our daughters, but he has a nephew to spoil. He loves teaching him lacrosse and playing with him. The two of them grilling in the backyard laughing at the girls in the pool, it brought him back. It gave me my husband back. This room, this situation, isn't your fault. I shouldn't have made you feel that way. I should be thanking you for being our family and not turning your back on him when he goes off."

I pull her into a tight hug, fighting the tears that threaten to fall. Indirectly, I have my family back as well. I have a big brother, a sister-in-law, and two nieces. Life has been muddy as hell, but maybe it's time to walk in the light.

"How are the kids doing?" I change the subject as I pull back from the hug.

"They're good. School is driving them crazy, as it should. We've got surprise quizzes, dances, dating, and of course gossip about who's doing what."

"Sounds like you're keeping their lives pretty normal."

"I'm trying, but they know he's missing at the dinner table. They know he's not around when they need boy advice. Will won't be there next week when this boy picks up our daughter for the school dance. She's struggling with that."

"Well, if she needs a replacement, I know a number of officers willing to fill in. I'm sure plenty of fierce-looking Marines would be willing to as well."

"That makes me feel very wealthy, but we both know it wouldn't be the same. He just needs more time to heal."

"I can be there if you want, scare the poor boy with my gun or something."

Mia breaks out into a deep belly laugh for the first time since her husband ended up here. "Will once promised me that you two would be dressed in your uniforms with guns at the ready. Something about heading to the shooting range and would this boy like to come."

Our laughter fills the room before an alarm goes off on my cell phone.

"Go, take care of business," Mia says.

I hug her goodbye, thankful for the distraction and hopeful conversation.

The trip to the hospital was good, but I have to sit down with Marlow and have a serious conversation about this case. Maybe Captain Udall's murder paused the case, but now it's time for a full-court press. I drop my keys on the table, grab a mug, and pour myself a cup of fresh coffee. One of my current roommates must have made it. The door opens, and Victor walks in wearing the same clothes as the night before. The two of us stare at each other awkwardly before he smiles and walks past me.

"Steele, is that you?" I hear Marlow from the living room.

"Grab some coffee and get your ass in here."

Walking into the living room, I almost drop my coffee cup. The whiteboard we have hanging around the house is covered with what I assume is Marlow's handwriting. Strings connect various pieces of furniture to the board. Marlow stands in the center of it all, her hair pulled back in a tight ponytail. It's a stark contrast to her normal perfect part with free-flowing hair. She bounces around the obstacle course barefoot, in jeans and a button-down shirt. Gone are her heels and power suits. What the hell happened while I was gone?

"I'm here. Mind telling me what you've been up to?" I say.

"Your new captain grilled me about where we are in our investigation," she says as she moves things around on the coffee table in the middle of the room. "It annoyed me actually."

"Welcome to the club. Doesn't explain what's going on here."

"I was annoyed," she says. "So, I went back to the drawing board to where we were before Udall's murder. I made some phone calls and dug a bit deeper into the cold case files."

Now she has my attention. I duck under some strings, barely balancing my coffee along my way to the center of the mess.

"Tell me what I'm looking at."

"Okay." She drops the remaining papers on the coffee table. "I went through the old files you copied. There were no connections between location, age, victims, or really anything. The only thing tying them all together was a gun."

"The same gun that was used to kill Judge Killian. All of this is in the reports. Without the gun, we can't connect anything. We need a ballistics comparison report," I say with a bit of confusion in my tone. I really don't know where she's going with this. Plus, I am emotionally drained. Not a good combination right now.

"Yes. And they were all digitized even though they were cold cases. That in itself is a miracle. The fact that they were also all transferred into our cold case locker, also suspicious."

"Not really," I say. "During various moves, our precinct had the largest temperature-controlled environment. I don't know how or why specific ones ended up there, but they did. Maybe the original precincts had a flood or some issue. Who knows how New York handles it—as long as they do."

"Captain Udall requested they be transferred." She hands me a requisition form with Udall's signature on them. I read over the page carefully. He requested they be transferred the minute we found the body of Judge Killian. Why was he being so secretive? It's simply not possible he had anything to do with these crimes. That wasn't his way, so there has to be a reason.

"I know what you're thinking," she says. "I don't know why he requested them, but I'm certain he had nothing to do with it. So, I called in some favors from the Bureau." She hands me another file. It's full of pages detailing Udall's life.

"You had them run a background check on him?" I ask.

"I didn't need to. We have them on all NYPD captains as per regulations. What I needed was to find the connection. It kept me up all night. There never was a case that crossed paths with the cases connected to the gun. That being said, he went to high school with Merthyl Williams. Mr. Williams is the father of Kesha Williams."

"Our murder victim from Nassau County," I say. Now I'm intrigued.

"Last seen with her girlfriend Vanessa Goertz outside a club in the city. Her father kept investigating and pulled an old high school buddy into the fold. Now, based on the captain's notes, he wasn't going to pull anyone into this side project until he had a solid lead." She pulls out some files which were buried under a stack of paper.

"How did you get those files? Logan said he was still working on them," I say.

"Quid pro quo. He wanted to chat with his girlfriend on a secure line, and I wanted the information. He's probably still working on the FBI files and the rest of the laptop now. He sent me these files as soon as he found them." She smiles as I scan through the images, documents, and handwritten notes. Logan was getting closer to the weapon but not the person or reason behind it.

"He found the gun?" I ask, almost in shock.

"Not exactly. He looked at every case that ever came through involving a 9mm handgun, and then he had them test it against the bullet casings from the Williams case."

"He found a match," I say.

"Yep. Beretta M9. The case involved a self-inflicted gunshot wound. A Desert Storm veteran shot himself. The ballistics tech said the gun striations matched the casings. Considering the number of soldiers returning from war during that time period, it was enough to limit our search pool to a few thousand people."

"Still too large a net."

"Not when you cross-reference them with Garrison's corporations, Valez, and the M9." She slams a photo onto the whiteboard of a soldier in uniform, the last name Mendes printed on his uniform. "Jorge Mendes, killed in action on Christmas Day in 1990. His family requested all of his things. His gun was deemed unserviceable and sent with his personal effects to the family."

"If it was unserviceable, how the hell was it used in these murders?"

"Ask his nephew, Emilio Valez aka Tucker Winslow." She hands me an image of a young-looking Emilio with his uncle in full uniform.

"That makes no sense. If he died in 1990 and Emilio's in this photo . . ."

"He's thirty-one years old. He happens to look much younger, so when his false identity was created, it was readily accepted. No reason to doubt it truthfully. On paper he was a good kid, worked hard at his part-time job and school."

"You're telling me we've been sitting on this information and couldn't connect the damn dots?" I ask.

"I appreciate your emotions, but there were tons of people who dropped the ball on this one," she says curtly. She's right. There are hundreds of cases that cross my desk every year that I never look at twice. Some I never even read fully. You canvas, read what you can, and do what you can before moving on. If nothing breaks within the first forty-eight hours, it's almost understood the case is gonna be boxed up and put downstairs. Without the manpower, money, or time, some things will never change.

"Logan did a thorough search of Emilio Valez. Why didn't this come up?"

"That's where my people screwed up," Marlow says "The information we entered for Valez in our search was very specific. The birthday month was transposed to a zero-one instead of ten. Since we were being rather precise in our parameters, it spit back what we asked for. When we expanded our search to only our soldier and his connections, we did a lot of background checking and found what we needed."

I feel a sarcastic and not so nice comment on the tip of my tongue. My phone buzzes in my pocket, pulling that thought away. Logan has sent me a simple text message: "Get Here." Straightforward and to the point. I show my phone to Marlow and she nods and runs off.

This case finally seems to be coming together. I love it, but I'm a bit overwhelmed by it. I want this case to stick. I want it all to be black-and-white. I don't want anyone walking. Let these bastards who want to try and trim a few years off their sentences with information not wind up becoming informants. This whole thing reeks of lies, greed, power, and innocent blood. Another day in the life of politicians and the top one percent.

Marlow and I make record time getting back to the precinct. The place is busy as hell, and we immediately know something's up. Captain Zeile stands in the corner with a group of Feds. It must be some kind of heated conversation. The new captain's neck is red, and the FBI agent has a vein popping out in the center of his forehead. If we weren't in a hurry, I'd like to watch. See how the new captain handles himself in a pressure cooker situation.

Marlow pulls me by my left elbow into the elevator. We are headed down into the depths, unsure of what awaits us there.

The doors slide open, revealing more men in black along with a half dozen plainclothes officers. They start to push their way into the elevator car, barely giving Marlow and me enough room to exit. The two of us stare at the door. I can't be sure what she's thinking, but I feel like I was just on a rush-hour subway at Times Square. Not something I enjoy, nor is it something everyone needs to experience.

"What the hell is going on here?" Marlow asks. Her tone ensures no response from me is necessary.

Turning our attention to Logan's domain, every desk is being used and the main front screen has a large list of names on it. Every tech is chatting on their headset, and the cacophony of sound rushes to my ears. The noise is so deafening that I can't focus on any specific voice or word.

Shaking my head, I walk faster into Logan's office and shut the door after Marlow.

"I understand, sir." Logan holds up one finger, indicating we need to wait. "My team will keep track of it in real time."

He slams the phone down on the desk and rubs his temples. He looks awful, like he hasn't slept in a week.

"What the hell is going on?" I ask with a little more venom in my voice than I intend.

"All hell is breaking loose," he answers as he cracks his neck to the right, then the left.

"I can see that. Would you mind explaining it, please?" Marlow says, and I hear her "mother voice" come out in full force.

Logan walks over to the side of his office and pulls up the shades, revealing the main floor. He points to the main screen. A name blinks wildly before it is crossed out and dimmed in color.

"I decoded the entire FBI sheet from the New York area. What you see there is a list of every known associate, employee, and parolee involved in the entire scheme. The powers that be decided that we weren't going to vet the list before arresting everyone and anyone on that damn thing. So, since five this morning, my team has been tracking, monitoring, and assisting in arresting over one hundred people," he says. His voice is filled with exhaustion and frustration.

"How close to the top?" Marlow asks.

Logan walks back around his desk and falls into his chair. He snaps open his laptop a little harder than necessary. He spins the laptop around, showing us a diagram of various boxes too small to read. Marlow leans forward, blocking my view, and reads. I see her squint her eyes as she focuses on the screen.

"Can you make anything out?" I ask.

"Yeah. Lots of names I don't recognize, several I do, and a lot of empty boxes at the top," she replies.

"That's the long and short of it. We've managed to get all of those people on the chart, and we've organized them by how we assume they connect," Logan says as he leans back in his chair. "For all we know that chart is flawed and one of the lower guys is actually the head of the whole damn thing."

"You don't believe that," I say.

"No. I know the majority of those people are simply hired help," Logan starts. "They're the fall guys. Like the TSA agents at the airports, or the guys at the container facility in security. . . they're the everyday people who kept the operation running at the ground level. Then, you have a lot of names of former politicians from the five boroughs, Long Island. The list up there on the main screen—that's just here in the city. The Feds are handling the other lists, and from what I gather, many of the names appear here, there, and everywhere."

"Do you think Irving Garrison is the head or not?" I ask.

"He's not. Based on his past dealings, financials, and everything else we could dig up. Garrison's a high-level player, but he's not the top dog. The money trail is a dead end in other countries. I can't tell you where or when it started, but he was brought in around 1989 or 1990. And that's when his market shares dropped in his own company. Three months later, after being so close to bankruptcy, he suddenly has the capital to get involved with real estate, government fundraisers, and more," Logan adds quickly.

"The question is: Did he spend his early years doing research on all of these people or did he get pulled into something to get his ass out of trouble?" Marlow asks both of us.

"Frankie created a psych profile for him back when we were going after his son, Keith," I say. "He's a power-hungry man. He's used to getting his way and doesn't appreciate anyone rocking the boat. If he was brought into the fold, it had to be on his terms and with his ability to profit from it. Irving Garrison isn't one to put anyone or anything ahead of his own greed. He's lost his son to the police, his girlfriend is cleaning up his mess and might turn on him, and his other son is a cop killer on top of that. This has got to be screwing him up mentally."

"Add in your vendetta, and he's got his hands full," Marlow adds and stares at me. I know how she meant it, but this is neither the time nor place. I'm about to answer her harshly when an alarm sounds on Logan's computer.

"What the hell is that?" I ask as Logan frantically slaps at the keys again. His eyes dart around the screen as a smile slowly forms on his face. He writes something down on a piece of paper and hands it to me. It's an address in Connecticut. My eyes must convey my confusion, because Logan once again wags his finger in front of my face.

"I had software running in the background, checking all the cameras in the tri-state area. I also did some checking into the security at all the local airports. And then I sent a bulletin to all hotels surrounding the airports, just in case. If anyone saw him nearby, they would just have to click a link and type in their location."

"So, what is it?" I ask, impatiently.

"It's the hotel where Emilio Valez is."

"Do they know he's wanted in connection to a few murders?" Marlow asks.

"No, I just said he was an EDP who was missing from a local hospital. They were told not to contact or speak to the individual." Logan leans back and smiles. "Now, get on the road before I call this in. Local police will be there before you obviously, but hopefully Agent Karina Marlow can flash her FBI badge and take control of the situation." He looks at Marlow and snaps his fingers. His phone rings, and he waves us off and answers the call. As we start to leave, I hear the beginnings of the conversation from Logan to whoever is on the other end. Marlow and I move out in silence. The heaviness of the information we've just been given weighs on both of us. The case is coming to a head quickly. I'm praying it ends well. Too many people have died already.

The drive is tedious. Marlow and I sit in silence as we try to get out of the city and into Connecticut. Turning left onto Route 5, we see local police stationed all along the street. A small barricade stops us from entering the Airport Inn parking lot. We turn into the parking lot of a building next to it. On the other side of the street, we can see cars in the distance. Considering how recently they got the word, I'm impressed by the speed at which they got the roadblocks up. An officer taps on Marlow's window. She holds her identification badge against the window, ignoring whatever the officer is mumbling to her. He nods, points, and waves us in.

Looking in the side mirror, I see teams of blue moving the barricades further back. I'm sure they want to keep more people from getting into this lot. One look and it's easy to see this building gives them a perfect place to set up without being seen. The L shape of the structure allows them to hide their cars and the command center. Marlow slows the car down to park in a spot next to the building. We exit the vehicle, and Marlow goes into power mode instantly. She walks right up to the nearest officer and shows her badge once again.

"I need to speak to the officer in charge."

"Captain Hart, he's inside the command center." He points to a large trailer parked alongside the back wall.

Marlow and I walk over to the black box and knock on the door. It swiftly opens and a man in a white shirt stares at the two of us. His round physique, square-frame glasses, and the sweat on his brow tell us he's not used to this kind of situation.

"Captain Hart, I'm Agent Karina Marlow from the FBI and this is Detective Jasmine Steele of the NYPD."

"I was told to expect you," he says and immediately looks calmer. "Come on in."

The inside of the trailer looks like a smaller version of a command center for a terrorist attack unit. One side of the trailer is a wall of monitors, manned by three techs wearing headsets, ready to pass along information. Their eyes diligently watch various images, some infrared, to get a better idea of the civilian situation.

"Where do we stand?" Marlow asks.

"What we know right now is that Valez checked into a hotel room at one thirty this afternoon. We've been told it's a room at the back of the hotel, so he shouldn't be able to see the road or our cars."

"Or us if we have to come from the front side," I say to Marlow. I can see the gears working in her head as to how to approach this.

"Anything else?" she asks.

"We've blocked off traffic as far as we can. The surrounding buildings have been evacuated, along with as many as we could get to in the hotel with our plainclothes officers. Other than that, we were told to wait for you and Detective Steele." He places his thumbs in his belt and shrugs.

"Can we bring up a satellite map of the area?"

"Sure." Captain Hart leans on the shoulder of the tech in front of him. The man nods and begins typing away. In a matter of seconds, we have an overhead view of the hotel courtesy of Google Maps.

"As you can see, there's four buildings. The one in the lowest right corner of the land is toward that grove of trees. We tapped on the windows of all inhabitants and told them to vacate. We asked them to leave their cars so that it didn't look like a mass exodus."

"Good idea," I say as the captain points to the next building.

"The building closest to it—this L-shaped one," Hart says, "is under renovation, so it was already empty. The building directly off the road in front of that L-shaped one is the main office. They're keeping us posted if Valez comes in or calls for anything from room service. The final building at the top shaped like an S is where he's staying. He asked for a room in the back closest to the tree line. We're assuming that's in case he has to run; he'd want cover."

The captain points to the line of trees outside of the building. My eyes move to the right of his hand and notice an open green space similar to a golf course and then another set of trees; beyond that there's a highway and a densely forested area. If he manages to get away from us, we could lose him in the woods or in the house of an innocent homeowner.

"We can't let him get out of the hotel. If he gets through us and into those trees . . ." I start.

"He could end up anywhere," Hart says. "This is a small town. The people here are calm and trusting. We don't lock our doors at night, and Valez could hurt any one of them on the way out of town."

"Is there a way to alert the local people without tipping off our perp?" I ask.

"We have the emergency alert system, but we don't have a way to remove specific buildings from the broadcast. We would have to cut the connection to the hotel and hope he doesn't notice his television going dead," the captain says.

"It's a risk I'm willing to take. We can't have any innocents getting hurt. Call the front office and see if they can turn off the feed for the television and let the emergency network do their thing," Marlow says as I stare at the map. I notice a small building north of the hotel with no description.

"What's that building there?" I point to the map and the tech zooms in. Childcare Center pops up on the screen and my heart sinks. We have children in the area. "We need to evacuate that place now."

Hart talks to an officer behind him. The man flies out the door before I can read his name off his uniform. I assume they'll call the team on the other side of the roadblock. They wouldn't want to risk being seen.

"So how do we handle this?" I ask Marlow.

"We have the element of surprise for now, but that won't last long. It might not even be to our advantage. The question is, do we care how we bring him in?" she asks.

"You mean dead or alive?" I ask, and she locks eyes with me. "I want him alive. He needs to face a judge, but more importantly, he might have information for us."

"Then we hit him head on. We call his room and we try to get him to talk. We place officers at the tree line to cut him off, and if forced to, we shoot to slow him down. If he can't be subdued and poses a direct threat. . ." Marlow pauses and looks at the monitors in front of her. "Shoot to kill."

Captain Hart grabs a phone off the wall of the command center. He punches in the hotel's number.

"This is Captain Hart, connect me to Mr. Valez's room," he says before holding the phone out to Marlow.

"You have a history with him, you talk." She grabs the receiver and tilts it with the receiver facing the ceiling. I lean in, getting as close as possible to hear the other side of the conversation. We don't have the ability to put it on speaker phone, so this is going to have to do.

"Hello," the boyish voice radiates through the phone.

"Mr. Winslow? This is Detective Steele." Thoughts flood my mind as to what he's going to ask me. How did I find him? What do I want? There are so many things that can trigger him to run, guns blazing, toward the trees. He's already killed an officer, possibly more if he was behind the game store bombing. The acid in my stomach starts to bubble up my throat.

"Yes, detective, how can I help you?" The innocent voice causes the hair on the back of my neck to stand up.

"We've been investigating your work associate's murder for some time now, and I know that Captain Udall said he would keep you safe. He passed away recently, and I felt it was my responsibility to take over that job." I roll my eyes at no one in particular. What the hell am I saying? He knows this is bullshit, I can hear it in his tone. He's playing it safe and waiting for me to make the first mistake.

"I see." His voice drops a bit, and I hear some muffled noise in the background. I grab Marlow's hand and shake her a bit. She leans back and looks at me. I mouth "running" and she immediately understands what I said.

"Tucker?" I ask.

No response.

One of the techs raises his hand in the air to get our attention. His screen very clearly shows Emilio walking outside of his hotel room. I drop the phone and run out of the trailer with Marlow right behind me. Unholstering my gun, we round the side of the building.

"We're sitting ducks if we come straight at him. If he turns the corner, he has a clear shot, and a vest isn't going to stop a headshot," I say to Marlow, and she weighs our options. We're stuck here until the other officers do the job. Not ideal, but it's our reality.

"Suspect is leaving the hotel room." One of the officer's walkie-talkies springs to life. "Heading down the stairs on the north side of the building. Waiting to engage."

I tap Marlow on the shoulder. I motion to run around the building and head for the action. If he's on the north side, he won't have a shot. The two of us set up with our guns raised and hurry across the lot to the first building.

"Get down!" I hear an officer shout from the side of the building. Marlow and I continue to move forward. "Police, get down!" the same voice screams again. It's obvious Emilio isn't about to listen.

Marlow and I turn the corner and face the building with Valez's hotel room. One shot echoes across the area. Marlow and I run full speed to find safety against the building. Another shot rings out, and I hear glass shattering. Looking around the corner of the brick building, I see Valez leaning against a car. Officers block the parking lot and the tree line. His only path is to go back up the stairs and possibly commit suicide.

I walk away from Marlow and up the back stairs. If he rushes up the stairs, I'll meet him. I hear Marlow calling after me in a hushed tone. I quietly move up the stairs and lean against the door. I curse myself for not having anything to check around the corner. I slowly lean out from my safe haven just in time to see Emilio's back to me as he shoots wildly. I raise my gun to shoot and aim at his knee before thinking better of it. If I shoot him, he goes to the hospital, and if Marlow wants to bring him in, he can't be harmed.

I take a deep breath and silently start running toward him. He turns around as I'm rushing at him full speed. His arm moves upwards, gun in his hand. This was a stupid idea, but I'm all in now. I slam into him full force, knocking his body hard to the ground and dislodging the gun from his hands. It slides along the walkway as I feel a knee come up into my side. The pain shoots through me hard and fast, and a gasp of air exits my lungs. My forearm presses firmly on his throat, trying to force him to stop. Another jab into my rib cage and I'm sure I'm going to breathe shallowly for a few hours. His fists hit anything they can come in contact with. The kid is bigger than me. Nothing I can do but hold on and keep him struggling to breathe.

I hear footsteps on the stairs, and the sound of the military grade boots at full speed. It's not long before I hear various clicks of metal and screaming orders. I feel metal in my hand as someone hands me a set of handcuffs. An officer comes to the side of me, and once I slide off to the right, he forces Valez face down on the walkway. Pressing my knee hard into his back to keep him in one place, I cuff his left hand hard.

"Emilio Valez, you are under arrest for the murder of Captain Tyler Udall. You have the right to remain silent. Anything you say can and will be used against you in a court of law. You have the right to an attorney. If you cannot afford an attorney, one will be provided for you. Do you understand these rights as I have said them to you?"

"Yes."

"You want to tell me what the hell happened?" I ask.

"With what?" he asks.

"Everything." I pull him up and look into his eyes. They dart around, taking in the scene but slow down to rest solely on me. The realization of what I'm asking is sinking in. He smiles slowly and confidently.

"I'd like a lawyer." That ends any chance of him speaking. Damn law says that anything he tells me from now on is inadmissible in court. I know if I ask him anything now, he would be truthful. I also know everyone here would deny he asked for a lawyer. He shot at us and is now smiling; we'd all lie to get justice. Tyler Udall wouldn't do it that way. And neither will I.

I push him against the wall hard. My hands fly around his body, frisking him for any other weapons than the gun Marlow is currently bagging up as evidence. I feel a hard object in his chest pocket.

"Officer, a bag please." The officer hands me a small plastic bag. I turn it inside out and reach into the pocket carefully. I pull out a knife, dried blood on the handle. Carefully, I turn the bag right side out to prevent contamination from my skin. I wonder if it's the captain's blood. Emilio stares at me as I do this, his eyes vacant, almost sad. I'm not sure if he's sad he got caught or for what he did. I complete my frisk and find nothing else. I push him toward the stairs, back to the cruiser and New York City. Marlow thanks the local police as she follows behind me. I don't know if he's going to talk, but it is going to be a long ride back to the city.

Chapter Twelve

After a long, silent trip back to the city, Marlow and I would rather call it a day, but the new captain is up our ass. We pull into a reserved parking spot and lean back in the car's seats. I'm so tired. Between the letdown from the adrenaline rush and our inability to get Emilio Valez to talk, I don't have the want or energy to deal with anything else today. Marlow turns the engine off and looks over at me. Her skin is pale, almost gray, and her hair is all over the place. We look like a haggard set of crazed fools.

We drag ourselves into the conference room. Logan, Victor, Lillian Brown, and Captain Zeile are already there waiting. I have no idea why the entire team needs to be here. We'll give Brown the gun, but there's no new dead body to autopsy. I don't get this whole "huddle the whole team together" thing at work. I prefer my living room without a captain overseeing how we decipher things. He also wouldn't get to see how often we throw shit out our asses to try to make sense of randomness. Plus, there's alcohol and pizza with bacon and we don't like to share.

"Detective Steele, Agent Marlow, thank you for making such good time. I know you two must be exhausted."

We silently plop into chairs at the large mahogany conference table. Logan jumps to his feet and rushes behind us. Before I can register what has happened or ask why, there are two cups of steaming coffee on the table in front of each of us. Logan smiles at me before sitting back down. He knows this case is heading to its climax, and Frankie will soon be home. Then, it's withdrawal and herbal tea for me.

"Now that we're all here, get me up to speed," Zeile says, mostly to me and Marlow.

"We recovered this M9 at the hotel when we arrested Emilio Valez." Marlow places the gun, still in its collection bag, on the table. "Doctor Brown should be able to run a ballistics test to verify if it's a match to the previous cases."

I set the knife in the plastic bag on the table next to the gun. "I found this in his pocket. It was bagged and tagged like the gun, so there shouldn't be any contaminants," I say.

"Shouldn't be?" Brown asks.

"We did everything by the book, doctor. We're just both very tired," Marlow answers for me.

"Valez go to central booking?"

"Yes, sir, we brought him straight to Rikers Island. He was processed and is being held there until arraignment," I say.

"Did you get anything out of him on the way back?"

"Not a peep. At the motel he asked for a lawyer in front of several witnesses. He should have a public defender later today. We can interrogate him then," Marlow says.

"Doctor Brown, would you please take the two items and start your analysis? And make sure they are entered correctly into the database. You can box them up as well."

"I'll let you know what I find." Brown stands, grabs the two sealed evidence bags, and heads out the door on a mission. It seems like everyone is on edge with this new leader of ours.

"Victor, anything else to add?"

Victor looks around the room, confusion on his face. He's already submitted his reports on all the victims. I'm sure Zeile has read it more than once. His question to Victor makes me uneasy, but I can't say why exactly.

"Not really, no. Autopsies are done, evidence cataloged, reports written and filed."

"Very well. Thank you for your time."

Victor stands and walks to the door.

"On your way down, please let Doctor Brown know that I'm having Valez's clothing brought over from Rikers. I want a full workup on everything. I know she's got a great staff, but if you're not busy, feel free to step in and assist her. This case is all hands on deck," Zeile says as he spins his chair to face the door.

"Yes, sir," Victor says with a smile as he exits the conference room. It's just the three of us and the boss now.

"I've noticed a spike in online chatter about Garrison's money," Logan says. "I keep trying to trace where these payments originated from, but the feeds bounce all over the place before they randomly end somewhere. One ended in the middle of the Bermuda Triangle in the water. We know he's funneled money as well as his earnings from his business. We know he's the money man who pays the employees."

"For all we know there are multiple Garrison-level people all over the world. If we are thinking full-out conspiracy, this could be a global thing with a group of people running the show," Marlow mumbles as she sips her coffee.

"She has a point," I add before Zeile can speak. "I hate Garrison as much as the next guy, but we know he is a small cog in a bigger machine. How big, who it involves, and what its main purpose is . . . unknown.

Personally, I don't care. We have to focus on the main people we are able to arrest and prosecute. Let Marlow and her team handle the rest. Right now, we need to get Alexa Valez and Garrison."

"How do you plan on doing that?" Zeile asks.

"Irving Garrison has been underground for months," Logan says. "No one's seen him. There's no activity on any of his accounts or credit cards. All his cars and real estate holdings are being watched. Nothing's doing. It's like he vanished into cyberspace somewhere. I've gone online, sent out BOLOs, searched hours of video footage, and he's not on it. No airports or bus terminals. I don't know how the hell he managed to run."

"I know it hasn't been very long, but he has to be somewhere," Zeile says "A man that high profile doesn't simply disappear. He has to have help. One way or another, his face will pop up again, and when it does . . . we'll be waiting. In the meantime, Logan, keep digging into everything you can. The rest of your team is gonna be busy vetting all of the arrests, so you're on your own for now. Just keep working."

Logan nods his head, stands up, and walks out.

"We've got Alexa's son," Marlow starts. "And while it's a long shot—the longest of shots, really—she might be willing to come in when the news runs the story. If she calls, we might be able to get her to flip on Garrison in exchange for immunity and a new identity. All lines of communication are remaining open, but it really is in her court." Marlow tries unsuccessfully to hide a yawn. Captain Zeile opens a file and slides each of us a piece of paper. There is a name on the piece of paper, but no image and no more detail.

"Aneesa Arias? Who's this?" I ask.

"She's one of the women recently apprehended in the raids. She was released a few hours later; Feds are quiet on why. She was previously convicted of fraud and served thirty months in federal prison. She worked closely with Valez as she was—get this—her aunt. We tried to get more information, but she was less than helpful."

"Considering the situation, I'm not surprised at her lack of help. How is it we're just finding out about their relationship now?" I ask.

"She's married, has two kids, and never went by to her maiden name. She also happens to have been born here and not in Puerto Rico. Even her crime wasn't connected back to the Garrison family until we dug into his financials. Without the decoded list, the connection might never have been found," Zeile states dryly.

I look over her name. "Aneesa Arias," I say, more to myself than anyone else.

"Do you know her?" Zeile asks me.

"No, but the cap—" I stop myself. "Captain Udall had an appointment scheduled with the initials AA and BD. If this is who he was meeting, her reluctance to help makes sense."

"So, we go talk to the aunt." Marlow rubs her eyes and blinks several times.

"I suggest the two of you grab a few hours shuteye downstairs before heading to Rikers. Emilio Valez has to know something. I'll let the district attorney know we're talking to him. Keep the lines of communication open. Have to give them the feeling of transparency," he says.

"He's going to want a deal," I say.

"Well then," Zeile says as he stands and straightens his tie, "tell him you'll see what you can do. He'll have a lawyer with him. It's his job to decipher your promises. After you're done there, go grab lunch at Alexa Valez's aunt's diner. See if she's willing to chat with the two of you."

He leaves Marlow and me sitting at the table, both of us half out of it. She looks down at her coffee and yawns loudly, and I can't help but laugh out loud at her. It's been that kind of thirty-six hours. We've been running nonstop since yesterday morning. Time to crash in the smelly pit of metal bunk beds for a few hours. Then shower and put on the same clothes from the night before.

Three hours in a room that reminds me of college. Three hours with my eyes closed begging for some rest. Three hours feeling life seeping into my dream world. At what point do dreams spill over into the conscious plane? When do the nightmares of sleep begin to seep into the ether around you? It's times like these when I need to rest that my mind is a torrent of activity. To shut it down is paramount to putting a bullet in my head. Three hours of silence . . . it is pure torture.

"We're here," Marlow says from the driver's seat. Our trip through the city passed me by like a blur, in a blink of an eye. Looking around, I see the buildings directly in front of us. Marlow crossed the bridge into Rikers Island without having to take the bus. How did that happen?

"No bus?"

"FBI doesn't have to play park 'n ride. I know that's how it's done for everyone else around here, but we've got priority right now." She exits the vehicle and I slowly follow.

"Frankie interviewed here once," I say as I take in the surroundings.

"And?" Marlow asks, truly interested as we walk through cars on our way to the holding cells.

"There was a riot the day she interviewed, so one of the other medical personnel had to pick her up by the shuttle buses. She said security was really tight, and the only thing keeping you from the inmates was a thick door with metal on the glass. She wasn't too fond of the layout, walking a mile to the cells, which was scary since there had been a riot that very morning. The staff irritated her too. She said something about everyone being guilty regardless of their mental capacity. She never was one for quick judgments. Hell, she still yells at me for jumping to conclusions, so you can imagine how she feels about grouping people together instead of case by case."

I smile, thinking about our conversations gone by. I really miss my family.

"I can't wait to meet this girl of yours. If she's anything like you say, we'll get along just fine," Marlow says. She pulls open the door of a large brick building, and I walk inside and am struck by the contrast, by the lack of light. The fluorescents flicker from old fixtures attached to the ceiling. There are metal bars on everything. Cold, bleak, and dreary smacks you in the face just inches within the first door.

An officer taps on a window at the end of the small entryway. We both walk over, and she points to a sign above the barrier. It reads "Present ID for Entry." A metal drawer pops out from the wall and the two of us place our badges inside. The woman closes it hard and grabs both items quickly. Her eyes dart from the identification up to our faces. I'm sure they get several hundred people through these doors on a daily basis, but Fort Knox it isn't. Sadly, that is the nature of the beast. Every time you try to make something more secure, you open up more vulnerabilities. Just looking around the room, I can easily see a few.

The drawer flies open with our badges inside. We take them back, and a loud buzzing sound greets our ears. A door to our right clicks open. The two of us walk through it, and there stands two more officers and a metal detector. Removing all metal, we walk through the machines with ease. One final window at the end; we sign in and leave our weapons locked up. Can't have an inmate taking control of the situation and being armed.

Finally, after walking through a maze of tunnels, doors, and metal bars, we end up in an interview room. The heavy door locks as it closes. One metal table, bolted to the floor. Minimal light. Dark, chipped paint all over the cinder block walls. I grab one metal chair and find it moves with ease. Thankfully, it isn't bolted down. There are two odd metal hoops on the table, I assume to attach handcuffs to.

One wall has the two-way mirror within it. I'm sure there will be a few officers in there making sure we don't say or do anything detrimental to their jobs. Can't blame them. They're outnumbered and work hard to keep some kind of peace.

The door opens and a young woman walks in. Her outfit is clean and newly pressed, her shoes shined, and she carries a very expensive-looking briefcase. She sets it on the desk and looks up at Marlow and me. She smirks as she pulls the chair out and sits down. A few seconds later, the door opens again, and Emilio Valez enters. With each step, he drags the ankle chains along the floor. A longer chain connects a set of chains around his wrists. His hands look red and irritated. The officers push him in a chair and attach his chains to the hooks on the table. Marlow and I sit in chairs across from them.

"My client is here as a courtesy," the woman says.

"Courtesy or not, he's not going anywhere for a long time," Marlow replies and smiles coldly back at her.

"If that's the case, then he'll be going back to his cell," his lawyer says.

"My gut said you were innocent from the very beginning," I say. "How did I get it so wrong? Was it how shocked you seemed? How you manipulated everyone? I can't put my finger on it."

"It was easy," Emilio starts. His lawyer places her hand on his forearm and whispers something to him.

"We'll talk, but we want a deal," she says.

"He murdered at least one cop," I say. "A well-respected captain in the NYPD. You'll be lucky if he gets a chance at parole." I'm not going to sugarcoat it or try to lie and not get caught. Based on everything we know about this kid, which isn't much, he knows killing a cop was a deal breaker. I'm sure he could plead down the murders of his friends at work, or even the drug deals, but not the other murders.

"Who needs parole?" He speaks up. His lawyer leans over again, but he stares right at me instead. "She can't do anything to me now, can she?" he replies to his counsel while staring at me.

"What do you want, Emilio?" Marlow asks.

"Tell me, detective, does your nephew still play shooter games? Does he beat you? How's his aim? I'm sure in the game it's pretty good, but if it meant his life . . ." Emilio smiles at me, and I feel a shift in the room.

"It wouldn't get that far," I reply.

"Oh yes, because his auntie would shoot me down in cold blood. Wouldn't you?" His eyes are dead, almost vacant and unrelenting. There's a chill starting at the base of my skull slowly radiating down my spine. This is not the game I was expecting or wanting to play.

"Without a second thought," I say, trying to stop the stutter that wants to come out.

"Why don't we let these two women leave us alone. I'm sure we can have a much nicer conversation without them," he says and leans back as far as the chains will allow him.

"I have to advise against that," the woman speaks up again.

"I agree with her," Marlow interjects quickly.

"It's fine. You two can stay on the other side of the glass with the rest of them," I say as Marlow looks at me in disbelief. I'll be stuck in a room with a man chained to a table. He might be attached to the metal, but the nightmares he can create go far beyond this room. As the two women leave, a creeping fear slowly begins to take hold. I've been in hundreds of interview rooms, and this is something I've never felt before. God, I wish Frankie was here right now. The door slams shut, and I bounce a bit in my chair from the suddenness of the sound.

"Detective Jasmine Steele. Can I call you Jasmine?"

"No," I say. "And I'll be the one asking the ques—"

"Oh, come on now, Jasmine. That isn't the way to get what you came here for." His smile unnerves me.

"Where is your mother?" I ask simply.

"Wherever she is," he replies coldly.

"Let's talk about the video store."

"Let's." He leans back, a smirk never leaving his face.

"Did you kill the employees you worked with?" I ask, trying to change the subject.

"Of course I did. Did you enjoy the fireworks? Heard you had a bit of hearing trouble after," he replies again.

"An officer died in your fireworks," I add.

"Collateral damage in our line of work is always a possibility." His smooth voice causes the hairs on my arms to stand up.

"Why did you torture the victims?" I follow up quickly.

"They refused to do as they were told. They ignored my calls. There was a pickup, and they weren't doing their job. I found them fucking on the back room desk. If that was more important than my work, then they deserved to be punished."

"But why not just kill them? Why torture them?" I ask again.

"Jasmine, sometimes it's not 'why' the kill, but the 'how' of death. I wanted to see how far the body could go. How would the blood spray? The body and all its inner workings is rather fascinating. It was also a message to the others. Needed to get some folk's attention. No more deviating from the path," he says, his tone never shifting.

"Others?"

"There are always others around the state, country, you name it. You didn't think this one little store was the beginning and end all, did you? Come on now, Jasmine, you're smarter than that."

He snickers.

"Where is your mother?" I try again.

"He didn't scream you know. Your captain? I half expected him to. I guess I cut his throat a little too deep. He just gurgled. It was sad, really. Such a strong and powerful opponent knocked down to such a small, childlike sound. I expected more." His monotonous tone unnerves me. I want to reach across the table, grab his shirt, and slam his head into the table. I want him to feel the pain he has caused so many people.

"Why did you kill him?" My voice wavers a bit, and Emilio picks up on it and smiles at me. He senses weakness.

"Why does a bear kill salmon when they head upstream? It's how they stay alive. He was catching up to me, and I figured what's the worst that could happen? It doesn't matter now anyway."

"You're openly admitting to killing them all?" I say, looking for him to accept the murders.

"How many is all, Jasmine? You begin to lose count after a while. Some you remember like a beautiful sunny day, but most fade into the nothingness of desire as their life pours out of their skin."

He leans forward and gets as close as possible to me. "I would have loved to watch your girlfriend bleed beneath me. Maybe let your nephew play his games while she begged for release. You couldn't draw your gun fast enough, Jasmine. That's what you don't understand. You might try and catch everyone in every case that comes across your desk, but someone like me will always be out there waiting," he says calmly.

I look him over once more. His eyes burn into mine, and his body appears relaxed and loose. This is the true Emilio Valez. He's a psychopath. He manipulated everyone, and we fell for it. I push my chair back.

"No, wait, Jasmine. Leaving so soon? C'mon, stay and chat." His monotonous voice taunts me.

I stand, ignoring his pleas to talk more. I bang on the door, and within seconds it opens. I walk out the door quickly, without a second thought. I hear Emilio screaming after me. His voice echoes around me, but the words never reach my mind. It no longer matters what he says. He has no desire to help us catch his mother. We're a means to distraction, and I don't want to play anymore.

Marlow pops out into the hallway and looks at my face. Her mouth moves, but I just close my eyes. I need to manage the emotions swirling within me before I can speak. The only way to erase the image of Frankie bleeding out is to close this case.

"Brooklyn," I say as I head down the hallway. Marlow nods and walks beside me. I don't know if she's ever faced someone like Emilio. I've been played, and it feels like shit. My gut let me down. It won't happen again.

The sounds of a local diner—something my mother and I used to enjoy. The two of us, would sit over eggs and bacon discussing what was new with us. It was something I always looked forward to and miss so much. Watching the waitresses flying around the room, ensuring coffee cups are filled and plates are removed quickly to stay on top of everything. It's organized chaos. Sitting at the counter, a cup of warm coffee in my hand, I try and absorb the environment. I let the warmth of my memories bring me some strength before facing the rest of my day. I hear Marlow talking to the waitress. She's probably asking for Arias.

"Sure, honey, wait one minute," I hear the waitress say in response. I enjoy a few more seconds of my personal peace before shutting everything off and entering work mode. Sad thing to do, but no human being can really handle this much death and not have an off switch.

An older Hispanic woman walks over toward us. She politely refills my coffee cup and looks at Marlow. The agent nods and is rewarded with freshly brewed coffee poured into her half-empty mug.

"I know you ladies aren't here for our pie. How can I help you?" she says and sets the pot down on the counter.

"Are you Aneesa Arias?" I ask quietly so as to not disrupt the other patrons or cause a scene.

"Yes, I am. If this has anything to do with yesterday, just forget it. I have a lawyer and if I need to, I will call him," she replies. Her face is calm and her voice strong and determined.

"Not at all, ma'am," Marlow says and raises her hands in a show of submission.

"We aren't here for anything you've done in the past, Mrs. Arias. I'm curious if you were planning on meeting Captain Tyler Udall?" Her face changes when I mention his name. There's no doubt in my mind she meant to meet him.

"Terrible thing, what happened to him," she says quietly. She refills my half-empty cup of coffee.

"Would you tell us what he wanted with you?" Marlow asks.

"Probably the same thing you want. My niece Alexa."

"From the information we've managed to gather, the Garrison and Valez families are rather dangerous. Why come forward?"

"Before he was killed, Tyler promised to help my daughter. She got in with a bad crowd and can't get out. I just wanted to get her into a rehab we could afford."

There's an ache and a helplessness in her voice that any parent would understand. We'd put ourselves in front of a moving train to help our kids.

"I promise to do the best I can to help you, if you can tell us what you know," I say before sipping some of my coffee.

"I don't exactly know what to tell you, truthfully. She's my niece. She got involved with the wrong crowd like my daughter. She pulled us all into it, and now it's finally crashing down," she replies. Her hand shakes as she picks up the pot to place it back on the warming plate.

"I understand that, ma'am," Marlow says. "We were just hoping you could tell us more about her. Maybe there is something in her childhood we missed. Anything that seems unimportant to you could be vital to us."

The woman turns around again and closes her eyes. I see the strain of years of hard work written on her face: Her crow's feet are deep and well-worn. The darkness under her eyes from lack of sleep. The slight hint of gray at her hairline. She's a woman who, based on everything I've read, has struggled to survive. She turned her life around when she got married. She has a son and a daughter; I hope she'll fight to do what's right now. Live by example and not hide from these people. We can't offer her much, but I pray the desire for justice is enough.

"Give me a minute and we'll talk in the corner by the restrooms. I can't promise you anything, but I'll tell you what I know." She walks away from us. Marlow and I walk over to the area by the restroom. We grab a secluded table that is hidden from most of the patrons and settle in.

"What are you thinking?" Marlow asks me. It takes everything not to laugh since my instincts seem to have taken a vacation during this case. "One mistake doesn't negate your feelings," she says, forcing me to stop my self-deprecation.

"She's been around the block. Either of her own volition or someone else's doing. She looks older than she is, was struggling with her right arm, and she stands slightly hunched forward. Probably the years of hard work here," I say simply, not giving anything away.

"Thanks for the physical evaluation, but I was hoping to discuss more than that," Marlow says as she sips her coffee.

"She's angry," I say. "Probably at the police for yesterday's incident, but it could be deeper than that. She seems family-oriented; she's got a necklace around her neck with charms inscribed with initials with gemstones in them. Maybe they're her children's. Either way, she moves forward in her life and here we are dragging her backwards. I can't blame her for being edgy. Your take?"

"She's tired. Like you said, we're bringing up her past and it could be causing issues in her life. One way or another, she might be willing to talk simply to get us all the hell out of her face."

Aneesa walks over and politely sits down. Her cup is piled high with a large cone of whipped cream on top. She takes the spoon from the table, scoops up a small amount, and sticks it in her mouth.

"Had to give up coffee so many years ago. Found a love for hot chocolate that I never had before. I blame my husband for the whipped cream part, but it's something we share to this day," she says as she takes another spoonful in her mouth. "Alexa never liked something like this. Felt it was a waste of time. Even when she was little, everything was fast-paced and organized. She once cleaned up my kitchen. I couldn't find my measuring spoons for weeks."

"Sounds like a normal kid," I add to the conversation, hoping to keep her moving on the same train of thought.

"I never asked your names," Aneesa says as her eyes focus on the cup in front of her.

"I'm Detective Steele and this is Agent Marlow," I answer.

"Feds working with the locals. My niece must be hitting the shit hard."

"Excuse me?" Marlow asks.

"She was such a love when she was younger. Sure, she had some issues, especially with the cleaning, planning, and making us all follow a list, but she had such a big heart. Her daddy, he was a mess when he got into a bottle. Got himself mixed up with the wrong people."

"We know her father was a trafficker. She used drugs and alcohol when she was a teenager," I say. My hope is she'll move the memories a little closer to the present.

"Her daddy had a shipping boat," Aneesa says. "He would take frequent trips to New York, make deliveries in Brooklyn, and come back down. He was constantly on the water and made a good living, but then he started having issues making his times. Was late and started losing clients. Turned out he was drinking on his runs and got caught by the Coast Guard. When he finally returned home, he was penniless and had a family to support. He made deals with the locals and started running drugs."

"He was a boat runner?" Marlow asks for clarification.

"Yes, if they couldn't get the drugs to Miami, Alexa's father would ship it direct to New York. He always made the run so no one was the wiser. Not to mention the amount of drugs in Puerto Rico was so abundant, it was easy to get it off the islands."

"Did he ever start using?" I ask.

"No, he was a liquor man. Always at the bottom of a bottle. He could drink a paycheck in a few hours. It was a talent in his mind, I'm sure. The men would have killed him if he dabbled in the cargo. My sister told me he was drinking more than he made. We both assumed he started skimming off the top and selling on his own."

She takes a sip full of whipped-cream-infused hot chocolate. "She was scared for herself and Alexa. We started planning a way to get them out of the house and to the mainland."

"We know Alexa was taken, so she never made it to the continental United States. Can you tell us what happened?" Marlow asks.

"My sister called me on the phone. He was drunk and yelling at them again. I told her to pack and come over. We would all share a room and figure it out. Maybe get police protection if we could. She said she would come when I heard a loud bang. The police said that must have been when they knocked the door down. I heard my sister screaming for her life and then two shots. Her voice never came back over the phone again. Alexa, she screamed for her daddy, and I heard him slurring his words. He begged them to leave his little girl alone."

"Did you call the police?"

"My neighbor had come over when she heard me yelling into the phone. She called," Aneesa says, her eyes glassy. "I heard them making all that noise. I know what they were doing to her. I heard her father whimpering like a fool, doing nothing but watching. I knew my niece would never be the same again."

"Did you expect them to take her?" I ask.

"No, that was a surprise. I expected to find them all dead, but the man in charge that day liked her. He took her under his wing, used her body, and taught her how to play the game."

"When did she meet Irving Garrison?" Marlow asks.

"I'm not sure. I felt the pressure of the local gangs coming for me. They knew I was related, so I fled to the mainland on a boat. I fought my way through hard times and started working here," she says as she plays with her mug.

"But Alexa found you," I say, stating the obvious.

"Yes. She had a young boy in her arms. I told her I wanted nothing to do with whatever she was into."

"But you did it anyway," Marlow adds, and Aneesa nods.

"She dropped an envelope in front of me. There was so much cash in bills I had never seen before. I was desperate and behind on my rent. She promised I wouldn't have to hurt anyone, just get information to and from specific locations. I didn't know some of the documents I was delivering were forged, but I always knew it wasn't legal."

"Did you ever meet Irving Garrison?" I ask.

"Once. He was playing with Emilio on the floor of Alexa's apartment at the time. Real fatherly. Told me about his other son in the police academy. Said he was very thankful for all my hard work. Made the hair on my neck stand up. He shook my hand so firmly he almost broke my fingers. I swore if I ever saw him again, I'd look the other way."

"Is that why you never mentioned this to the police officers?" Marlow asks as she scribbles notes on a pad in front of her.

"My little time working with them got me a sentence. I was going to prison for fraud, Agent Marlow. I didn't know how long I'd be in prison, but I knew Alexa and her boyfriend didn't play games. That handshake was enough of a warning. I kept my mouth shut and did my time. When I got out, thankfully my job and apartment were still here waiting."

She sighs loudly. "I'm sure they had something to do with it, but I didn't want to know. I just wanted to go back to my old life."

"I understand. Can you tell me more about this place in Brooklyn?" I ask, going back to an earlier point in the conversation.

"Building 820 in the Navy Yard. It's a massive open warehouse where I did most of my pickups. They had containers in there filled with whatever they smuggled. They had rows of rooms along one wall and lots and lots of people working there, like it was a normal storage place. I swear if I knew there were people in those things, I would have called the cops right then," she says, her voice rising in fear.

"I don't doubt that, Aneesa, and it's okay. You said it yourself; you were in deep and needed the cash. We're not here to bust you on anything. We just need to know everything you remember," I say.

"It should be empty now. Cops seized most of the stuff when they shut him down. That's what the papers say anyway. Can't trust much of nothing from them," she finishes.

"Does Irving Garrison strike you as the kind of guy who'd just abandon a warehouse?" I ask Marlow.

"I didn't know him well enough. I do know if there was an inkling of a raid, he had a plan. There were escape routes, meetup points, weapons at the ready. I doubt he would hide there though. He'd rarely be there, and Alexa was in charge most of the time." Her eyes widen as she understands what I'm asking. The two of us stand up. I open my wallet and give Aneesa a twenty-dollar bill and my card. "Detective, my niece isn't perfect, but please don't kill her," she begs.

"If something happens, you call me."

The two of us sprint out the door, and I frantically dial Zeile's direct line. After three rings, he finally picks up and answers with a chipper voice. "Captain Zeile speaking."

"Cap, it's Steele. We have some information about an old warehouse of Garrison's in the Brooklyn Navy Yard. Marlow and I are in route, but we need backup just in case. Have Logan access satellites and do a heat image of the area. See if anyone's in there."

"Brooklyn Navy Yard? That's a big place. Got anything to narrow it down?" he asks.

"Tell him focus on Building 820."

"I'm sending backup and I'll call the yard. They should be able to close off the area to local traffic. You do not go in until we know more. There are civilians in there working. Do you understand me?"

"Yes, sir." I end the call and hop in the car with Marlow.

"What did he say?"

"Wait for backup, don't go in, the usual. Logan's gonna get us what he can."

She doesn't wait for me to put my seatbelt on before we're peeling out of the parking lot and fighting the traffic. It will be an hour before we're even close to the yard. We're probably stuck there until nightfall. Easier to get closer when the moon shines above you. The sunlight will make us that much easier to spot.

Forty-five minutes later, Marlow whips into the yard and asks the attendant where building 820 is. He starts to give her a hard time about entering the lot, and she simply flashes her badge. It's nice having the all-access pass sometimes. He points in a general direction as Marlow drives through the gate. We immediately notice a batch of patrol cars hidden behind a building. We pull up next to them and park. I get out of the car and show my credentials to the nearest officer. A few other officers come to the two of us and stand almost at attention.

"Anything we need to know about the building?" Marlow jumps right in with questions.

"It's been under renovation since last year, but since political debates went on nearby, they put it on hold and started working on other ones. We've isolated a soft perimeter and have officers staked out on all sides of the building," the male officer says.

"You are?"

"Officer Finley, ma'am."

"Agent Marlow, not ma'am. Now who's in charge here, Finley?"

"You are, Agent Marlow. Word we got from headquarters was that we were to secure the area and wait for you and Detective Steele," he says.

"If the debates were nearby, the Secret Service had to investigate the building beforehand since it was empty. Did they leave any updated reports?" I ask.

"Yes." Finley walks us over to a small folding table with some scattered pages on it and a laptop that looks like it could survive a war. He opens a file and displays it on a screen. "They pointed out that two of the loading bay doors had been sealed permanently from the inside. The yard plans on reopening them, but they haven't gotten around to it yet. The upstairs floors are blocked off from the main floor."

"Does anyone have access to the upper floors?" Marlow asks.

"Not that we can tell. The rear doors were bolted shut while they dealt with asbestos issues. The only entry points are one door on the side and one in the back. Both could be covered; one or both of them could have an alarm or be booby-trapped. We can't be sure until we get closer," Finley answers.

My phone rings and I answer it quickly.

"Is the building unlocked?" Marlow asks.

"We're not sure," he replies.

"Steele," I answer, my voice more authoritative than ever. Easier to cover up the nerves.

"It's Logan. I did some scans and managed to find out that someone has been going in and out of there. Whether they are inside or not at this point . . . can't help you with that. The walls and ceiling of this place is like a fortress," he says.

"Can you confirm it's Valez?"

"Not with certainty. Based on images from the street cams though, it's possible. They made sure to hide their face from all cameras, but one's a woman, and the height and build are pretty close to Valez's. I also checked the scanning records for when people enter the lot. The ID is legit. And probably stolen. The yard has a policy of reissuing the same cards if you have a letter from your job and ten bucks."

"So, we're going in blind?" I say.

"Be careful Jazz," Logan says. I hang up and turn toward Marlow.

"What's going on?" Marlow asks.

"We have no confirmation she's in there or that it's even her. We have no real way in or out in case she blows the place with us in it. Not to mention we're running off a hunch instead of evidence. We're not making this easy on ourselves. We can wait for nightfall, or we can go in now."

"We can be seen if we go in now. Too easy for them to take an uncontested shot," Marlow comments.

"Not if only one of us goes in."

"You're out of your fucking mind," Marlow says harshly.

"We need answers. If she's in there, I'll radio you. If not, then we can move on to the next stop," I argue.

"She'll kill you before you get a chance," Marlow says.

"She's been calling me just like Keith Garrison used to. She'll talk to me," I say, trying to sound more confident than I really am.

"You're wired at all times. We record everything, and if you mention your family, we're storming the castle. If the doors are locked, you turn around and we storm the castle later tonight. Understand?" she says firmly.

"Do I have a choice?" I ask.

"No," she says.

Marlow turns to bark orders to the other officers. I remove my jacket and unbutton my shirt to my waist. If this wasn't such a serious endeavor I'd be a little shyer about flashing everyone around me. A small receiver is slammed into my hand, and I see Marlow standing there. Her mouth continues to move, but I block her out. She manhandles me as she attaches the wire to my chest before tucking the almost minuscule box in my back pocket.

My breathing slows as I button my shirt. My eyes focus on each button as if forcing my mind to stay on one thing at a time. If I go in there with my head a mess, it's over.

"You got it?" Marlow's words finally break through my focus. "You mention Chase and we crash the party. That's your safe word."

"Yeah, got it," I say as I feel my cell vibrate in my pocket again. "Steele," I answer meekly.

"He's fully awake! Jasmine, he's awake and talking!"

I hear the joy in Mia's voice and Will trying to talk over his wife and daughters. "That's amazing news, Mia. Thank you, I needed to know that," I say with little enthusiasm in my voice.

"Jasmine, what are you doing?" I hear the noise in the background fade out. I assume she left the room to yell at me. "You can't tell me, can you?"

Silence.

"Whatever it is . . . promise me you'll be safe," she pleads.

"I have to go now." I hang up the phone before I can say anything else. I hold it out to Marlow, who puts it in her jacket pocket.

I grab the bulletproof vest Marlow has in her hand and toss it over my shoulder. My shaky hands Velcro it shut. I pull my suit jacket over the top of it to give it a look of normality.

"You know this idea is shit, right?" Marlow says. I nod and tap her on the shoulder.

Without another word, I walk past her and the other officers. I will be alone with only my thoughts until I hit the side door of building 820. Normally my brain is so busy that even at yoga I struggle to shut it down. Yet here I am counting my footsteps. This is not how I envisioned my day going.

One foot in front of the other. Keep moving. Focus on the task. Primary objective is simple: stay alive. I talk to myself to calm the nerves, but I'm not sure it's helping.

I arrive at the door, pull on the handle, and the door swings open. That makes me happy and scares the crap out of me. No lights are on in the building; only the waning sun from the outside filtering in through the dirty windows illuminates the space. I leave my gun at my side. If she is here and can see me, I don't want to seem like a threat.

"Police. If anyone's here, I need you to vacate the premises." My authoritative voice bounces off the walls. I see the rows of rooms Aneesa was talking about. I wonder how many people have been through this building before. What illegal activities have run rampant here? With this much space, it could be anything and everything. I wonder if they were doing this when the Navy still controlled this port. Were they functioning right under the government's nose? My mind wanders as I reach the center of the room. The wide-open space, rooms along the wall, and a loft built high above give a myriad of places for Valez to hide—or to shoot from.

"Police," I say again.

"I heard you the first time, detective." Valez's voice echoes throughout the room. I turn around slowly, trying to find her location.

"Alexa?" I ask.

"No, it's your dead mother. Come now, detective, let's not play stupid. It's beneath you," Valez says. Her voice resonates in the somewhat empty factory. She must be up in the loft area for her voice to carry like that.

"Okay," I say. "It's just you and me. No one else. I'm armed, but it's in my holster. What about you?"

"I'm armed and pointing it right at your head."

I hear her voice to my right and cock my head to see Alexa leaning on the metal railing of the loft. "One move and I could remove you from our existence."

"That would really suck for me," I reply.

"There must be something really wrong with you. How many times do you need to be in a life or death situation before you wake up? Maybe it's not the situations; maybe it's the cop in you. Maybe you want the life or death thrill. You need it to breathe."

"Maybe," I say. "Then again, I'm not the woman holding the gun. Maybe you need the thrill of the kill to make your day better? With everything you've been through, maybe you need to take someone out to forget your own pain."

Valez laughs loudly, and it bounces all over the room. The sound slowly echoes down to silence.

"I don't like to kill anyone or anything. It's not the best part of this job. Not much is though. It was supposed to be a means to an end. A way to get out of Puerto Rico and have a life for my son." She taps the gun against the railing, and I see she's lowered it. "I love what I do, detective. I make people happy by supplying them with what they need, or rather, want. Women, men, animals, sex, drugs—you name it, and we can provide it. All a perfectly simple job with imports and exports. It's just a business, Jasmine."

"People were beaten, raped, killed, starved, tortured, and whatever else they could think of."

"What they do with the product when it leaves our warehouse is none of our concern. Irving and I had an understanding, and we kept to it. You, though, you were the anomaly. One stupid mistake by his eldest son and you were brought into our lives. Why do you fight so hard?"

"It's my job. It's the oath I took," I say. I turn again, and I'm nearly facing her.

"It has to be more than that. The police in my country take an oath too," she says. There's a sadness, a loathing, in her voice. What is that? Then I realize: her aunt called the police, but that didn't stop her from being abused.

"What happened to you was inexcusable, Alexa, but this needs to end without bloodshed," I plead.

"That night only made me realize my body was merely a tool. My mind was a force to be reckoned with, and my limbs became my weapons. The police didn't just watch them; they took turns as well. It's how it is with that kind of corruption. Not so anymore. I made sure of that. Even in the darkness, a light can be seen. If I looked close enough, I was able to see that light."

Valez slowly walks down a flight of rickety wooden stairs. They creak with every step, and part of me wishes they would collapse beneath her. I'd easily be able to stop everything. She raises her gun and keeps it on me. Her eyes are more focused than before, which sets off an alarm in my brain.

"What will you do if I shoot you, detective?" she asks.

"Writhe in pain on the floor. You're not going to shoot me, Alexa," I answer.

"One shot to the head and you're free. Isn't that what you wanted not too long ago? To be free from the responsibilities of life in general? To find your family and spend the afterlife with them? You're so sweetly gullible. There is nothing else, detective. After this, we simply evaporate into the ether. It's as if we never even lived in the first place."

She stops on the fourth step from the bottom and takes aim. Her thumb raises, and I hear her pull the hammer back.

"Why wouldn't you just shoot me when I walked in? You don't want to do this, Alexa," I say.

"Wanting and being forced to are very different things. My son's life hangs in the balance," she says. There's a new quiver in her words, an uncertainty.

"He's in Rikers Island pending trial. He made it clear he has connections inside. He's safe among his people," I say. I know it's a lie; no one is ever truly safe behind bars, no matter who you know.

"He's not safe anywhere as long as his father is alive," she says, and again I think I hear some sadness in her voice. "But you, you are the price he demands of me to keep my son alive. You once thought he wanted your friend, but it was always to get to you. Hurt you, harm you, and now kill you."

Far off to my right, I hear a soft shuffling. I see the flash simultaneously as the shot is fired.

"No!" I scream.

The shot catches Valez in the leg, and her gun clatters away on the stairs. She crumbles to her knees and makes a desperate but unsuccessful attempt to grab the railing and rolls the final four steps to the ground. Blood gushes from her thigh. I see Marlow approach, but it's from the other side. So, who fired the shot?

I quickly strip off my suit jacket and wrap it around her leg. I tie the sleeves together tightly as a tourniquet. Marlow rushes over to me, and I see her grab the gun forgotten on the ground. She grabs her walkie-talkie and calls in for a bus to our location immediately.

"Let me die," Valez weakly begs.

"Can't do that," I say. I keep the pressure on her leg as my hands turn red.

"After all I've done to you. What's wrong with you, Steele? Not normal. . ." Valez leans back and raps the back of her head on the ground repeatedly. Officer Finley grabs her head, gently preventing her from hurting herself further.

Marlow leans down and handcuffs her as she recites her Miranda Rights. I can feel the blood pumping slower out of her leg. She's about to pass out. We're running out of time. As I hear the ambulance in the background, I crank down another turn on the tourniquet and lean into the wound with all my weight.

Marlow screams a string of profanities at an officer. He hangs his head down. I see the gun in his hand. He fired without provocation. Without my call. She could have shot me the second I walked in. She wasn't going to shoot. She wanted us to shoot her, and we did.

The paramedics show up and push me aside. The two women work on Valez. They stick needles in her arms and call out numbers to each other. I have no idea what they're doing.

I raise my hands up to my eye level and I see the blood.

I've seen plenty in my time on the force, but this blood makes my stomach roll. One of the paramedics stands and grabs my hands. They want to know if I have any injuries. I shake my head, indicating that I'm okay. My mind, it flashes, and all I see is my brother's body, the blood on the floor forming a pool. Just like now. The cement in front of me turns brownish-red as Valez's life force streams out of her.

An EMT streaks in with a gurney. The paramedics pick up Valez and place her on it and rush out of the building. Two officers grab me and pull me with them outside. The blood is slowly drying on my skin, staining it. Before I know what's happening, a paramedic in the back of the medical wagon pulls me up and forces me into a seat. She buckles me in as the officers close the doors. They bang slightly and the ambulance jerks in motion. Sirens are blasting. I can't stop thinking about what Valez said. Why was I surrounded by blood and death? Did I need the adrenaline to survive?

The paramedic looks at me and continues talking. I just blink. I don't have the energy to reply. She grabs my arm and wraps a rubber cord around my bicep. She taps my arm, and a vein pops to the surface. In one swift motion, a small needle enters my arm and I feel the bile rise up my throat. I hate needles more than blood. I throw up onto the floor, only slightly embarrassed. The EMT ignores my biological release and stabs another concoction into the IV feed. It isn't long before my eyelids feel heavy and my head lolls to the side.

Chapter Thirteen

I peel open my eyes and can tell by the sleep in them I've been out for a long time. I try to raise my right arm, but it's restrained. I swing my left hand over and feel the IV still there. Shit. That means I've been given lots of drugs. Yet another entry into my file. And probably a month of Sundays on desk duty. I lean toward the window and see a sunset in bloom. Or is it a sunrise? How long have I been here this time?

Every part of me feels like it weighs so much more than it normally does. I feel like someone has set a bag of rocks on my chest and my stomach and my thighs. I let my eyelids drop back shut.

"Open your eyes, Steele," Marlow says. I'm grateful to hear a friendly voice I recognize.

"I don't want to," I drawl out.

She slides my eyelids back and the bright sunlight of the room blinds me. I recoil and cover my face. I hold my hand over my eye and spread my fingers to peek through them. I slowly let in light to allow my eyes to adjust. When they do, I see that Marlow is sitting on the edge of the bed, her eyes dark and gray.

"What's going on?" I ask her as my voice clears the sleep away.

"It's been a long day," she says.

"How long have I been out?"

"Forty-eight hours. Your body needed rest since you haven't been sleeping," she answers.

I sit up, fighting the ache in my body from being in one position for too long. I'm relatively wide awake and more coherent now.

"Valez?"

"Alive and in the prison ward section of this lovely establishment."

She rubs the back of her neck, and I see the tension as her muscles flex.

"What aren't you telling me?" I ask. "If it's my family . . ."

"No, according to Logan they're fine. We contacted Frankie. Took me a few hours to convince her not to come home. She may still show up. Stubborn like her wife." She smiles as she says the new pronoun for Frankie.

"Then what?"

"Emilio Valez was killed in Rikers. Homemade shiv. He was stabbed in the kidneys while in the shower. Guards didn't hear a thing, and when they found him, he had already bled out."

"Does she know?" I ask.

"Yes. She's accepted our plea agreement. As long as she cooperates, we keep her safe and hidden. If at any time she breaks the agreement, she goes into a federal penitentiary for life without the chance of parole."

"She accepted that shitty deal? She's becoming an informant for the government. With the information she has on the other players, she could have asked for immunity."

"She did," Marlow says, and the shock must be written on my face. "Someone told me that justice has to be served, so we refused to give her a sweetheart deal. She needs to know she can pay for her crimes at any time. The agency guaranteed not to use our clause indiscriminately, but she also understands she can't play us for fools. Keeps us both honest, I hope," Marlow says.

"I want to talk to her." My words cause her to stop moving and stare right at me.

"You've been getting antibiotics pumped into your system—"

"In case she has some blood disorder like AIDS or Hep C? Yeah, I know. It's protocol." I reach over and pull out my IV and bend my arm up. A trickle of blood rolls down to the point of my elbow. I slide out the side of the bed opposite Marlow and start looking for my clothes.

"In the bottom drawer. I had Logan watch over you while I went to the house. Made sure everything was safe, grabbed some clothes, and came back."

Marlow reaches for some gauze and tape off the nearby table. "Here, damn it, before you bleed all over everything." She expertly rips a length of stretch tape and tacks it to the side of the table, roughly straightens my arm, and presses the cotton ball in the crook.

"Hold," she says. And I push down on the gauze while she grabs the tape and finishes taping the gauze to my injection site.

"Frankie must be angry." I open the bottom dresser drawer and grab a long-sleeve shirt, jeans, and undergarments. Marlow turns away to offer me privacy while I change.

"Nah, she's just worried. She's not here to protect you. What do you expect?" Marlow says, talking up at the ceiling.

"Tell me about Valez's injuries before the nurses come in wondering why I disconnected everything," I say. I dress as fast as possible.

"I told them you'd be out of here the minute you woke up. They were fully briefed. They didn't like the idea, but the docs already said you could go home once you woke up. You just expedited the process. As for Alexa Valez, the bullet pierced the femoral artery. She was damn lucky. The bullet somehow managed to plug part of the hole it created. Your tourniquet probably saved her life. She had extensive surgery, blood transfusions, and the other medical jargon. End result: she survived, but it was a damn miracle."

"She awake?" I ask.

"She's been in and out since the surgery. I assume that means we're making a trip upstairs?"

Saying nothing, I slip on my boots and tie them. Throwing on the leather jacket that was in the drawer, I head out of the room. I see the nurse on duty stand up and place a clipboard on the edge of the counter. I look at it and see they're discharge forms. I turn my back toward Marlow, who shrugs her shoulders.

"Feds have a lot of pull when we need to. Doc said you could go when you woke up; we had the papers ready for when you did. Besides, I'm paying attention to you or face the wrath of your girl."

Marlow passes me as I sign the forms. The two of us walk up the two flights of stairs to the prison ward floor. I show my badge to the guards, and they let us through the main gate. One at a time, the metal gates open; we step inside and they close behind us. Systematically, they click and slam. It's a very claustrophobic feeling as you get further through them. I know each area needs to be cornered off with various directions, but the rat in a maze analogy sits in my mind. The final gate is opened by an officer with a key. I nod my thanks and follow Marlow down the hallway.

She stops in the doorway of the first room. The view out the window faces the city, and the new Freedom Tower is perfectly framed in the square space, the bars the only hindrance to the full image. I take a few steps in and realize Marlow isn't following me. She stands at the doorway and turns her back to us. She's giving me privacy to talk to Valez, but why?

"Detective," I hear Valez whisper. I turn my attention to the woman lying frail on the bed in front of me. Gone are her confident facial expressions. Her eyes are red and puffy, I assume from crying. Her hands look bonier and thinner than before. Everything about her looks less threatening. She's become mortal.

"Valez," I say.

I pull up the guest chair and take a seat next to her bed. She leans her head to face the window.

"It's such a beautiful view, isn't it?"

"It is. I preferred the original," I say, remembering the twin towers.

"Me too, but change comes whether we like it or not," she says. She raises her eyes to meet mine. "The doctors said you were instrumental in saving my life. I want to know why. Why did you keep fighting?"

"Excuse me?"

"I know I have information you want, but why put yourself at risk? One of the nurses told me you were downstairs unconscious. They were pumping you full of meds apparently. I told them to test my blood. See if I have anything that could make you ill," she says as she yawns. The thought comes that I ought to find that nurse and arrest him. The last thing they are allowed to do is share personal information about anyone to an inmate. He should know better.

"I don't know," I answer. "It felt like the right thing to do at the time."

"You're contrarian," she says. Her voice drops and a single tear falls down her face. "My son has paid for his crimes. I'll pay for mine."

"Where is Garrison? I need to know. You at least owe me that," I say.

She gingerly reaches over to the side table and grabs a pen and paper. She writes down an address. Below that, she writes a string of numbers with letters and a time listed next to it. Her hand shakes as she hands me the note before dropping the pen on the bed.

"What's this?" I ask.

"You gave me my life. I'm giving you what you want. Revenge, or maybe acceptance, I truly don't care. I've got nothing left but a lifetime to think. Please, just let me sleep now." She lays her head back and says nothing further. I take the hint and walk to Marlow outside the door. I hold up the sheet.

"What's that?"

"An address to where, I don't know, and some numbers with a time. Maybe Logan can make sense of it. Valez acted like this will lead me to Garrison. Either way, if it's where Garrison is, we need to take a minute and regroup. I'll be shocked if he's alone."

We make our way out of the prison ward. I've seen this address before, but I can't pinpoint where. Once I can shove it into a GPS, I'll figure it out. On the way back to my house, I'll call Logan and have him check things. Once he figures out what we're up against, we'll head out.

***

A keypad with six digits. That's all that keeps Chase out of my armory. I'm sure he could easily figure it out. I type in the code, pull the handle, and swing open the heavy steel door. Inside are more guns than I or any other cop really needs. I grab my thigh holsters and attach them. I always did love the Lara Croft/*Tomb Raider* look. I check my everyday Glock 9mm—fifteen in the clip, one in the chamber—and put it in the right holster. I slide open the drawer in the safe and grab a second Glock, check the clip, and chamber a round. I slap it into the left holster.

I grab the bulletproof vest off a hanger next to the safe and slip it on. The Velcro seals with my hand's pressure. I feel the tightness coming back to my chest when I realize I'm heading back into the fray. I need a break, but it's never the right time. I grab a belt with several black pockets and clip it to my waist. Reaching in the back of the safe, I pull out a steel box. I dump the contents onto a nearby desk and a half dozen empty clips clatter out. I grab a box of ammo and, in a routine I've done a thousand times, rapidly load bullets into all of them. I take all the clips and place them in every empty pocket on the belt.

"Jesus, Steele, where did you get all this?" Marlow asks.

I hand her a belt that matches mine and shove the box into her other hand. There's no time to talk right now. After typing the address into the GPS, we know Garrison is hiding out at the container terminal in Brooklyn. It makes sense, as the walls are closing in around him. This is his only play to try and get out of the country and not be detected. If he pays cash, it's as easy as pie; someone is bound to take a score that big. My phone rings.

"Steele," I answer. I see Logan's name on the screen and hit speakerphone. As usual, he sounds like an excited teenager.

"It's a container number. He's shipping himself out in five hours."

"Ship's destination?" I ask.

"Cuba," Logan says, and his tone shifts dramatically. I understand why. "Thanks."

I hit end on the phone and slam the safe shut with a loud clang. I open my dresser drawer and reach all the way into the back. Grabbing a small black box, I hip check the drawer closed. Flipping it open, I pull the ring out. I feel Marlow looking at me, but I say nothing. I put the ring in my jeans pocket before heading out of the room. Running downstairs, I hear Frankie in my head telling me to stop what I am doing and think about things. I open the fridge and grab two beers as Marlow's footfalls follow me into the kitchen. She drops the box with a few clips still inside on the counter. I place them on the table and fall into a seat. I pop open a beer and look at her. Marlow shakes her head as I take a long swig.

"A beer? Right now? Jesus . . ." Marlow hesitates a second before she pops the other bottle open and drinks.

"We need a game plan, one that we can win, and I need to calm my nerves, hence the beer."

"You were in the hospital a few hours ago. You shouldn't be drinking," she says and grabs my beer. She pulls out a bottle of water from the fridge and places it in my hand. Then I watch as she takes a final swig before pouring both beers down the drain.

There goes my liquid courage. One sip won't affect me at all, but she's right. I open the bottle and chug the ice-cold water. The chill hits my teeth, causing pain to shoot through me.

I slam the empty bottle to the table and look over to Marlow, who's leaning against the counter. I'm sure Logan has already notified the higher-ups about what's going on. Even with all of those men around us, all that manpower, we still might be outnumbered or outgunned. Unlike the men that work for Garrison, should his men be manning the ship, we have a legal obligation to protect the innocent at the shipyard. His ship will be leaving at a peak time of day. That means any number of civilians and workers can be walking around that area.

"He's heading to Cuba," I say.

"I heard. Perfect place for him to recover."

"Regardless of our recently improved relations with them, there's still no extradition treaty," I say.

"Nope."

"If we don't get him before he gets on that vessel, we lose him."

"Theoretically, yes. We still have the Coast Guard, and worst case the Navy could come into play."

"Stop a vessel bound for Cuba?" I say. "That would open the doors for an international incident regardless of the reason. Their government is none too fond of ours, remember?"

I grab Chase's iPad, which has been sitting on the kitchen table since he left. I turn it on, enter his passcode. I launch the maps app, type in the address, and click satellite view.

"You know this isn't the most up-to-date or accurate, right?"

"Yeah, the number of containers change every day. The layout for this location is very specific though. And they have fixed buildings already in place. Maybe we can get a better idea of how to approach safely."

I zoom in on the site and see a small building off the main road, a parking lot, and what looks like a huge metal shed on either side of it. Three areas of dock space for ships to unload form a C around the main land mass. There are three main rows of containers: one really long one on the top dock, smaller ones on the left and right dock, and another massive one by the main building.

There are two smaller solid structures between the office building and the first row of containers, as well as two small cargo container areas by the parking lot and metal shed. It's a massive amount of space, and at any given time it could mean cover for the police, or we might be in the open.

I guess it all depends on what's there now and if the ship heading to Cuba is off loading or loading up. That's it. I hand the iPad to Marlow, and her eyes scan the area.

"It's not going to be easy," she says. "If we have the element of surprise, it will help a lot."

"Then we go in silently. No sirens, no loud walkies."

"Garrison's guys are gonna be professionals."

"Of course. Whether hired guns or just workers, they're gonna be focused on getting the work done. Distractions aren't going to work. Hell, a hurricane probably wouldn't work."

I rub my eyes as a migraine begins to form.

"That's our plan then," Marlow says. "Logan gets us the current image, and we hide behind containers before announcing ourselves and taking them all into custody."

"Awfully ambitious," I say with a smirk.

"Work with what you have, Steele. If I've taught you nothing else while here, it's to accept what you've got and use it." Marlow grabs the box and heads out the door to the car.

I flip the tablet back around and go to the home screen. There, staring back at me, is an image of Chase, myself, and Frankie dressed up as characters from the *Mass Effect* universe on Halloween. She had no idea why she had to be blue, let alone why Hadley's makeup people were putting prosthetics on her head. It was a gift for Chase really. He wanted me to be Commander Shepard, the leader of the ship. Frankie was Liara, Shepard's soulmate in my play-throughs, and he got to be a Krogen and smash things. Needless to say, he loved running headfirst into the pile of pumpkins we had carved that week. Poor kid would have got a concussion if we hadn't stopped him.

"He's such a good kid," I say aloud. "I wish you could see him now, Henry. You'd be so proud."

The screen dims to blackness and I know it locked back up. Closing my eyes, I hear my mother telling me to slow down. "Just focus on your breathing," she would say. "Feel every beat of your heart. Feel the life pumping within your chest. Feel your essence expand within you and accept your truth." My eyes pop open at that moment. She never explained to me what that meant, but at this moment I understand. My truth, my reason for saving Valez and others . . . It's not to be different. It's not to be difficult. It's to ensure that the world is a little bit safer for the woman I love and a nephew who has me whipped. Simple in essence, but accepting it is a separate beast altogether. This overwhelming calm flows from my head all the way to my toes. Control what you can, Steele. Put the rest of your faith in your team and your abilities. Nothing else you can do.

The horn honks outside and I walk out the door. I silently pray to my mother to watch over me. May she bring us all home unharmed to our families. This time is just as dangerous as any of the others, but it feels like this time there's more on the other side. So, I have to be sure to come home.

***

The silence at the dock is overwhelming. No one says anything as we march by. The officers nod and continue to gear up in the relative safety their trucks provide, parked behind the main building. Marlow and I walk up to the main group. Captain Zeile and a few other high-ranking officials huddle and whisper back and forth. I know we said silence, but seeing grown men whisper and use hand signals isn't something I see every day. Marlow slaps my arm to bring my focus back.

Zeile walks away from his officer buddies and waves us over to the main table.

"Okay, you two are going to be the leads. Your job is simple; you are to capture Irving Garrison. Everyone else's job is to ensure the two of you succeed. We have a small window here. The ship isn't leaving right away, but we want to ensure the least number of casualties," he says while pointing to his charts that I can't read.

"What's the cover look like?" I ask.

He flips out a blown-up satellite image on a tablet. He zooms in and, with a small pen, highlights the path he wants us to take.

"We're lucky." He points his pen to the first row of containers. "We've got full coverage. Few ships made drop-offs in the morning on their way further up the coast. The first row in front of the storage unit building is completely full. Thirteen containers wide, two deep, and four high. There's no walkway through them so we have to go around."

"If we go around, we'll be spotted," Marlow says.

"Not necessarily. The row in front of it is broken into two sections. The one on the left is full at six wide and three high. The one on the right only has four of the six filled and one in height." Zeile points to the layout on the touch screen.

"That seems to be the easy part," I say, pointing to the row directly in front of the cargo ship.

"Out of thirteen possible spots, only seven are being used, and they also run one container high."

"What's this on our left?" Marlow asks, pointing at a collection of squares north of the boat.

"Owner said they stack the old wood pallets there until they dispose of them. It might provide some cover, but you would be more exposed," Zeile answers.

"The boat?" I ask.

"Harbormaster," Zeile says as he steps aside.

An older man with a long beard and calloused and dirty hands from a hard day's work rolls out a blueprint sheet. The old and worn documents look like they were shoved in a drawer for eons.

"The vessel was built in 2004, but it's a workhorse with very little room to hide. From the stern to the bow, she was meant to carry as much cargo as possible. She's been unloading a bunch of containers on her trip back home, so the center of her deck is somewhat full. They have most of the weight in the center of the boat, so the starboard and port should be clear to move about." He points to various points on the blueprints.

"That leaves us out in the open," I say, looking over the plans.

"Yes and no. It's definitely something you have to consider. Most likely the individual you are looking for is in the deck house here," he says, and points to the tall structure toward the stern of the boat. "It's six levels. Top floor is where the captain pilots the vessel. From there down is the galley and living quarters. The lower you go, the smaller and more cramped the living spaces." He rolls up the blueprint and looks at us.

"Garrison would be toward the top floors," Marlow says. "Entry points to those floors?"

"Steps on both port and starboard sides of the ship," the harbormaster adds.

"Ways onto the actual vessel?" I ask.

"They have two gangways set up. One bow, one stern. You can see for yourself on the security camera feed."

He hands me a small tablet showing the various camera feeds on the lot. The gangway in the stern is lower than the bow. Might be easier to enter, but both entryways are very risky.

"We'll be monitoring these feeds to be your eyes in the sky," Zeile says. "In the meantime, we have snipers hidden on top of the storage and main buildings. We've stationed uniforms along the first and second rows already. Mostly to ensure no one got close to us, but also to be ready when we storm the boat."

"They obviously have a crew and several guards on board. Are they Garrison's or civilian company men?" I ask.

"Sadly, we believe it's a mix of both," Zeile replies.

"Shit," Marlow and I say in unison.

Zeile takes a breath, and a grim look crosses his face. "We have to do the best we can. We won't know who is who. If they raise a gun, do what you have to do. Simple as that."

"Collateral damage?" Marlow asks.

"Not ideal, but there is nothing any of us can do if it escalates that far. The two of you will have to infiltrate and search the best you can. Once it's safe, we'll bring more on board to help. Logan will also have eyes in the sky should he be seen above deck, as well as infrared scans to pay attention to the two of you."

"How will he distinguish us from them?" I ask.

Zeile reaches into his bag and grabs two round semicircle-like items. He hands one to each of us. Spinning it in my hand, I truly have no idea what the hell it is.

"According to Mr. Pevy, these are personal cooling systems. I don't know how he did it, nor do I care. He said they will give you a different look on the camera so he can tell you apart. That's all I care about. Make sure your earbuds are in so we can all communicate with you if there's something you should know. Turn them on and go to the first group of officers. I know this is going to be a play-by-the-hip op. Udall trusted in you, Steele. Don't make me look like a fool for doing the same. Now move out." With that, Zeile walks away. The entire team of higher-ups walks into a command center trailer. Safe from the flying bullets, of course. Frustrating as hell, but it doesn't change the job we have to do.

"You ready for this?" Marlow asks me as she places the cooling thing around her neck, slides the earbud in her right ear, and flips it on.

"Not at all. You?" I reply as I gear up as well.

"Nope. Let's try not to get shot." She smiles.

"Works for me," I say with a smirk.

I grab my gun from my left leg and verify it's loaded. Marlow does the same. We walk up to the first row of containers, confident in the height to hide our approach.

"You think they know we're here?" Marlow tosses out.

"I want to say no due to all this shit piled here. Part of me though thinks they could be playing it coy right now. Who knows?" I answer.

We meet up with five officers lining the closest row of concealment provided by the containers. I look over to the young faces and see discomfort in them. They're ready for orders, and I'm sure they have been trained to handle anything. They just look very ill at the moment. Like the feeling you get when you've got to make a speech in front of a room full of people but you don't want to; it's like that. Marlow stands with the rest of the officers and looks at me intently.

"Agent Marlow is with me; the rest of you split in half. Meet up with the other officers in the next row. Once there, Marlow and I are going to move forward on our own to the stacked pallets. Once we do that, we will announce our presence and pray for a quick resolution. If that fails, you will protect yourselves and your fellow officers. Make sure you pass this information along to the other officers stationed in the next row. Everyone goes home tonight, understand?" I say with more confidence than I have.

They all mumble in response, and I hold my gun at the ready. It's time to move. Crouching down to minimize my height, I turn the corner and rush to the next row of containers. I meet with the next group and repeat the same game plan I told the others. I look over at Marlow; she's holding her pistol in her hand waiting on my mark. I nod to her, and she rushes from behind cover and over to the pallets. Counting to ten Mississippi in my head, I follow suit.

I look through the holes of the palettes and wonder if this was such a great idea. One properly placed shot or a lucky one and we're hit. Marlow taps me on the shin, and I see her almost lying on the ground. I lie down near her, making myself as small as possible.

"This is the police. You're sur—"

Before I can finish my thought, gunshots sound out, shredding the pallets and caroming off the first row of cargo containers behind us. Like we fully expected, this is going to end in blood. Peeking through the wood, I can see the front gangway and several individuals running onto the dock. The back gangway seems to have been abandoned. That's either luck, idiocy, or like Marlow said before—a trap.

I hear a few shots from our snipers followed by splashes of water. The gunfire erupts on both sides now, sounding like an orchestra of violence. Marlow fires a few shots off while I survey the stern part of the boat and surrounding dock. Machines, more pallets, and a crane—that's the ticket.

"There's a crane before the gangway. If we can get to it safely, we should be able to get aboard," I say as Marlow cranks off another few shots.

"Then let's go," she says as she pops up and runs over to the back of the crane, discharging her weapon as she goes.

I follow suit, focusing on my firing as I try my best to make it to cover. The sniper fire echoes loudly over the riot, and I turn my head to the left quickly. A man falls to the floor of the dock; his shot at me would have been uncontested. Getting to the crane, I catch my breath and look over to the gangway; no one is on it.

"They'll be waiting on board," Marlow says.

"We stick together," I answer.

Breaking out into a full sprint, I cross the remainder of the space onto the dock and up the gangway. I hear Marlow a few steps behind me.

"You can't be here!" a voice directly to my right says. He swings his fist and connects with my face, knocking me into the nearby stairs. I hear Marlow engage in a fistfight as I look up to see another crew member running toward them. Sliding my foot out, I trip the man. He and I get up at the same time, and my fist swings as hard as my brother taught me. It connects with his gut, and he falls over instantly. I swing my leg up and kick him in the face, knocking him out cold. I taste blood on my lip as I turn to see Marlow finishing off the other guy with a flurry of punches to the temple and cheeks.

"Which side you want?" she asks.

"We stay together," I adamantly state.

She begins walking up the rusted metal staircase, slowly and methodically, her gun pointed ahead of her, ready to fire at anyone who is a threat. I follow closely behind, ensuring no one else has a clear shot from the deck. The ship's horn sounds, and I hear the engines revving up.

"They're trying to leave port!" Marlow says as she quickens her pace.

We push open the door on the fifth floor. We begin to walk through the length of a hallway with one door on the left and one further down on the right. The captain exits his cabin at the end of the hallway and stares at us for a second before bolting. Marlow rushes after him, and I follow suit until I hear the door open and close behind me. Looking back, I come face to face with Irving Garrison. He stops and smiles as if taunting me. I raise my weapon, but before I can say anything, he too is running. Without giving it a second thought, I chase after him.

I fly down the flights of stairs to the main deck, taking two steps at a time to keep up with him. He runs along the starboard side of the boat and makes a left into the center of the main deck. I rush along the starboard side in hot pursuit. The gunfire on the dock continues at a vicious pace, but it seems further away to me than before. I stop at the corner and peer around the bend. The containers have been oddly spaced, stacked together in the middle, then stacked toward the sides to allow movement in the middle of the deck. More places to hide.

I make my way around the corner, and two shots pop off. One hits the container next to me; the other pierces my skin. I fire a few rounds off and return to my original place. Looking at the side of my leg, I see where the bullet grazed my skin. Blood drips out slowly and the pain is palatable.

"We've got you surrounded. There's nowhere to go, Garrison. Just give it up," I say.

Silence.

I try again. "You turn yourself in now, the FBI might be willing to cut you a deal. You get to spend the rest of your life in club fed."

Silence. I peer around the corner again and make a break for the next row. A crew member turns the corner, gun raised, and I put two in his chest before he can respond. He stumbles before falling over the railing and into the water. The ship's horn sounds again. It feels like we're moving. Running out of time.

I follow along the containers to the starboard railing, hoping to see who's around the corner. I see Garrison running between the containers, and I immediately run full speed toward him. He fires his gun over his shoulder, missing wildly. I duck behind the second to last row of containers on the long boat. My back slams against the metal, and I feel the skin bruise. I turn along the starboard side and open fire where I saw Garrison last.

"It's over, just end this now!" I scream. I'm getting tired of running.

Gunshots ricochet from the metal I'm leaning on and some lodge in the deck boards. The unmistakable sound of clicking rings in my ears. He's run out of bullets.

"Why'd you wait so long? You should have run sooner. Hell, you could have been in Cuba for months." I turn the corner, gun raised. I don't see him right away and turn my attention to the starboard side of the containers.

I hear a faint grunt followed by a rush of footsteps. Before I can respond to the approaching attacker, I'm hit at the waist. My gun falls out of my hand and clatters to the deck. The railing slams against my back like a baseball player swinging for a home run. I punch the body holding me as we race toward the water.

Garrison releases his hold and pushes away from me just before we hit the water. My left shoulder pops out of joint on impact. My back feels like it's been broken, beaten, and bruised. My lungs burn as I force my mouth to stay shut. My legs kick, but the bulletproof vest holds me down. My right hand shakes and fumbles to rip open the Velcro straps. Screaming underwater as I move my arm, I release the entire breath I was holding. Not a smart move.

Frantically, my legs kick to the surface as fast as humanly possible. Breaking the plane of water into an oasis of oxygen, I breathe in deeply with every gasp. It's then that I remember I'm not alone. Spinning around in circles while treading water, I see nothing but the normal waves of the harbor. Where the hell could he be?

In an instant, I'm pulled underwater again. Garrison climbs up my body, pushing me further below the surface. His arms wrap around my throat in a headlock, forcing me to fight my instinct to breathe. I punch his forearms, but he barely budges. Feeling the urge to breathe overwhelming me, I elbow him in the groin. His arms release enough for me to latch down on his forearm.

I bite down hard and shake my head from side to side. I need to break skin, get him to bleed and go on the defensive. He fights me, pulling his arm, pushing me hard. I release his skin and taste the blood in my mouth. My body naturally expels the blood-filled water out of my mouth as I gasp desperately again.

I feel my ponytail being held in a fist and another hand pressing down on my scalp. I reach up with my left hand, punching at anything I can reach. Every swing sends an incredible, searing pain through my shoulder. My fist finally connects with something bony and the hold on my hair loosens. My vision clears, and I see Irving propelling himself out of the water again. He pushes me back under hard before I can grab another breath.

There's a serenity that comes over you as you start to drown. I don't know if it's because your body is overwhelmed with the stimuli of dying or if it's the sensation of being back in the womb. Either way, you feel free. Your mind begins to wander as your limbs begin to feel weak. Each punch is slower. My head thrashing about is more sluggish than before. Then I see images of my family. The ones I fight for.

My legs swing up in the water slowly. I manage to bend in half as my legs wrap around Irving's waist. In a split second, I squeeze tightly and pull him under the water. His grip on my head loosens and I push myself off of him to spit water out of my mouth as I desperately fill my lungs with air. He punches my legs repeatedly. I feel his body shaking. I could easily kill him right now as I squeeze my legs tighter.

I reach down and grab his shirt tightly. I pull him to the surface and wrap my right arm around his throat. He fights; I can still take him out. He struggles and kicks. He head-butts me once, and we both sink below the surface again. I have just managed to get us back up to breathe when I hear several clicks. The two of us stop moving and look up to see the Coast Guard with weapons pointed at the two of us.

Garrison simply raises his arms out of the water. The case is done. Everything is done. Henry and Belinda can rest now. I can rest now. I feel his weight pulled off me as he is lifted aboard. After they cuff him, two men lift me out of the water. My left arm screams at me with each twist or turn. I look over at the man who was indirectly responsible for so much torment in my life.

"Why?" I ask with so much emotion laced behind the one-word question. With everything that's happened, I want to know the meaning behind his actions. I hear the boat pull up alongside the main dock. They grab Garrison, and I jump up to face him.

"Answer me," I ask, almost begging.

Silence. He makes eye contact, and I think I see a smirk form. That's a mistake. A big mistake. I rear back and head-butt him with a ferocity that nearly lifts me off my feet. I hear the satisfying snap of nose cartilage breaking. Blood begins to pour.

"You were supposed to be right behind me," I hear Marlow say. I turn to see her waiting on the dock for me. With her help, I step off the boat and onto dry land. I hear the boat rev back up and pull away from the pier.

"I thought you were supposed to be behind me," I toss back at her.

"Maybe Logan should have had these stupid things have communicate between the two of us." She laughs.

"That would have been logical," I say, looking out at the water.

"Bus is waiting to take you to the hospital. I don't care what you say, but this time you're there for a few days, if not more. I'm also getting Logan to call Frankie and get her on the first plane back. I'm not getting blamed for this," Marlow says, pushing on my injured arm, trying to hide the slight fear in her voice.

"Are you okay?" I ask.

"We're not dead. We get to see our families. Some of our guys are critical, but so far, no fatalities. That's what I call a good day. Now come on."

"I'll be there in a second," I say, and she leaves me be.

Continuing to stare out over the waves, I feel the last few years roll over me. Tears fall from my eyes, but I don't shake or wail. It's as if relief has finally found me. Reaching into my skintight jeans, I pull out the diamond ring. So much was tied to this ring. Henry and I went out to buy it together. The night I planned on proposing, he and Belinda died. I lost myself and Frankie after that. There I was on the precipice of freedom . . . and this ring brings back the weight of it all.

I wind up and throw the worst lefty toss into the water. A bolt of pain shoots down my shoulder into my arm. The ring makes a slight plopping sound before disappearing forever under the surface. I could have returned it. I could have given it away. So much I could have done, but the negative would always be with it. Water is cleansing. Water washes away all the torment. My mother always told me that if you throw a rock into a lake, the water will ripple and eventually calm but the lake is forever changed. That's me now. That ring, these experiences have forever changed me, but it's time to move on. I turn away from the water and head to the ambulance.

$$***$$

It's been ten months since Garrison was arrested. His mainland bank accounts are still frozen, and Logan also managed to close all of his overseas accounts. Without a dollar to his name, Irving Garrison has the best lawyer the city of New York can provide. The kid he has is good. Better than a piece of shit like him deserves in my opinion, but the law is the law.

Once everything here had settled, Marlow flew back to Seattle. She sent me pictures of her family at the airport holding up various welcome home signs. Of course, her kids texted me with an image of her kissing her husband. It was cute, but probably not something she wanted to share.

Will had a solid six months of intense physical therapy with me nearby working on my shoulder. He's managed a full physical recovery, but he's still seeing the department shrink. Can't blame him. He was knocking on death's door but managed to come back. He still has to be cleared for active duty and pass his reassessment test. He's got a village of friends and family helping him out every step of the way. I'm sure his desk duty will last only as long as he desires it to.

"I'll be there in the morning," I say into my phone. The district attorney wants to go over my testimony again, as if I could forget anything.

"Steele, I need you to speak to Detective Everts. He's not returning my calls," Barbara Prince, our newly appointed district attorney, says.

"The man just wants to spend time with his family. Give him a little leeway, okay?"

"He's had ten months. The judge won't grant more time because he's making up for being shot."

I hear the frustration in her voice. I get it, I do. This case is big, and the FBI are waiting in the wings to take Garrison to federal court. Prince has promised to work her butt off to get an honest and fair trial. Agent Sharp promised justice. Either way, pressuring us to run around like sheep when we need a break doesn't work. The office might feel the stress of winning, but they wouldn't have even had a chance without us grunts.

"I'm gonna let that go and not say what I'd like to. I'll talk to him, but not for you or your fucking department. I'll make sure he calls you tomorrow."

"Thank you." Her voice is calmer.

"One more thing. You might want to remember that without us grunts you wouldn't have anything. Maybe think about that before you talk to my partner again."

Before she can answer, I hang up. I have better things to do than sit here and get into a pissing match. Getting out of my car, I walk into the park. The smell of exhaust, the sound of the cars, and the pressure of the city slowly falls away with every step I take. Chase's laughter floats on the breeze and reaches my ears. I missed his laugh when he was away. He tells me stories of ice cream trips, movie marathons, and forts being built with the agents assigned to protect them. Part of me is jealous for missing out on those moments, but I am so thankful he has positive memories about it all.

"Aunt Jazz!"

Chase runs up full force, slamming his body into mine. His arms wrap tightly around me as I lean down and hug him back.

"You're late," he says and looks up at me.

"I know, buddy. Work stuff."

"Can you stay?" His pleading eyes bore a hole right through my heart. God, kids really do have us adults wrapped around their fingers.

"Yeah, little man. No more work for the rest of the day."

His big smile washes away all the stress from my day. He hugs me tightly again before running off toward Will. My partner stands by the grill, one hand on his hip, the other holding the spatula as if he was a British soldier on guard of the grill. Chase stops next to him and assumes the same position. People say I'm a big kid. They haven't seen Will and Chase when they want something. Well, more like when Chase wants something and his best buddy Will tag-teams the parental units.

Walking over to the bench, I sit down next to Frankie. Her eyes are closed, and her face is raised toward the sun. She's stunningly beautiful. I lean back and try to calm my racing heart.

"What are you thinking about?" she asks.

"Nothing much," I lie. My eyes focus on Will and Chase a few feet in front of me.

"Jasmine . . ." She grabs my right hand and winces in disgust. "Your hand is cold and clammy. You're either lying or really nervous."

"I know you found the ring in my drawer." I hear her body shift against the wooden bench next to me. I swear her eyes are burning into the side of my face.

"I, well . . ." she stammers.

"Henry and I went to a store and I saw it. When I bought it, I knew we weren't ready to get married anytime soon, but I had to get it. Henry, he was all about me having it for the right time. I remember asking my mom what the hell I was thinking. She just told me I was finally letting my heart make some decisions. When I was ready, I planned everything out and was nervous as hell. Then my phone rang. I stood you up that night."

"The night Henry died," she says, barely above a whisper.

I take a deep breath and ease it back out through my nose. I have a lot to say. A lot to apologize for. My mother has been right in the past, so maybe letting my heart do some talking isn't such a bad thing.

"When my phone rang and they threatened Chase, I lost it. I made promises to my brother, and I couldn't keep them. Not really. I felt vulnerable, lost, terrified that whoever it was would be right around the next corner. When Keith Garrison was chasing me down, I wanted to die. I figured if I was gone, he would leave you and Chase alone."

"That wouldn't have solved anything, Jasmine. Chase would have been devastated. Hell, we were both a mess the entire time you were in the hospital. Not to mention your friends would never have stopped until they caught who took you from us. It wasn't going to end until Irving Garrison was caught."

"Then I fell down the rabbit hole, Frankie. I just had you back. I couldn't get that nagging voice out of my head. I had to figure it out. I had to find him. I had to stop the wheel. I know I'm not perfect, and I know you were angry at me for sending you and Chase away. I know it hurt you that I stayed behind."

"I could have helped you. We're a team, remember?"

"You're Chase's other mother. If something happened to me, he would be safe. I know that sounds cold, but that's the nature of my job, Frankie."

I feel her lean back on the bench. She knows I'm right, but she doesn't have to like it. Reaching into my pocket, I hold onto my prized possession tightly.

"You've always grounded me. Didn't matter how dark I went or how lost I was; you always pulled me back. When you found that ring, my heart was racing. I kept thinking back to the night I decided to propose. The night my brother was killed. It was such a beautiful ring, but there were so many bad things attached to it. Yet, I couldn't get rid of it. All this time it just sat in my drawer. I couldn't look at it or even imagine it being on your finger."

"I understand," she says as a hint of sadness in her voice betrays her true emotions.

Pulling my hand out my pocket, I rest it on my thigh as I take a deep breath for courage. Exhaling slowly, I open her palm and place a small diamond solitaire on it. It's nothing fancy. Not like the first one, but this one means more to me than anything I could buy. We're not those people anymore. My eyes remain forward, vulnerability and fear preventing me from looking at her.

"I can't promise you my job won't be dangerous every day. And I can't promise you that I won't occasionally lose my way. What I can promise you is that I will protect you and Chase until I have no breath left. I promise to protect this city and make you proud. With the same ring that my father proposed to my mom many moons ago, I promise to love you for as long as I live. If you're willing to take a chance on me, that is."

I feel her moving next to me, but my fear keeps me from looking at her. Giving her my mother's ring—getting rid of the old one—it was a massive step forward. Rejection at this point would break me. Her hand glides to my cheek and she pulls me to face her.

"Jasmine, we're both truly imperfect people. But I would love nothing more than being flawed with the love of my life."

Before I can reply, her lips gently touch mine. All the fear flows along my skin and into the bench away from my heart. She's always had a way of doing that for me. Frankie is perfect to me, and I can't wait to marry her. I don't think either of us have a clear idea where our lives will take us. I just know I have the person I need to keep me grounded while I continue to do my job. That's the one thing I am sure about. Crime never stops, but Will and I will do our best to slow it down a little. Because there is so much more to life than just being a cog in a machine. There's family, love, and hope.

THE END

Author's Note

I normally don't write notes within my books, but I wanted to take a moment of your time to thank you for reading my novels. My writing is a very personal thing. Associates of mine swear they can see me as Jasmine Steele and my wife Sheila as Frankie. I have said in many interviews that she is part me and part who I wish I could be. Creative types always put some of who we are into what we create. It's the nature of the beast. It makes me smile, but I try to let her be a somewhat separate entity.

There is one character that is truly based on someone I knew. Jasmine's grandmother was truly based on mine. Her pug was named Tuffy, not King. She was strong, intelligent, loving and accepting of all her family members. She came over to this country with my mother after surviving the war in Germany. She and my grandfather, who passed away in 2009, built a life here in New York. They worked very hard to provide and always instilled that work ethic in me and my brothers.

The reason I bring all this up. . .she passed away before this book was finished.

People ask me what the hardest part of writing Steele Intent was. My answer has always been Chapter 8. That was only half of the truth. I had a significantly hard time writing Chapter 11 where Jasmine talks to her grandmother. That was purely Kimberly talking to her Oma. I dreaded the day I lost the oldest musketeer in the trio of mom, me, and Oma.

From the moment she made me pancakes to the last time I saw her, she was always supportive. She might not have understood what I was doing, why I was doing it — but she always asked if I was happy. That was really what mattered — my happiness.

The last moment I saw her, she had been sleeping for quite some time. I sat next to her, smiled, and told her I loved her. She opened her eyes and smiled back. That was her goodbye to me . . . and just like her, it was perfect for me.

Like my Oma said, life is more fun when you have happiness within you. May you all find it and thank you for allowing me to have it by writing.

About Author

Kimberly Amato is the author of the Jasmine Steele Mystery Series and Enemy. Having won awards for a TV Pilot she co-wrote & produced, she dove headfirst into writing novels. Always creating, jotting down new ideas & unafraid to try new genres, Kimberly writes mysteries, crime, romance, sci-fi & more. Beyond that, she's a podcaster with her wife, Sheila, for the show Forever Fangirls reviewing TV and film on streaming services and in theaters. Kimberly enjoys keeping in touch with her readers. You can find her by using the links below or going to her website KimberlyAmato.com.

amazon.com/stores/Kimberly-Amato/author/B00RKJDIXA

bookbub.com/authors/kimberly-amato

facebook.com/thekimberlyamato

instagram.com/kimberlyamato

Go to the link below to stay up to date on new releases and more!
https://www.kimberlyamato.com/newsletter

Also By Kimberly Amato

THE STEELE SERIES

Steele Intent (Book 1)

Melting Steele (Book 2)

Breaking Steele (Book 3)

Cold Steele (Book 4)

Steele Shield (Book 5)

Steele Influence (Book 6)

STANDALONES

Enemy

www.ingramcontent.com/pod-product-compliance
Lightning Source LLC
Chambersburg PA
CBHW020956180626
46814CB00003B/1118